ABERDEE
SILVER LININGS

SILVER LININGS

MILLIE GRAY

BLACK & WHITE PUBLISHING

First published 2015
by Black & White Publishing Ltd
29 Ocean Drive, Edinburgh EH6 6JL

1 3 5 7 9 10 8 6 4 2   15 16 17 18

ISBN   978 1 84502 997 5

Copyright © Millie Gray 2015

A CIP catalogue record for this book is available from the British Library.

ALBA | CHRUTHACHAIL

Typeset by RefineCatch Limited, Bungay, Suffolk
Printed and bound by Nørhaven, Denmark

AUTHOR'S NOTE

This story tells of one family's life in Leith during the Second World War. Although it echoes some of the writer's experiences and personal feelings, and uses the attitude and spirit of the people of Leith, the characters portrayed in the book are wholly fictitious and bear no relation to any persons, living or dead. Many of the street names, localities and other details from that period in Leith's history have been preserved, however.

This book is for my husband, Bob, who in 2008
believed I could write a book that people would wish
to read. Now, seven years on and a bestselling
author, here is my seventh offering.

ACKNOWLEDGEMENTS

Firstly I must thank Rachel and Alastair Donald for allowing me the extended loan of their precious copy of *Leith-Built Ships on War Service*, which is the wartime history of the firm of Henry Robb Ltd.

I also acknowledge the contributions by the following that assisted me in my research for *Silver Linings*: Alice Lauder, Margaret McIntosh, May McIntyre, Mary Gillon and Jack Martin.

I am also very grateful to Diane Cooper for her initial editing of the work.

Finally I wish to thank the team at Black & White Publishing, especially Karyn Millar for her excellent in-depth editing, Laura Nicol for her PR, and Campbell, Alison and Janne, who give me such wonderful support and advice. Without their assistance, 100,000 people would not have read a Millie Gray book.

1

13 MAY 1940

Johnny Anderson, who was eager to hear the news broadcast, was annoyed when the radio started to splutter and crackle so loudly that it distorted the newsreader's voice. After viciously banging the top of the receiver, which only served to enhance the interference, he turned abruptly. 'Kitty,' he roared through clenched teeth, 'for goodness' sake, can you no keep that bawling bairn quiet? Och,' he continued with disgust, 'does nobody in this house understand that I want to listen to this broadcast?'

'That right?' his sister Kate chuckled.

'Aye, it is,' was his impatient retort, as he waved his hands in the air. 'I mean, do I have to spell it out to you just how very important it is that I hear exactly what Winston Churchill said to the parliament today?'

'Important to you, is it?' goaded Kate. 'Well let me tell you, sonny boy, all he said was that he'd nothing to offer the whole country except . . .' She hesitated so as to savour the moment before slowly simpering, 'Blood – toil – tears – and – sweat.'

Johnny's jaw dropped. 'He never did,' he slowly drawled.

'Oh, but he did,' was all Kate replied.

Turning to his mother, Jenny, he suggested, 'She is joking, Mammy?' Jenny shook her head. 'But she just has to be,' was his emphatic reply.

'No I'm not,' Kate almost sang.

'And I hope you bawled right back at him through this broken-down contraption that cost me a fiver – aye a whole bloody fiver, and me a man that breaks his back working sixty-five hours a week.' Johnny now looked around the room before continuing. 'Aye, sixty-five hours, that's what I toil each week to come out with less than a bleeding fiver in my hands.' He now turned back to the radio and viciously thumped it again. 'Now where was I? Oh aye, that you told that Churchill, in no uncertain manner, that we more than welcome him, and all the rest of the bloodsucking blinking upper class, into our world – the world of the fucking working class.'

'Language, Johnny!' Jenny exclaimed. 'You are in your home, not standing with your feet in the sawdust of some downtown pub.'

Johnny gave a contrite nod to his mother before she said in a more conciliatory tone, 'As you know, son, I don't often agree with you, but you're right: we in the working class will cope because we've never known anything else but blood, toil, tears and sweat.'

'But now we have a wireless are we no . . . ?' eighteen-year-old Bobby tentatively asked.

'Have I no already explained to you, Bobby, and everybody else in this bleeding house,' Johnny emphasised, his eyes challenging everybody in the room, 'that when I asked you all to chip in to buy this second-hand Defiant radio—'

'Which is well named because since it came in here it has decided to be defiant and only play when it suits it,' mocked Kate.

Ignoring Kate's observation Johnny continued, 'That now we are at war with Germany it is essential that we are – and that means especially I am – kept up to date with all that is going on.' Johnny began to strut about the living room. 'And what is also of significance is that this war is an opportunity for us workers to get off the bloody dole and get proper recognition for what we contribute to the wealth-making of this country. That means we should all be singing from the same hymn sheet and that is why I am urging all the workers to join a trade union.' He sniffed deeply before adding, 'And no just them that are employed in the shipyards, like me a plater, or the riveters, fitters, turners, shipwrights, hudders-on, blacksmith strikers, catch-and-fire boys, welders, painters . . .'

Johnny paused to think and make sure he hadn't missed a trade out. This gave Kate an opportunity to suggest, 'And the draughtsmen and management?'

'Aye, the draughtsmen, but no the bloody management that always try to hold us hoi polloi down and keep us in the place they think we should be.'

'Come on, Johnny,' Kate expounded. 'Do you ever stop to consider that your continual hassling of the management and threatening them with walkouts might have a bearing on the dichotomy that forever exists between you?'

Johnny's response to her was to snort before responding, 'Well, Kate, unlike you I've not been well educated and then swallowed a blooming dictionary so I dinna ken what dichotomy means – but what I do ken is that the management and us trade unionists just cannae get on the gither.'

Kate sighed long and loudly, allowing her rolling eyes to survey the ceiling.

'So back to what I was saying,' Johnny jubilantly went on because he thought he'd got one over on Kate, whom he judged to be in Leith Provident's management's pocket. 'So that means we need to get all the workers – ye ken the actual ones that will be doing all the back-breaking toil, so we can win this bloody war – into a trade union.'

'So that's the real reason that we all had to chip in to buy the radio, and by the way its union seems to have told it only to work when *The McFlannels* and their like come on,' insinuated Kate.

'I like that Molly Weir, Kate. Ye ken, she's the one that plays Poison Ivy in *The McFlannels*.' Jenny chuckled.

'For heaven's sake, Mammy, surely you ken fine we didn't get the wireless so you could be entertained while you're doing your ironing.'

'That wasn't what you said when you asked me to chip in so you could buy it.'

Johnny ignored his mother's comment and went on to further point out to her and Kate, 'No. We got it because we could be told things first hand like.'

'They've put a penny on a pint of beer and one and threepence on a bottle of whisky to help pay for the war effort?' teased Kate.

'And here, did you ken that from next week meat's going to be rationed?' Jenny chipped in.

'Aye, right enough that's going to happen,' Johnny agreed, nodding his head. 'But on the bright side I did hear, from a reliable source in the Steamboat pub, that we will still be able to get as much tripe as we like,' he added with a knowing wink.

Kate's laughing response to the tripe was to flash her eyes to the ceiling before following her niece, Kitty, who was trying to soothe the now hysterical one-year-old Rosebud, as she dragged her out of the living room.

Frustrated, Kitty viciously kicked open her bedroom door

4

before she bent down and lifted the screaming infant up. Without warning she then tossed the toddler on to the bed.

'Careful, careful, Kitty,' Kate remonstrated. 'She's still just a baby and what's for sure is that she, poor wee soul that she is, didn't ask to be born.'

Kitty, who was now slumped down on the floor with her arms around her knees, surprised Kate when she became convulsed with sobbing. 'You're right, she didn't,' Kitty spluttered through her tears, 'but can't you understand that I at fifteen didn't wish to be saddled with her and her puking and her shitty nappies?'

Getting up from the floor, Kitty began jabbing her index finger towards her aunt while she mouthed vehemently, 'The prime minister says we can expect nothing else now but blood, toil, tears and sweat and here was me hoping that somehow I could break free from my bloody awful life.' To vent her anger she lifted her foot and kicked out at a rag doll that was lying on the floor. 'Aunty,' she continued, 'can't you see I'm nothing in this house other than a drudge – a wretched slave that's ignored. It's as if I don't count. Don't have an opinion. Nobody ever asks me what I think. I'm just the invisible one that does the cleaning, shopping and cooking. And now that everything is going up in price I won't even be able to skim enough from the paltry housekeeping Dad hands me to get my weekly visit to the pictures with my pal Laura.'

Rosebud, who had been picked up by Kate, was now snugly cuddled up against her breast and the child's beautiful little face relaxed into a smile as sleep overtook her. Deciding that it was Kitty, her beloved namesake niece, who now required consoling, Kate gently laid Rosebud on the bed, and once she had wrapped a shawl about her, she then turned her attention to Kitty, who had plonked herself down on the floor again.

'Look,' Kate started as she patted Kitty's head, 'Churchill was right to say what he did. But he should have started with, "No matter what, there will be some silver linings along the way, there always are. In reality, however, we are facing a satanic foe and all I can offer, as we wrestle with it, is nothing other than blood, toil, tears and sweat." Now come on, Kitty, admit it, we have always had some silver linings even in our darkest days. It's how we survive it all.' Kate lovingly patted Kitty's face before adding, 'Remember back to a few weeks ago when Rosebud took her first steps, she walked towards you and we laughed when she called you "Mama".'

Instead of Kate's advice having a calming effect on Kitty all it did was upset her further. Eventually, when Kitty's tears were exhausted, she sniffed. 'See next week, I won't even have my pal Laura because she's going down to Coventry to work in a munitions factory – and before you say I could go with her, they wouldn't be taking on a lassie with a snotty bairn tugging at her skirts.'

Kate wanted to say something to ease Kitty's suffering but when she said, 'Be honest with yourself, Kitty, you wouldn't really be happy if you gave up on Rosebud, now would you?' Kitty's response was to wail even louder.

Eventually the scalding tears started to subside and, wringing her hands, Kitty whined, 'Oh, Aunty, I turned sixteen today and nobody has even said "Happy Birthday"!' Tears started to well again and spilled over before she continued. 'I know you can't understand how bad a sixteen-year-old like me can feel. You've never known the feeling of being trapped and your life somehow over before it really began.'

KATE'S STORY

Kitty's words jolted Kate into reminiscing back twenty-five years to when she had been a happy-go-lucky sixteen year old. Staring directly into the mirror that fronted the wardrobe, she saw nothing. Not even her own ghostly reflection. Reluctantly her thoughts slowly drifted to summon up the secrets of her heart – to look back to the wonderful carefree hours she had spent with the love of her life: handsome and charming eighteen-year-old Hugh Brown.

Their close friendship had developed throughout their childhood. Kate's mum and dad were great friends of Hugh's parents. Every Thursday night the two couples played cards at each other's homes, and the children were encouraged to keep quiet and get out the Ludo and Snakes and Ladders boards. For years Kate and her brother Johnny and Hugh and his brother Matt had played together and enjoyed each other's company. But life had to move on and childish games had to be put by. This had meant that the older boys, Johnny and Matt, no longer stayed at home on the whist nights. Johnny's interests were in the trade unions and he was forever at evening meetings held in offices just round the corner from the tramcar depot in Leith Walk. Matt, on the other hand, had started to court a green-eyed lassie from Blackie Road. Up in the world he'd gone from Glover and Ferrier Street, where the Andersons and Browns were housed.

Kate smiled to herself as she remembered how she'd always been jealous of the Browns' house in Glover Street.

Now this was not because they had a big front room, a kitchen with a coal-fed range, a cold-water tap, a box room that their granddad slept in and a small lavatory for their exclusive use. After all, her family were lucky enough to have similar accommodation in Ferrier Street. No, it was because Glover Street was the first street you came to after you had come through the Hole in the Wall at Crown Street, just off Leith Walk. The other reason, which she now acknowledged was the more important, was that she and Hugh could lean out of the front-room windows and observe life in the raw that was forever going on in the street below. As they grew and matured, their arms, shoulders and legs, at first accidentally and then intentionally, would rub together. Kate quietly giggled as she remembered the pleasure she had felt in their innocent but reckless intimacy.

Biting on her lip her thoughts then wandered to 1912, when both families started going to the Gaiety Theatre down in the Kirkgate in Leith on a Saturday night. Life was so colourful there. When the picture jumped into her head of the smartly dressed orchestra rising up like spectres through a trapdoor in front of the stage, she tittered. Once the band was assembled and had started to play she was always immediately transported to a land of make-believe. The actors would then come on to the stage and she had especially enjoyed when her favourite actor convincingly took on the role of the 'baddie'. Even today, twenty-five years later, she remembered his portrayal of 'The Demon King'.

That was until her illusions were shattered when her mum had sent her to buy some sausages from the butcher at the foot of Leith Walk. She had just bounced into the shop when a vision before her filled her with horror. Now, her fright was not due to her seeing a dead pig hanging from a hook by its neck. No, it was the sight of the handsome, debonair Gaiety band leader's bloody hands ripping the kidneys out of a lamb. She had inhaled deeply to get over the shock but, when she averted her eyes, her misconceptions went into free fall when she looked directly into the eyes of the man serving behind the counter. 'Oh, no,' she screamed inwardly when she was confronted with none other than the bloodied 'Demon King' himself. Yes, there he was, her favourite actor, serving Leith's thrifty housewives with offal and then, with a licentious wink, he started to throw free marrowbones towards the customers who pushed each other out of the way in an effort to catch one.

Kate later discovered from her mother that all the people employed in the Gaiety Theatre only worked there part-time. Mum, with relish, had gone on to elaborate that the butchers were very lucky to have a talent that could be used to entertain people because that meant they were able to earn a bit on the side, and so help ends meet.

Back in the present, Kate glanced across at Kitty, who was now relaxed in sleep. She shrugged as her memories went swiftly back to the Gaiety Theatre of her youth.

She could not help but laugh out loud when she remembered how all working men wore 'Paw Broon' caps. These hats were removed when they entered the theatre, which resulted in every man then exposing a red rim tattooed on their foreheads. This badge of honour was the effect of years of labouring outdoors. On theatre nights the red badge was soon joined up by an alcoholic flush creeping up their faces. This was because on every level in the theatre, except the gods, there was a bar, and when the bell rang to say the show was about to start, or the interval was over, men downed their pints with such speed that colourful inebriation swiftly registered on their faces.

Kate now gave an involuntary shudder before screwing up her nose when she recalled how the smell of the beer from the bars mingled with the stench of the urinals. Indeed, at no level, no matter how much you had paid for your ticket, were you protected from this distinctive odour washing over you and no amount of Evening in Paris perfume could whiff it away.

Her mood changed and she chuckled when she remembered that everybody in Leith, except the cashier at the Gaiety – a rather dim, stout woman, who took the entrance money – knew that the rather accommodating Mrs Greenhill, who wore the biggest cape you have ever seen, was the mother of ten differently fathered children that she took everywhere with her. Nonetheless when she arrived at the pay desk she only purchased two tickets. One was for herself and one for a child that she was holding firmly by the hand. However, when she walked away from the cash desk, to mount the dangerously steep concrete stairs of the theatre, she appeared to move like a centipede. People gasped and sniggered when Mrs Greenhill banged her chest three times and then as many as up to sixteen feet could be detected marching in unison under her cape. When they arrived at the first floor a deep cough emanating from Mrs Greenhill then signalled that six of the feet should break free from under the cape and scramble up the remaining two flights of stairs to the gods. Once they reached there they took off their coats and spread them down on the benches, thus indicating to other customers that these choice front seats were reserved for the rest of the family, when they finally arrived.

Looking down over that twelve-inch brass rail, which prevented you from falling over into the Grand Circle's upholstered seats, Mrs Greenhill would collapse down on the wooden bench and then loudly declare it to be a scandal that she was sent up here after her paying full first-rate prices for her children and herself to watch second-rate shows. 'Does the management in here no ken that I suffer from vertigo?' she would holler and swoon. When it became evident that no one was going to bother about her fainting she would quickly recover and grab the handrail before going on, 'And that three of my bairns are noo addicted to Brasso because, when the acts are boring, they take to sooking this bleeding banister?'

Kate now willingly recalled that she had been a blonde, willowy eleven-year-old when the Gaiety began to have competition in the form of moving pictures. She vividly recollected how excited everyone was when the Leith Picture House opened in Lawrie Street, down off Constitution Street, in 1911. Dear, attentive, thirteen-year-old Hugh, who was an artisan apprentice in the shipyards, saved enough from his meagre weekly pocket money so he could treat her to a visit to the picture house.

By the time she was thirteen, and the First World War was looming, every Saturday night she would be burying her head into Hugh's shoulders as *The Perils of Pauline* serial saw the heroine Pauline become a poor damsel in distress, faced with dangerous actions that were threatening her very life. One serial lasted a whole twelve weeks, so poor Hugh had no other option but to treat Kate to a visit to the Leith Picture House every one of those weeks so she could make sure Pauline survived the daft weekly cliffhangers. Kate shook her head, because now, at forty, she accepted the storylines of the *Pauline* films were always flimsy and that they relied on sensationalism. She also acknowledged that Hugh was not impressed by silly movies like *The Perils of Pauline* but he would shake with laughter at *Brewster's Millions*. As time went by Kate's taste in films took on a developing air of sophistication and she became enthralled by films like *The Old Curiosity Shop* and Cecil B. DeMille's first shot at directing, in a film called *The Squaw Man*.

The last film Kate and Hugh sat through, before he marched off to war, starred a newcomer, Charlie Chaplin, in the thankfully hilariously funny film, *Making a Living*.

Tears now streaming down her face, Kate stood up and lifted a pillow from the bed, which she then placed under Kitty's head. 'So, Kitty, my dear, you believe I never knew sorrow.' She huffed and grunted and then whispered, 'Never knew sorrow? My dearest Hugh was a big man in every way. At seventeen, when he marched off to war, he was six feet tall, a gentleman, and I loved him. I wish,' she continued, 'I could forget just how much we loved each other – lay to rest the memories of the plans we made for when he would come marching home victorious.'

Sinking down on to the basket chair, Kate allowed her head to bend over and she cradled it in her hands. Rocking backwards and forwards, she now thought of that fateful day, 22 May 1915, when the 7th Royal Scots, Leith's own Territorial Army, which Hugh had joined, set off for the front line. A train which they had boarded tragically ended up in a disastrous rail crash at Quintinshill, near Gretna. A simple error by a signalman led to the troop train colliding with a stationary passenger train. What was worse, before anyone could stop it, an express train from Glasgow bound for London ploughed into the wreckage, resulting in an uncontrollable fire. Between the collisions and the consequent inferno, 418 people were left either killed or injured.

When news of the worst rail tragedy ever to happen in Britain filtered into Leith, Gladys Brown ran panicking to her friend, Jenny Anderson. Throwing open the Andersons' door she screamed, 'Jenny, Jenny, all our braw laddies hae been killed. And not, mark you, in the blinking war, but in a blasted train crash here in Scotland.'

The noise of the slap that Jenny had made across Gladys's face was still reverberating around the room when she pulled hysterical Gladys into a strong embrace. Holding her in her arms, Jenny looked towards Kate and whispered, 'Dear God, Kate, it seems Hugh's been killed. Quick, get Gladys a cup of hot sweet tea and lace it with a dram.'

Kate did hear her mother's request but the thought that Hugh might be dead riveted her to the spot. With fists so tightly clenched that her knuckles were white she thought back to only the night before, when she and Hugh had walked hand in hand through the Links. They talked and talked about nothing except their future together. Hugh vowed he would come back and then they would tell their families of their love for each other and they would marry. They had even spoken about emigrating to America. All the films they had seen in the Leith Picture House had inspired in them the belief that they could go out to the Land of the Free and make a go of it there. After all, Kate had argued with Hugh, hadn't Dunfermline's Andrew Carnegie gone from rags to riches in 1835, emigrating to America and becoming the richest man in the world when he sold the empire he had built up for $480 million in 1901?

Buoyed up by Kate's enthusiasm Hugh conceded, and readily agreed, that they would make it in America and they would not be greedy. Just one million would satisfy them. After all, who really would ever need more than that?

All over Leith people were huddled together into whispering little groups. They were impatiently awaiting news of their loved ones. At the Leith 7th Battalion Royal Scots' Drill Hall in Dalmeny Street, from where the lads had left earlier that day, lists of the names of the dead were eventually posted on the outside billboards.

'Kate, you push yourself into the front of that rabble there and see what it says,' her mother brusquely commanded.

'Oh, Jenny,' Gladys pleaded, 'what will I do if it says . . . I mean, how will I break it to Dodd?'

Jenny's only response was to tuck Gladys's arm firmly under her own.

When ashen-faced Kate returned she inhaled two deep breaths before spluttering, 'Oh, Mum, thankfully our Hugh's name's not on any of the lists.'

'So it looks as if he's okay?' was her mother's quick response.

'He might be,' Kate replied with less enthusiasm, 'but the lad who posted the notices was also saying that the lists are not complete.' Changing her tone Kate went on. 'But, Mum,' she almost sang, 'he also said some, might be as many as fifty or even a hundred, have survived.'

'That right?' Gladys cried as she wrestled herself free from Jenny's grip.

Kate nodded. 'And they will either continue their journey onwards or come back here, and then after a while, they will be sent back off.' She said no more to her mother and

Gladys, but she inwardly screamed, *Back to the bloody useless war again!*

The next morning, 23 May 1915, the rosy dawn found Kate sitting on a bench in Leith Links with her arms wrapped tightly about herself. She had been there all night praying and hoping. A long sigh escaped as she looked over the lush grass that had begun to take on a ghostly appearance when a thin mist started to drift upwards from it. Sheer exhaustion was seeping away any hope she had had about Hugh and, as despondency overtook her, she wondered if the phantom haze swirling at her feet was an omen. Lifting her eyes she stared long into the distance. Her heart jumped into her mouth. 'Who can that be?' she gasped. The tall figure was at one moment striding quickly towards her and then it was shrouded in the mist.

Eventually, the running upright figure was so close that the haze could no longer swathe it. All that Kate could make out was that it was a man dressed in a military uniform. She also noted that he was not wearing a regulation cap, a uniform irregularity which encouraged the filtering rays of the morning sun to light up the highlights of his gingery blond hair. 'Hugh!' she cried, half rising from the bench. 'Is it really you?'

In three quick strides he was pulling her towards him. She was so overcome that her head reeled, her knees buckled and her tears cascaded, all of which took him by surprise. Instinctively he wished to comfort his beloved so he gathered her up into a tight embrace. As the warmth of his body radiated through her, she was grateful to acknowledge that this was no dream, no ghost – it was her Hugh, in person. He had survived and he had come immediately to look for her. Finding her was easy for him because he knew that she would be nowhere else except in the part of Leith Links that was their own special place.

Steadying herself, she rigorously patted his chest before she fell against him again. It was only at that moment that she realised just how much she had missed him – and he had only been away for a night and a day.

'Come on, love,' he whispered as he stroked her silken hair. 'I'm not back for long so let's not waste a minute.'

She hesitated but only for a short time. Then lifting her eyes to meet his she blurted, 'Oh, darling, I want you so much. Really want you. So much so that I am very sorry I said no to you last night before we parted.'

He laughed. Rocking her back and forward he teased, 'Are you saying I should look forward to tonight?'

Her thoughts were now in turmoil. She tucked her head under his chin. This gesture allowed him to gently stroke her cheeks and he smiled when he felt the fire of the passion that was now soaring within her. He smiled, knowing that tonight they would make passionate, true love for the first time. Quickly his thoughts turned to where he would take her. He loved her so much that he wanted their first union to be in a lovely place. A quick roll in the long grass that surrounded the railway along the Seafield track was not good enough for his darling Kate. Behind a tombstone in Seafield Cemetery was also a definite no-no.

Kate, on the other hand, felt fear arising within her bosom. The terror that she tried to control was not that she would be letting her mother and church down when she allowed Hugh to make forbidden love to her tonight. Oh no, she was scared this promised one night of passion would be all that she would ever have.

* * *

Later that evening they sought each other's hands when they alighted from the tramcar on Princes Street. Hugh had already explained that they could not book in anywhere in Leith where they might be recognised. He went on to explain that, this being the case, in the early afternoon he had nonchalantly sauntered into the Imperial Hotel on Cockburn Street and booked them in for one night in the name of Mr and Mrs Hugh Brown.

On reaching the Imperial Hotel's reception area, Kate hung back as she did not wish the receptionist to see how young and childlike she looked.

Treasured memories of the only night they had spent together rose up within Kate now and swamped her every thought. She just couldn't believe that twenty-five years had passed since she had waved goodbye to Hugh on that draughty train station platform. The pain of their parting was as raw and as real today as it had been on the morning after their wonderful night of love-making. They truly hadn't wasted a precious second of their stolen time together – in fact they were clinging to each other so much that they hadn't even had time for breakfast. Indeed, they had to scamper down the brae so that Hugh could catch the very early morning train that he had been instructed to board.

Often Kate wished she hadn't dissolved into tears when she had clung to Hugh for the last time. Somehow she thought he should have remembered her smiling instead of seeing her scalding tears as they gushed from her eyes.

Kate had kept looking warily at the guard who had been poised to blow the whistle that would signal that Hugh should jump aboard. She vividly remembered Hugh fishing in his pocket for a handkerchief to wipe her sodden eyes, cheeks and nose before whispering, 'Thank you, love, for last night. And know something, darling, it won't matter what happens to me in this war because I will remember every detail of our time together. Believe me, last night's memories will see me through whatever befalls me.' He had grown pensive then and, increasing his grip on her, he tenderly whispered, 'Now, my sweet, don't you worry because I was careful and got off at Haymarket every time, so I did.' This remark meant nothing to Kate but to others in Leith who were acquainted with the facts of life it meant that Hugh had been careful not to go full steam ahead into Waverley and therefore put her in the family way.

Reluctantly her memories jumped to how she had watched her beloved Hugh board the train that would take him out of her life forever and all she had been able to do was stand on tiptoe for one last goodbye kiss. The accursed whistle blew and then the train slowly began its departure from the station. Before she knew it the puffing locomotive had vanished in a swirl of smoke and steam. Even although the train was gone from sight Kate had continued to stand and frantically wave and wave until the guard finally said, 'He's awa, hen. Noo is it no time you got yourself hame to your mammy?'

However, canny Kate didn't go straight home because she didn't wish her mum to find out that she hadn't spent the night with her pal Sheila. Sheila always called in for her in the morning so they could walk together to their work in the Leith Provident Department Store. If Sheila turned up on Mummy Anderson's doorstep looking for Kate, in no time at all the cat would be out of the bag. Two and two would be put together and made up to at least seven and Kate would be on the next train to Glasgow, where she would be sorted out by her mum's elder sister, Aunty Katherine – a fate that no one should suffer.

Well, reasoned Kate, *that being the case and as the hour is still early I could call in for Sheila at her family home in Lorne Street. That would also give me plenty of time to work on Sheila and prime her as to what she should say, if she was asked, about where I spent last night.*

Kate had no doubt that Sheila would cover for her. After all, how often had Kate lied for Sheila, who was forever going up to the Corner Rooms Dance Hall and making merry with sailors when her mother thought she was at a Band of Hope meeting banging a tambourine?

Sheila and Kate had linked arms as they strolled down Leith Walk and then on to Great Junction Street. 'Do tell where you really spent last night?' Sheila kept on urging.

'Nowhere except in Leith Links and there were plenty of people about there.' Crossing her heart before snuggling closer into Sheila, Kate then elaborated, 'Believe me, Sheila, even if I was going to do what we must never do until we are churched, I couldn't have done it in Leith Links last night. Honestly, you should have seen all the people milling about. Going on and on they were about the disaster.' Kate had giggled. 'And there was Hugh trying his best to make mad passionate love to me but the bench that could seat five always had six nosy parkers squashed up on it just gaping at us.'

Thinking back to that time, Kate was not convinced that Sheila had believed her story. They were both juniors in different departments in Leith Provident Department Store. Sheila was in the chemist part while Kate was employed in women's undergarments, where Miss Stivens was the manageress and buyer.

Recalling the very name of Miss Stivens always caused Kate anxiety. So getting up off the floor and going over to gaze from the window, she wrapped her arms tightly about herself. It was as if she was trying to prevent Miss Stivens from invading her person.

From her first week of employment in the store people had whispered stories about Miss Stivens. The main story seemed to be that Miss Stivens had had an affair with a married man which had resulted in her having a child. The child was now the same age as Kate but she was in boarding school. Sherry Stivens had been residing in North Berwick with her wealthy widowed mother when she found herself pregnant. Unable to cope with such a shocking scandal her mother had immediately sold up in North Berwick before Sherry's fall from grace became evident. Up until the baby was born, mother and daughter squirrelled themselves away in Melrose. After going through a long and troublesome labour, Sherry refused to give her baby up for adoption. This annoyed her mother, who wished to relocate back to North Berwick and renew acquaintance with her friends there. Left with no other option, as she saw it, Mrs Stivens purchased a house in the Trinity district of Edinburgh for herself and Sherry. As far as the people of Trinity were concerned, the baby, who had been christened Helen, was Sherry's much younger sister.

The truth was Sherry Stivens had paid a high price for refusing to give up her baby. She was constantly at her mother's beck and call and she couldn't even go out for a cup of tea on her Wednesday afternoon off without her mother, her self-elected chaperone, trailing along with her.

When Kate arrived for work, the morning after the night

she had spent with Hugh, everything seemed so unreal to her. Kate recalled in detail walking into the store that morning and there must have been an air about her because it seemed as if Sherry Stivens knew where she had been and what she had done. Kate remembered standing in the small, cramped staffroom and Sherry looking long and hard at her before she softy uttered, 'You know, Miss Anderson, when a woman is in love and that love is returned by her suitor then that woman takes on an air of glowing beauty and a magic envelops her. Sometimes this results in her throwing all sense of decency and caution to the winds.' She hesitated before adding in an almost inaudible whisper, 'And the price for that could be exacted from her for the rest of her life.'

To say that Kate was startled by this announcement from Sherry Stivens was an understatement. She glanced up at the mirror that was hanging above the tea table to be assured that she looked no different from yesterday. She remembered thinking as she gazed at her image that she was right, there was no beautifying variation in her appearance. In fact, she felt that she looked so sad and dejected that she reasoned there was no way anyone could think she looked enchanting and sparkling.

Nothing more was said by Miss Stivens, but within three weeks Kate was panicking. Hugh had said he had been careful not to get her pregnant – alas not careful enough! All too soon Kate accepted that soon she would have to break her mother's heart and own up to being pregnant. Why, she thought, was it that when a young lassie got into a scandalous mess that somehow the shame fell on her mother? People would judge that Kate had not been brought up properly. Every day that passed Kate wanted to shout, 'It was me that indulged in sinful acts – not my mother. My mother does not deserve the red face and humiliation that I am going to heap on her!' Kate also knew that if Hugh realised what had happened he would somehow get home to her. Make it all right for her and their baby.

The idea that Hugh could come home to rescue her reputation was tragically beyond his control because during the latter part of June 1915 he and most of his battalion were led like lambs to the slaughter at Gallipoli. Kate had been inconsolable when she learned of Hugh's death. She couldn't bear to be in the house with her mother, who was going to feel so wronged when she confessed. How was she going to find the courage to tell her dearest mother that she was pregnant with Hugh's baby? She had been grateful that it just happened to be stocktaking that heartbreaking weekend. This had meant she would be out at work both Saturday and Sunday and on Monday . . . Well maybe, just maybe, she would find the courage to speak to her mum.

Sherry Stivens and Kate were up in the attics of the department store going over the records and they seemed to find that six whaleboned corsets and half a dozen pairs of pure silk knickers were missing. To be truthful, Kate, who was now feeling wretched, wasn't in the least bit concerned about the corsets having been spirited away. Nor, unlike Sherry Stivens, did she have any interest in who was wearing any of the six pairs of silk knickers. Rising laboriously up from the floor she sighed deeply. All she could think of was trying to ward off the faint feeling that was now overwhelming her. Instinctively she knew she was going to fall backwards down the steep worn wooden steps of the attic and she remembered holding out her hand to Sherry in the hope she would grab it. Sherry did at first appear as if she was going to take hold of Kate's outstretched hand and save her. However, without any warning, a perplexed look of sorrow and regret crossed over Sherry's face. Clenching her fist tightly she then withdrew her hand and clasped it to her chest. These actions, of course, resulted in Kate tumbling down and down into merciful oblivion.

Kate also remembered Sherry holding her as they waited for an ambulance and she knew she did not imagine it but Sherry's tears washed down on her as she whispered, 'You and your mum would not have coped. This is a godsend of a way out. Believe me, it is.'

How, wondered Kate, did Sherry discover her plight? It was one thing that she had stumbled upon the truth, but why did Sherry judge that because Kate's family had not the resources of her family that the child would be better to stay unborn? Of course, the baby – Kate and Hugh's child – would have been called bastard and Kate herself labelled a whore and easy meat. Kate knew all of that. In addition, if she claimed that Hugh was the father then Hugh's parents would have been deeply offended that she was besmirching the memory of their hero son. They would have proclaimed that she was nothing but a lying whore who had accused their son when he was incapable of defending himself. It would also have meant the breaking up of the important and long-time friendship between the Anderson and Brown families.

Now, still standing, and gazing unseeing from the window, Kate shrugged. No use going over and over that awful year, the year to end all years when she lost the love of her life as well as the right to be a mother, and these two happenings had left her filled with deep melancholy.

Turning, she looked down at her niece. Poor Kitty just sixteen and saddled with Rosebud. Wouldn't it be right, she thought, for her now to take the burden from Kitty and accept the responsibility of rearing the toddler herself? Was this not an opportunity to get retribution for all she had suffered?

Having made up her mind to suggest to her brother, Johnny, that Rosebud would be better off being brought up by her, she lightly tiptoed from the bedroom.

Striding back into the living room, Kate found Johnny had just finished brushing his hair. Without uttering a word he then proceeded to put on his jacket. Kate immediately pulled on his sleeve whilst sharply uttering, 'Here, brother dear, where do you think you're going?'

'Over to the Learig pub to wet my whistle,' retorted Johnny as he swept Kate's hand from his jacket.

'No, no, you're not,' Kate decreed, 'because I want to speak to you.' Kate glanced around the room. 'As a matter of fact I want to speak to everybody in this house.' She hesitated before emphasising, 'Right now.'

'What about?' huffed Jenny. 'And if you're going to go on again about me not doing enough for the war effort, then let me tell you, I bloody well am. I mean, who do you think keeps the welcoming stations going?' Jenny, who was obviously offended, sniffed long and loudly before continuing her tirade. 'None other than the churches' Women's Guilds, of which I am proud to be a full participating member.' Jenny, her eyes now ablaze, exhaled through gritted teeth. No one spoke because they knew she was not finished and no one was brave enough to stop her from concluding her sermon. 'So that means three nights a week the women in South Leith Parish Church are up there making soup, sandwiches, tea and just talking to the laddies and lassies before they catch a train out o' the Caledonian or Waverley stations and only God kens if they will ever come back alive.'

Johnny acknowledged his mother's war contribution with a nod of his head before making for the door. 'Johnny,' screeched Kate, jumping in front of him to bar his way, 'didn't you hear what I said? Come on now, we as a family have a big problem that we have just got to get sorted out.'

'That right?' uttered Johnny before he allowed a derisive cackle to escape him. 'Well let me tell you, Kate,' he continued loudly, 'the only big problem in here . . . is you. So if you don't mind, get out of my way.'

'No. We have to talk about Kitty and her being saddled with a year-old bairn.'

Roughly pushing Kate aside, Johnny blustered, 'And I hope you're no laying the blame for that at my door?' Kate could only shake her head so Johnny went on, 'And let me tell you before you go on and reorganise all our bleeding lives, you should have been in Robb's this afternoon. Ye know, that's the shipyards where I slave to provide for this household, and you would have seen what a bloody problem is!'

Johnny's eyes glassed over and he visibly sagged. In his mind's eye he was seeing the brave *Cossack* destroyer limping into Leith Docks. His thoughts now blocked out everything except his remembering how the *Cossack* had had the bad luck to be in the North Sea and get herself rammed in the blackout. 'The blasted merchant ship didn't see her,' he mouthed. 'Only thing that saved her from being cut in two was her super-mounted 4.7 gun turret.' Johnny's head was now swinging from side to side and he said quietly, 'All these brave young sailors – just bits of bairns really they were.' His mother and sister could see and hear now how thinking over the events was obviously unnerving him. 'Ye wouldn't believe it,' he hoarsely whispered, looking directly at his sister but seeing her not, 'but there were men, including me, openly weeping as we watched her struggling into berth. Up to six feet down by the head she was and her mess decks completely awash. Completely engulfed they were.' He brushed his hand roughly under his nose before continuing: 'Oh dear God, some of the young lads hadn't been able to escape. Slaughtered they were and their broken bodies are tangled up in the bloody wreckage, so they are.' Tears were now racing profusely down his cheeks and he could only go on haltingly. 'Told you, I did, they were just bits o' bairns so they were, but we'll treat them – as best we can – with respect.' Johnny now looked at his own sons before muttering, 'Because they were all some mothers' sons, so they were.'

Kate and Jenny were also shaking their heads now. They could see that the events of the day had completely gutted Johnny. Kate thought that they should have known when he said he was going over to the pub on a weeknight that there was something sorely amiss. He only ever went out to the pub at the weekend.

Blind to his mother's and sister's reaction, Johnny sniffed loudly. Then he inhaled deeply before continuing. 'When we start in the morning the first thing we will have to do is cut the poor souls out with the oxyacetylene cutting plant. Then it will be full speed ahead on to the repair and that will take us four or five weeks, so it will. The *Cossack* captain, that de Pass bloke, says that the poor smashed-up wreck of a ship still has urgent war business to attend to. Went on to say that no matter what, we will have to get her ready to sail again as soon as possible.' Johnny rubbed his chin before sarcastically chortling, 'Suppose that means that we will have to do the impossible once again and get her shipshape in four weeks and no five.'

'How will you manage that?' Kate asked.

'Just means that for the next month or so the hale of the repair yards will be concentrating on the *Cossack*.' A long, tired sigh escaped Johnny before he added, 'That also means life will be what's come to be normal now. All of us tradesmen taking it in turns to work twenty hours a day, which will include us donning our Home Guard uniforms at night because we are the only blooming thing that stands between the Gerries and you lot!' Johnny now had his hand on the door handle, and as he pulled on it he turned to face Kate directly again. 'So, dear sister, you deal with the problems in here as I, and all the lads in the yards, have got our bloody hands full – and not only in the day but in the bloody night as well.'

Kate submissively stood aside. She accepted that Johnny and his mates in the yards had more than enough to cope with so she would have to find the solution to Kitty's problem herself. *After all,* she thought, *we just have to win this war. And we in Leith have to give the brave sailors every chance that we can to get the food in or we will be starved into submission.* She drew herself up before accepting that she and the rest of the family would have to do all that they could to make life easier for the men in the shipyards. Kate acknowledged that, like Leith folk had always done, they would need to accept the blows that would come their way in this war. But, as in the past, no matter what was thrown at them they would always gather themselves together, get themselves shipshape again, and sail on with their lives.

KITTY'S STORY

If you asked Kitty Anderson what kind of a childhood she
had had, she would shrug simply before uttering, 'Up until
I was thirteen it was better than any princess's.' This
statement really did ring true because Kitty was the adored
only daughter of Johnny and Sandra Anderson and she very
diplomatically took after both of them. To say she was
beautiful would be an overstatement but she was strikingly
handsome. Her crowning glory was her platinum-blonde
hair that was like her father's, but instead of the tight ring
curls, Kitty's hair flowed down in deep waves. It was just a
pity that her nose also resembled that of her father's:
whereas a man could get away with a puffy, slightly-on-the-
large-side nose, on Kitty it seemed to detract slightly from
her femininity. This one drawback, however, was hardly
really noticed by anyone because she had inherited her
mother's most unusual glinting green eyes and her tall,
willowy, slim but busty figure. This, along with her mother's
bubbly personality, with which she was also endowed,
resulted in no one failing to be anything but enchanted
by her.

To be truthful, there were times that Kitty's two older
brothers, Bobby and Jack, and her younger brother, Davy,
could have seen her far enough. Like the time when Kitty
was just turning fourteen and leaving David Kilpatrick's
School in Great Junction Street. That was when Sandra had
announced at the tea table that she was determined that
Kitty was not going to be factory fodder. She was positive
that, unlike her brothers Bobby and Jack, who were
indentured apprentices, her Kitty would find life on the
factory floor just too coarse.

Aunt Kate, who was now manageress of the ladies'

underwear section in the superior Leith Provident Department Store in Great Junction Street, was then summoned by Sandra to be reminded that family was family and that it was her duty to offer Kitty, who was called after her, a position in her department.

Kate had only been appointed to the post of manageress and buyer of women's lingerie a short twelve months ago. That was when Sherry Stivens' mother had died, and not only was Sherry released from being punished for having given birth to a daughter out of wedlock, but she also had inherited the grand house in Trinity and a considerable fortune. Sherry, without giving the statutory period of notice, had resigned. 'No more,' she declared, 'will I spend my days trying to push a fifty-inch waist into a twenty-six-inch corset – and as for hitching up belly-kissing sagging bosoms, I've had more than enough.' Turning to Mr Jameson, the store's manager, she added sweetly, 'So, sir, don't bother sending on any due wages to me because I'm setting off to tour Europe. Imagine it – little old me sitting by the banks of the River Seine sipping coffee.' The picture that Sherry painted of her whiling away her time in foreign parts was dashed, however, because hadn't she forgotten to tell Hitler of her plans. If she had then perhaps he would have put his plans to invade Poland on hold – or postponed them forever.

To say that some of her staff, especially Myra Ford, who had two years more service than Kate, were put out by Kate's elevation to department head was an understatement. This being so, there was just no way Kate would dream of upsetting the apple cart further by engaging in nepotism. A long pause had elapsed before Kate tentatively said, 'Look Sandra, I do love your – I mean our – Kitty dearly but I am

not brave enough to cope with any further staff resentment
. . .' Before she could explain further Kitty had flounced
into the house.

'Mum,' Kitty crooned before anybody had time to speak.
'Know what?' Sandra and Kate both shook their heads. 'I
was sent by the school today for an interview at Oxo's
offices in Constitution Street and I start there on Monday
as,' Kitty now worked her fingers to indicate that she could
type, 'a clerkess/typist.' Kitty grimaced and inhaled and
quickly exhaled loudly before adding, 'Only problem is
they pay a . . . monthly salary.'

'A clerkess/typist,' Sandra spluttered, grabbing hold of
Kate's hand. 'Did you hear that, Kate, and a monthly salary?
Oh, oh, now that must be a first for Ferrier Street.' Suddenly
Sandra's eyes widened and her hand shot to her mouth.
'Kitty darling,' she hoarsely whispered, 'you didn't say
where you really lived? I mean, you did remember that it is
important when you go for interviews for good jobs to say
that you live with your granny in a bought house in Parkvale
Terrace.'

Kate had a quiet chuckle to herself. She was remembering
when she, her mum and dad had moved out of the 'stair
house' in Ferrier Street and into Parkvale Terrace. The
house was in one of the upmarket colony streets across from
Leith Links and round the corner from Vanburgh Place.

Some of their neighbours in Ferrier Street did think they
were getting above themselves by being able to buy a house
outright. Especially a house that had its own front door, an
outside coal box and a little garden where you could hang
out your washing or have the luxury of being able to sit and
sun yourself. The purchase of the house came about because
the three of them worked full-time and her mother never

allowed a penny to leave her purse unless it was under escort. Also, debt was shunned by the prudent, because there was no job security. Suddenly you could find yourself without an income and left with no way of paying your obligations.

The moving to Parkvale Terrace worked out for Johnny too because he and Sandra moved into the vacated house in Ferrier Street before the fire required re-stoking.

'Were you going to say something, Kate?'

Kate shook her head. 'Not really, Sandra,' she said, hesitating. 'It was just that, on second thoughts, I had decided that Kitty would be such an asset to any establishment and that I should employ her. And yes, there would be tons of flak coming my way, but it would be worth it.' She hesitated and sighed before adding, 'I'm just so disappointed now that Kitty won't be wishing to come and work with me when a firm like Oxo has offered her a position.'

Looking askance at her mum and her Aunt Kate, all Kitty did was chortle before saying, 'You thought that I, a proficient typist with a fifty-words-per-minute certificate, would want to spend my life selling knickers!' She huffed before she added contemptuously, 'You two should realise that there is life beyond Leith Provident's Great Junction Street store!'

Kitty had fitted in very well when she started to work in the Oxo offices and, being ambitious, she continued to upgrade her secretarial skills – she even sat for, and was awarded, the much sought-after Pitman's One Hundred Words per Minute Shorthand Certificate. This certificate was immediately framed and hung on the wall for all who visited the house to see.

Sandra, who was just so proud of Kitty and her achievements, always made sure that Kitty was smartly turned out in freshly laundered clothes. To say Kitty blossomed after leaving school was an understatement. On a Saturday, her half day off, she loved to treat David, her younger brother, to an afternoon up the town where they would go to see a film in either the Playhouse or Salon picture houses. That was not the end of the treat, however, because Kitty would then ask David, 'Well, will it be a pot of tea and bun in Littlejohn's café in Leith Street or will we really push the boat out and go to Mackie's on Princes Street and have a praline tart with our tea?'

Kitty felt really good about taking David out on a Saturday afternoon because there was an added bonus in that it meant her mother could have an afternoon all to herself to do whatever she wanted. Never, thought Kitty, did any mother sacrifice herself for her family the way Sandra did. Kitty was so grateful to her mother for providing the little extras in life, such as her fine clothes and meat for the boys' dinners in the middle of the week. This was all made possible by Sandra taking on a job as a cleaner in Lorne Street Primary School. She also took on another three-hour weekly job cleaning the Kennedys' house. These people owned the two upmarket shops on Lochend Road that sold groceries, fruit, vegetables and sherry.

Never would Kitty forget the day she felt her whole world change. It was a Saturday and she and David had just alighted from the tramcar at the foot of Leith Walk when David had decided, as he always did, to nip over to Costa's chip shop in Great Junction Street for a poke of chips. Kitty then pointed out forcibly, as she always did, 'But you have just had tea and a bun.'

'Aye,' replied David, giving her a wink and rubbing his stomach, 'but I'm a growing laddie and need more than a tart to stop ma guts frae rumbling.'

After she watched David scoot off, Kitty started to make for home. When she entered the house the fire was burning brightly in the grate and the table was laid for tea. Taking out a paper bag that was filled with tea-bread she had bought at Littlejohn's she laid it tentatively down on the table. Kitty then looked long and hard at her mother. For weeks now Kitty had tried to pick up the courage to say to Sandra that she was piling on the weight and that she always looked so sickly now. Today, thought Kitty, these problems were even more pronounced.

'Mum,' she hesitantly began, 'are you well enough? You're not looking great.'

Before Sandra responded she sank down on a kitchen chair. 'Oh, Kitty, I only have to get through another ten weeks and then it will be all over.'

'Oh, Mum,' Kitty whimpered, 'please don't say that you're going to be like Ella Jones and . . . die!'

'No. No, I'm not ill as such,' Sandra explained. 'It's just that I'm going to have a . . .' She now hesitated and giggled before finishing. 'A baby.'

Kitty's mouth gaped. Her eyes quickly widened and she began to shake her head. 'But, Mum,' she spluttered, 'you're thirty-six. Oh no, you just couldn't be doing things like . . . Well, what you do to have a baby with Dad at thirty-six!'

To add to Kitty's consternation Sandra started to titter. 'Kitty, I love your dad and he loves me and both of us so looked forward to having the house to ourselves on Saturday afternoon and being able to . . .'

'Oh no, Mum, you're not saying that with me and David going to the pictures and Bobby and Jack away playing football that you and Dad . . .' Kitty started to wretch before she spluttered, 'What am I going to say to the girls in Oxo?'

'Tell them the truth.'

'Mum, they all come from families of two or three and their parents act . . . decently.' Kitty sniffed. 'Don't you realise, Mum, that I won't be able to hold my head up when people know that my dad of thirty-seven and mum of thirty-six . . . No, I can't say it because the picture that is coming into my mind is so disgusting.'

'Don't be ridiculous, Kitty. There is nothing wrong with a man and woman being . . . em . . . loving towards each other.'

'That so? Well why, since I took my monthlies, have you been saying that I would find what you have just done with Dad revolting? And that I should never ever let myself be used by any boy for his gratification.'

A long 'Ahhhh' escaped Sandra and she hummed and hawed before she eventually said, 'In your case . . .'

'And why not yours?'

Flabbergasted, Sandra tried to think of a suitable riposte but she had been rendered speechless.

Kitty, on the other hand, was now in full flight but before she could tear into her mother again, Bobby, whistling loudly, burst into the house. 'We are the boys,' he chanted, grabbing Kitty around the waist and proceeding to dance her around the floor. 'Can you believe it? We whacked them five-nothing.'

Feeling relief seep into her, Sandra chanted, 'That's just great, son. And do you know how Jack's team fared?'

'Oh, they scored too.'

Donning her coat, Kitty smirked. 'Scoring is what this family seems to be good at.'

'I'm just about to dish up the tea, Kitty. Come on now, take off your coat and sit down. I made your favourite – potted meat and—'

Before Sandra could finish Kitty butted in. 'Quivering potted meat is the last thing I want to look at tonight. I am away to get myself a poke of chips.'

For the next six weeks Sandra tried every trick in the book to get her relationship with Kitty back on track. She even scrimped and saved so she could buy Kitty a pair of black-market pure silk stockings, but they were still lying in their wrapper on the dressing table. Conversation between mother and daughter was reduced to the bare minimum. Sandra was broken-hearted. Wasn't it the case that she had always been proud of the fact that she and Kitty were more like sisters than mother and daughter? There was also the added aggravation for Kitty in that Sandra seemed to be getting so big around her stomach that she waddled. The climax came when Kitty had just arrived home from work and Sandra excitedly said, 'Kitty, you will never guess.'

'You've decided not to have a baby,' was Kitty's sarcastic reply.

'No . . . well yes . . .' stammered Sandra, 'but because we are going to have another child, Edinburgh Corporation say we now have enough points to be rehoused and your dad just has to sign the papers and we will get a three-bedroomed flat up in Restalrig Road – you know, up the top of the brae round from your granny's house in Parkvale.'

Kitty just shrugged.

'Oh, Kitty,' pleaded Sandra. 'Are you not excited? You will have a room to yourself, dear.'

'Huh,' responded Kitty, 'that will only be until this brat you are going to have is bunged in beside me.'

The papers from Edinburgh Corporation regarding the renting of the house in Restalrig Road had been signed and the Council had awarded Johnny the key when Sandra went into premature labour.

When Kitty arrived home the house was in turmoil. The clay-pipe-smoking midwife, who had been summoned urgently, was ordering Jenny and Kate to keep up the supply of hot water.

'Why on earth did Sandra not book Grace Tosh for her lying-in?' Kate coarsely whispered to her mother.

'She did,' Jenny retorted, 'but as Sandra has gone into labour early and Grace was delivering for someone who had booked her I just had to take Aggie.'

'Oh, Mum. Are you sure she'll know what to do?'

'Of course she will, only last week she delivered triplets to a wifie up in East Restalrig Terrace and she was only expecting twins.'

Kate huffed. 'Fine, but Sandra doesn't look well. Mum, I'm so scared.'

These words had just been uttered by Kate when Kitty asked, 'What's going on?' She was now looking quizzically at her grandmother and aunt. 'I mean the two of you looked as if you'd lost a bob and found a sixpence.'

'Oh, Kitty, your mum is just about to bring a wee brother or sister into the world for you.'

Kitty slumped down on a kitchen chair. 'She just can't,' she blubbered. 'What I mean is she said it would be another four weeks. Another month would have given me time to think of what I'm going to tell the girls I work with. Aunty Kate, don't you realise how embarrassing this is for me?'

Kate looked dumbfounded. 'Kitty,' she snorted, 'don't be so silly at a time like this.'

'What do you mean, "at a time like this"?'

'Kitty, the midwife has not said anything but your granny and I are both worried. Things don't seem right.'

Swallowing hard, Kitty looked directly at her grandmother. 'I know that it's not right. I told her that. Told her I did that she was too old to be doing what she was with Dad . . .' Her voice trailed away.

'Not that kind of right, Kitty,' her grandmother haughtily responded. 'And it was right and proper for your dad and mum to love each other. Believe me, my lady, you are very wrong to think and say that it wasn't.'

Kate walked behind Kitty's chair and she began to massage Kitty's shoulders. 'Look, love, what Granny and I are trying to say is that there would appear to be complications with your mother's labour. But try not to worry as it might work out fine.'

'You mean the baby might die?' Kitty almost whispered as guilt began to swamp her.

Before Kate or Jenny could respond a dishevelled and blood-splattered Aggie Mack came into the living room. 'I've managed to haul the wee lassie out. And some job that was. But the mammy . . .'

'Sandra, my sister-in-law, is she . . . ?' Kate started to ask as panic began to gallop within her.

'Ah well, your Sandra or whatever . . . she's no so good. And it's no my fault,' Aggie said defensively. Lifting her soiled apron to mop her brow she then added, 'I wouldn't have taken the job on, no I wouldn't, if I'd known she was a bleeding bleeder.'

A sound like a wounded cat meowing escaped from Kitty. Before anyone could say anything or stop her Kitty dashed into the bedroom.

The scene that confronted her was so surreal. The broken gas mantle was giving out ghostly rotating hues of yellow and blue, which seemed to Kitty to accentuate the horror she was looking at. All she could see was her mother lying limp upon the bed. A queasy faint feeling overtook her when she noticed that Sandra's pallor was whiter than the bed sheets that covered her.

'Mum,' Kitty whimpered. 'Please, please speak to me.'

Sandra's eyelids fluttered and her right hand began to crawl across the bedcovers towards Kitty.

'Kitty, my pretty Kitty,' she said in a weak, barely audible voice. 'Look, darling, at my side here, it's your baby sister.'

'No, I don't want to look at her. I just want you to say that you will not die and leave me.'

Jenny and Kate were now also standing by Sandra's bed and Kate leaned over and picked up the small bundle at Sandra's side. The baby was just so tiny and adorable that Kate had to say, 'Oh, Sandra, she's a wee beauty. Know what? Her wee face is so round, pink and perfect that she looks like a rosebud.'

Sandra tried to struggle up in the bed and with outstretched hands she indicated that she wished to hold the baby. Kneeling on the bed Kate placed the tiny bundle into Sandra's arms. Sandra smiled as she looked down at the baby. 'You're right, Kate,' she said in a small voice that was barely above a whisper. 'She is like a rosebud. So that's what I wish her to be called.' Sandra then closed her eyes and she breathed in deeply as if trying to find some strength from somewhere. Once she felt strong enough she held out her hand to Kitty. 'Kitty, my dear, pretty Kitty, you are going to have to grow up very quickly – and be strong.'

'Strong?' questioned Kitty. 'But I'm not strong.'

'Oh, Kitty,' Sandra slowly snuffled, 'all of us think we cannot be strong until we have to be.' There was a pause before Sandra added, 'You will be surprised where your strength will come from.'

Tears were now coursing down Kitty's cheeks and all she could say was, 'Mum, please don't tell me that you're going to leave me.'

An uneasy silence filled the room. Eventually Sandra sought Kitty's hand again. 'Darling, will you promise me something?'

'Anything, Mum. You just have to ask.'

'Then please swear to me that you will give up your job and rear Rosebud as if she was your own and . . . look after your father and brothers too.'

'Mum,' Kitty protested, 'you can't mean this. I'm only fifteen years old – what do I know about caring for a baby and . . . oh no . . . running a house too?'

'Kitty, I was only twelve years old when my mother died and I was taken out of school to keep house for my dad and two brothers. I managed and I was not as bright as you are.'

Before Kitty could answer, Johnny came rushing into the room. 'For Christ's sake,' he hollered, 'what in the name of heaven has happened here?'

Sandra tried again to struggle up. 'Johnny, my darling, it's a wee girl, Rosebud.'

Going over to the bed Johnny lifted Sandra up into his

arms. 'Love,' he whined as he stroked her hair, 'never mind if it is a boy or a girl, it's you that I want.' He was now weeping sorely. 'Please don't leave me,' he pleaded.

Sandra gasped. 'Johnny, please, please promise me that you will never marry again. I just couldn't bear it if my bairns were abused by a stepmother.'

Johnny nodded. 'I promise you that, but love . . .' Sandra did not hear his answer because death had silently stolen in and rendered her deaf and speechless.

Rocking Sandra backwards and forwards, Johnny began to look about the room. His mother and sister were awash with tears. He looked over to Kitty and just as he was about to ask her to come to him she jumped towards him and began beating him on the back. 'I hate you, Daddy. You forced my mum to do things she didn't want to do. She was too old to have another baby. And it's not you that's going to pay for this disaster. It's me! Don't you realise, Dad, that I'm going to have to give up my life to look after the little bitch!'

Jenny grabbed hold of Kitty and, birling her around to face her, she slapped her hard across the face. 'That's enough. How dare you speak to your father with such disrespect? And as to you being responsible for Rosebud . . .'

Before her granny could finish, Kitty interrupted, 'No, Granny, you won't take her on because I promised my mum, so I will look after her.'

'Kitty, my dear, there's no need for you to do that,' Kate said.

'Yes, there is. I made a promise to my dying mother and I will keep it. But I will never love her.'

It was now Rosebud's turn to protest and she did so by wailing loudly.

'She's hungry,' Jenny stated. 'But how are we going to feed her, because, as clever as Kitty is, she won't be able to breastfeed her.'

No one had noticed that the midwife had slunk back into the room. With a swift, silent movement she lifted her coat and as she donned it she looked at Johnny and asked, 'About my fee . . . it's due to be paid before I leave. And fifteen shillings is what I agreed with her.' Aggie indicated with a back jerk of her thumb towards Jenny.

Johnny leapt towards the woman and, grabbing her by the coat lapels, he hissed directly into her face. 'You are nothing but an incompetent bitch who has murdered my wife.' By now Johnny was violently shaking the woman. 'And now,' he continued as Aggie's false teeth wobbled in her mouth, 'you have the cheek to ask me to reward you with a pay-off!'

Realising that Johnny was about to completely lose control, Kate leapt forward. 'Johnny,' she pleaded as she got herself between him and the woman, 'get a grip. You'll end up arrested for assault.' She gulped before adding, 'Or worse, and that isn't going to bring Sandra back.'

Collapsing down on the bed Johnny spluttered, 'And who in the name of God in heaven asked her in here?'

Jenny, eyes bulging with fear, began to pant and wring her hands. 'Johnny, I'm so sorry, but she was all that we could get. The good ones were all out delivering babies and I just couldn't manage by myself. Sandra was screaming in agony. I didn't know what to do. All I knew was that our Sandra was in bother and I needed to get her help.' Jenny stopped to blow her nose and wipe her tears before whispering, 'I even had to say to Aggie here that I would pay her fifteen shillings instead of the usual twelve and sixpence if she would just come. Johnny, please try and understand that I was desperate.'

Kate, who was now trying to console her mother, looked directly at her brother before imploring, 'Johnny, for heaven's sake, try and understand that Sandra was in bother when Mum got here. She was frightened. She didn't know what to do when Grace Tosh, the midwife Sandra wanted, couldn't come. It was nobody's fault that she was attending to someone else at the other side of the town. Can't you accept our mum did the best she could?'

'Look here,' Aggie butted in as she extended her hand, 'I am a competent midwife. It was meant to be. It was Him upstairs that had decided her time here was over. And everybody kens when that happens nobody can save anybody.' Aggie stopped to wiggle her nose and sniff before saying, 'Besides, the older a woman is the more likely complications are.'

Inhaling deeply, Kate decided that as everyone was getting more upset by the minute, she had better get rid of Aggie. Signalling to Aggie that she should follow her out of the room, Kate went into the living room and picked up her handbag. Very quickly she was then able to press a ten-shilling note and two half-crowns into Aggie's hand, before bundling the woman out of the door.

There are events in life that stay etched in your memories forever. For Kitty one of the first of these lifetime memories was the day her mother was buried. It was such a heartbreaking affair that even the sky wept continually from dawn to dusk. Kitty, of course, did not attend at the graveside as it was thought that only men could cope with such grief. Kate, however, did attend the funeral but she was there to support her brother. Johnny, the tough union negotiator, wasn't coping well with the sudden death of his wife. Sandra's passing was affecting him so deeply that he seemed oblivious to the needs of his children. And as to Rosebud, he couldn't even look at her, never mind hold her.

So the poor motherless Rosebud became Kitty's problem. It was true her grandmother and aunt had assured her they would assist her all they could. But both women worked full-time so all they would be able to do was visit and assist the bereaved family every second night.

To make matters worse, Kitty's grief was compounded when her father returned from Sandra's burial and announced that the next day they would move into the house in Restalrig Road.

Saturday flitting, according to the rhyme, is short sitting. Kitty hoped that this was true. She had pleaded with her father to stay in Ferrier Street, or at least to come back if the move to Restalrig did not work out, but he was adamant that Restalrig was the future for his family. Kitty, however, was convinced that, since her mother was not dead a week, she and the rest of the family would be better placed to get assistance and understanding from their loyal, supportive neighbours in Ferrier Street.

Having said a very emotional goodbye to her friends in Ferrier Street Kitty was now pushing a posh but overladen, second-hand Silver Cross pram along the front of Leith Links towards Restalrig Road's steep brae.

Tears streaming down her face her thoughts strayed back to when her mum had purchased the pram. This steal of a purchase, according to Sandra, was made from a rather snooty lady in Prospect Bank, no less. Sandra had then gone on to elaborate, to the decidedly disinterested Kitty, that now they were going up in the world – especially now that Kitty was employed in a 'salaried' position – the new baby should benefit by having the best. Evidently a Silver Cross pram, the type favoured by royalty no less, would signal to the neighbours that the expected baby was extra special.

A protesting cry from Rosebud brought Kitty's reminiscing to an abrupt halt. Fishing in her pocket she pulled out a dummy-tit that she cleaned by sucking it in her own mouth before leaning forward and pushing into the baby's mouth.

The dummy-tit did soothe and placate Rosebud but it also brought home to Kitty just what a support system they had left behind in Ferrier Street. Hadn't it been the jovial, rotund Mrs Grant next door who had said to Kitty when she was trying to get Rosebud to stop her eternal whining to go out and buy a soother? 'Sure, lassie,' she had said, taking Rosebud from Kitty and pushing the child's face into her ample bosom, 'bairns should be snuggled into their mammy's breast and they don't always suck on the nipple for food. Naw, naw, lots of the time they just run their wee tongues round it and it comforts them. They like to know that they're with their mammy and when they get hungry the milk bar is available and within sooking distance.' Mrs Grant had lifted Rosebud's face up to her own and she crooned to her before she added, 'So, Kitty, this wee mite has no mammy to comfort her so away you run over the road to Johnny Aw Things' shop and get a dummy. Sure it will be a poor substitute but it's better than nothing.'

Kitty wanted to cry as she grieved for the loss of not only her mother, whose death had put her in this position, but also that of Mrs Grant and the rest of the neighbours that she had left behind. What, she wondered, would the folk at Restalrig be like? Three minutes later she would find out because there, a few steps in front of her, was her father and his cronies unloading a handcart in front of the tenement that was to be their new home.

Later that evening, once they had moved all their belongings into the new flat, Granny Jenny threw a shovel of coal on the fire and turned to speak to Kitty. 'Right,' she announced, taking a deep breath through her nose, 'that will heat the water so we can get Rosebud washed and settled.'

Kitty's disdainful response to her grandmother was to shrug. She wanted to scream, 'Granny, that little brat has only been in this world for a week and she has turned my life upside down. And why do we all in the family, except for Dad, have to dance attendance on her because she is a poor wee motherless soul? Don't you realise that my brothers and I are also motherless – and it's all because of her – so why don't you care about that!' But she stayed silent because she knew better than to take her granny on.

'Are you listening to me, Kitty?' Jenny demanded forcefully.

Kitty nodded.

'Good. Now as to getting on with the tea' – Jenny pursed her lips before continuing – 'no time for cooking now, so put wee Rosebud in the pram and walk her over the road to the chippie and get . . . Here, hang on till I ask your dad if any of his mates will be staying to eat with us.'

It was nine o'clock before Kitty found herself with only sleeping Rosebud for company. Granny Jenny had left after tea to carry out her duties at the forces welcoming centre. Aunt Kate had arrived after work but she was only able to stay a couple of hours as she was on fire duty at her work. This meant that she and a number of her colleagues slept there in case the building was bombed and set alight and they would therefore be there to deal with the blaze. Dad, of course, was over in what was going to be his new watering hole, the Learig tavern, just down the road. Kitty laughed inwardly. *So with my brothers being out socialising with their pals, that leaves me the only sucker left in here – well, two if you count Rose-blooming-screaming-hungry-bud!*

Lifting the poker she stirred up the fire. As the flames leapt she looked into them to see if she could see any pictures. She remembered how her mum, Sandra, had often sat with her and they would play the game of looking for moving pictures in the louping flames. She was so engrossed in her memories that the shrill ringing of the doorbell caused her to drop the poker and jump up.

Racing out of the room and along the hallway she called out, 'I'm coming. I'm coming. For goodness sake, don't waken up baby greeting face.' Hauling open the door, Kitty was surprised to see a rather plump dyed-blonde lady standing on the doorstep. 'I'm your neighbour from next door,' the woman explained as she brushed past Kitty and walked towards the living room. 'Is your mammy in?'

Kitty did follow the lady but she did not respond.

'Hoping that I'm going to get a pal in your mum, so I am,' the woman chuckled. 'Need to get a rest from old Mrs Dickson on the ground floor. Forever going on, so she is, about people sticking to their days of the drying green – and whatever your mammy does, she shouldn't get old Mrs D's back up by either not sweeping and washing the stair properly, or even worse, forgetting to do it at all.'

The woman now took out a packet of Woodbine cigarettes

and after lighting one up for herself she offered the packet to Kitty.

Kitty laughed. 'I don't smoke and my mum used to say I never should.'

Running her tongue around the inside of her mouth the woman looked long and hard at Kitty. Eventually she made some sucking sounds before saying, '"Used to say." What do you mean by that?'

Sighing, Kitty picked up the poker and hung it back on the companion set. 'What I mean is my mum . . . is in heaven . . . went there last week, so she did.'

'I'm sorry, hen. Didnae mean to upset you.' The woman went over and started to rub Kitty's back. 'I'm Constance Sharp, but everybody calls me Connie . . .' Before Connie could go on, however, a fretful wail emanated from the bedroom. Connie's mouth dropped. 'Is that a baby you've got in there?'

Kitty shouted, 'Aye,' as she dashed into the bedroom, lifted the protesting Rosebud up and brought her into the living room.

Connie's eyes bulged and her mouth gaped. 'You have a baby?' she exclaimed.

Kitty nodded. Unaware that Connie presumed she was Rosebud's mother, she then spluttered, 'Trapped with her, so I am.'

'Where's her father?'

'You mean my dad? Well he's over in the Learig but before you meet him I think you should know he takes no responsibility for Rosebud.'

Connie's mouth gaped. She wondered if she was hearing right. *Surely,* she thought, *this lassie is no telling me that her own father is also the father of his grandchild!* She gulped and blew out her breath slowly. Things like that, she thought, might happen in Leith but never here in upmarket Restalrig. She knew she should say something of comfort to this young lassie, and in truth she wished to, but what could she say?

Rosebud was now being fed from a bottle that had been heating by the fire and as she suckled Kitty inhaled before saying, 'My mum died last week giving birth to her and all she does is cry. Know something?'

Vigorously shaking her head, Connie relaxed as warm relief washed over her.

'It's me that should be doing the wailing,' Kitty went on.

'Am I right in understanding your dad's not having anything to do with the poor wee mite?'

Kitty allowed her eyes to roll in exasperation but remained silent.

Connie was shocked. In truth she was finding it difficult to keep the conversation going and she was surprised when she heard herself ask, 'Where does your dad work?'

'Robb's Shipyards. He's employed as a plater and in his spare time he's the main shop steward.'

Raucous laughter suddenly reverberated around the room. 'Don't tell me your pig of a father is Johnny Anderson, the bane of the yard manager's life?'

Kitty nodded.

'Well if this is not a turn-up for the books! My Uncle Willie, he's one of the cops on the gates, got me a start in the stores, so he did. Good pay, better than in the canteen.'

'Women work in the shipyard itself?' Kitty huffed.

'Aye, with most of the unskilled men being away at the war, women are now being employed in the stores to hand out the spare parts and so on.'

'That must be heavy work.'

'Aye, but it seems women can now be allowed to lift out the parts that are needed but are not deft enough to do the actual fitting. Anyway,' Connie hesitated as she threw her cigarette stump into the fire, 'wasn't I on duty last week when your dad called a strike. The whole yard was out. No work being done and all for nothing really.'

'Are you saying my dad called a strike over nothing?'

Connie nodded. 'One of the wee engineering apprentices thought he would have a go at hammering out a bit of steel plate in the dinner break and all hell broke loose when he was caught. "Everybody out," your dad hollered. Then he and the yard manager got into a huddle and it was agreed, yet again, that all apprentices would be given a quick lesson on industrial relations and demarcation. The result was that within five minutes we were all back to essential war work.'

Shaking her head, Kitty said, 'Connie, if you would like a cup of tea just you make it while I put Rosebud back down.'

'Tea? That's no a nightcap; how about I go and get the leftover Christmas sherry and we have a tot?'

'Oh no. You see, I don't drink,' Kitty blustered.

'Right wee Rechabite, so you are,' Connie chortled as she playfully elbowed Kitty. 'Tell you what, you put your sister down and I'll go back ben the house and get myself a sherry then I'll make you some tea.'

Kitty had just lifted the teacup to her mouth when her dad arrived back from the pub. 'What's going on here?' he demanded.

'Dinnae fash yourself, son,' Connie said, before throwing the last of her sherry down her throat. 'The lassie and me were just getting acquainted.' She now began to sashay sensuously over to Johnny. 'And you never know your luck, big boy, I could maybe take a shine to you too.'

Johnny jumped back as fear and indignation overwhelmed him. It would have been bad enough to have been compromised by a fast piece like Connie in the yard canteen, but in your own home, that was just not on!

JOHNNY'S STORY

Johnny snorted and his thoughts strayed to his own conduct when dealing with the opposite sex. Pursing his lips and cocking his head, he reassured himself that always he treated women, no matter whom, with the utmost respect. This behaviour had been instilled into him by his mother, Jenny, from when he had been just a greenstick teenager.

His meanderings now drifted back, as they always did lately, to when he had first fancied Sandra. He was just a gawky fourteen-year-old laddie then but as he partnered her in a Strip the Willow at the church's Saturday night youth club she awakened troublesome longings within him. He grinned as he remembered how she seemed to flirt with him as she twisted and turned her way up the male line of dancers, but always coming back to swing him, until he was dizzy with lust for her.

The dance wasn't to finish until ten o'clock so Johnny had hopes of being danced off his feet several times by Sandra. His hopes, however, were dashed at nine when Sandra donned her coat. At just thirteen she was a 'stand-in mother' and therefore responsible for her two younger brothers, whom she had warned to be indoors by nine o'clock. When Johnny realised that Sandra was leaving, he ran up to her and offered to walk her home.

As they dillied and dallied along the road they spoke

about this and that and nothing in particular. They had just turned into Sandra's street when Johnny pulled up abruptly and, seeking Sandra's hand, he stuttered, 'Would you like to go to the pictures with me? What I mean is, I might be able to scrape up enough to treat us both during the week.'

Pulling her hand from his grasp, Sandra teased, 'Oh, so I'm not good enough for the extra you have to pay on a Saturday?'

'Yes. Yes. You are,' he blustered in reply, 'but it's quieter in the flicks during the week so you have more chance of getting a chummy seat.'

'A chummy seat? Oh you are a gallus one, Johnny Anderson,' she chortled, giving him a playful poke.

To add to Johnny's discomfiture his face fired.

Laughing, Sandra said, 'But ken something, Johnny, Monday is a good night for me. My aunty comes and looks after the boys then and I get to have a wee bit of time to myself.'

'Monday?' Johnny became flustered and stuttered in reply, 'Look, could you no make it any day but Monday?'

'Why?'

'Monday night's the night I go to the union meeting.'

'Oh well, if the union meeting is more important than going out with me, let's just forget it.' Sandra then tossed her head before flouncing away from him.

'Look,' Johnny hollered after her. 'The union meeting is not more important than you and it never will be. But if we are ever going to be anything to each other then we will need the union.'

'Need a trade union! And what would they be able to do for me?'

'Everything. You see, the unions will fight for better rights for the workers, like me and all the lads in the shipyards. Surely you want a better life than . . .' They had now reached the East Cromwell Street entrance to the tenement where Sandra and her family were housed. Johnny lowered his tone and indicated with a jab of his thumb to the condemned housing before adding, 'Than this.'

'You're just a snob, Johnny Anderson,' Sandra indignantly mocked. 'So you've got an inside lavvy to sit your stupid backside on – so what?' She snorted. 'That doesn't make you better than me.' Sandra then turned abruptly from him and bolted into her stair entrance.

Johnny had made to run after her but her dad was hanging out of the first-floor window and he indicated, in no uncertain manner, that Johnny had best be going. Johnny hesitated. He did so want to run after Sandra but when a pail of ice-cold water cascaded down on him, he decided it would be best to make for his own home in Ferrier Street.

The union meeting always broke up about nine o'clock on a Monday night. The older men, those who were allowed to drink alcohol, would then adjourn to the Volunteer Arms over in Leith Walk and continue with their arguments there as they swilled pints. The young lads would then make for Costa's chippie.

On the Monday night following Johnny's clumsy attempt to woo Sandra, he was the last to leave the union meeting. He was just about to run after the lads who were going to the chip shop when out of the adjacent doorway emerged Sandra.

Johnny, still seething about being doused with icy water, growled, 'And what do you want?'

'Just to say sorry about what my dad did to you,' was Sandra's contrite reply.

'Huh,' was all Johnny answered, digging his hands deep into his trouser pockets.

'Well, if that's how you feel I'd best be going.'

'Wait. Would you like to share a poke of chips with me? I'd make sure they were doused in plenty of muck sauce,' the immature Johnny wheedled.

Sandra nodded and smiled as she thought to herself, *Now why did I not realise that the dashing Johnny would think a big dollop of cheap chippie brown sauce was what he should woo me with!*

From that Monday night on they had courted and, as he matured, Johnny became more and more involved in the union – so much so that he was nicknamed 'Red Johnny'. His mission in life was to get a fairer share of the country's wealth down to the hard-pressed masses of the working class. These people, his people, laboured like slaves to create the profits – profits that were then creamed off and enjoyed by the select few in the upper class. 'Bridging the gap' was his dream and slogan.

Years later, when she was nineteen, Sandra's dad died suddenly, which brought forward Johnny and Sandra's wedding plans. Just after the funeral Johnny had taken Sandra's hand in his and said, 'Look, sweetheart, for the next couple of years or so your brothers will need you to keep looking after them. You also need a main breadwinner – a man's wage coming in. So let's solve these problems by us marrying right now and me, now a qualified plater, moving in with you.'

This news was not music to the ears of Johnny's mother, Jenny. Indeed she was striving with the help of her husband,

Donald, and daughter Kate, to save enough to buy a house in a good district in Leith. Oh yes, Jenny prayed every Sunday that God would allow her to amass enough money so she could leave Ferrier Street behind. And now what was she hearing from Johnny? Surely he was aware that she had high hopes for him and that she wished for him to go up in the world. But here he was saying that he had decided to take what she deemed to be a very backward step.

Johnny always gave his mother credit for the brave face she put on when, at the altar in South Leith church, Sandra and he pledged themselves to each other. She had even lain on a lavish family celebration tea in Ferrier Street.

As the years passed, Johnny and Sandra were blessed with children and Sandra's brothers moved on. By that time Jenny had become more like a doting, grateful mother than an awkward mother-in-law to Sandra.

When Jenny's dream of buying a house outright came to fruition she had immediately asked the landlord of her Ferrier Street home if he would allow her son to take over the tenancy.

Sandra had given Jenny what she yearned for and was never going to get from Kate – four grandchildren. Within a year of Sandra and Johnny's wedding, Bobby had arrived, followed a year later by Jack. Ten months later the apple of Sandra's eye appeared in the form of Kitty, but she was not to be last. No, three years later, just when Sandra thought that her pregnancy days – which she enjoyed – were over, darling David arrived. The family seemed complete. Then out of the blue, twelve years later . . .

Johnny realised that he should also be thinking of Rosebud as his child. Shaking his head, as if to signal that he would never get over losing Sandra, the love of his life, tears started to gush from his eyes. He felt unable to control the overwhelming grief that had overtaken him. He honestly felt he hated Rosebud because he considered her arrival into the world a poor swap for her mother leaving it. Wiping his dripping nose with the back of his hand he wondered what Robb's foreman would think of him right now. Would he really still be wary of him? Or would he see that 'Red Johnny', the blight of his life, was in fact a man of straw? That he had only been able to appear to be the hard man, the skilled negotiator, because he'd had a woman behind him who gave him the confidence to fight for what he thought was the workers' rightful due.

'Dad,' Kitty had said gently, bringing him back from his memories.

'Yes, love,' he sniffed.

'What's wrong?'

Johnny just shook his head as he thought, *Oh, Kitty, do you have to ask? Your mum was my life and it is so, so hard to go on without her.*

'Please don't cry. You see, Dad, I don't think Connie was really making a pass at you. It was her way of cheering you up.'

'She's a . . .'

'Rough diamond,' suggested Kitty, who advanced over to hug her dad and tell him how badly she felt about losing her mother. She also wished to say that she thought they should move back to Ferrier Street. These thoughts came to an abrupt end, however, when they were interrupted by the hungry, demanding wails of the week-old Rosebud, the baby who had brought such turmoil and anguish into the lives of her father and sister.

Johnny shook his head, huffed and exhaled, because these

still-fresh memories were all from a year ago. Now here he was, in 1940, still grieving for Sandra – a grief that was accentuated by the dreadful realisation that he was partly to blame for her demise. What was also swamping him right now was his belief that he was failing – not only as a father but also as chief shop steward.

2

APRIL 1941

'Will you get a move on, Kitty? We're going to be late, seriously late, for the beginning of the big picture, and believe me, the State Picture House isn't going to hold off starting the film because of your dithering.'

Kitty snorted and huffed before replying to her old school pal. 'Laura,' she began, 'unlike you I've not just got myself to think of. Don't you realise it was so good of old Mrs Dickson to agree to come up here to babysit R-r-r-rosebud? It's a struggle for the old buddy to get up here from the ground floor.'

'That right? Well let me also say I am home on compassionate leave for only a week . . .'

'Compassionate leave!' Kitty gasped. 'But there's nothing amiss with your mum and dad.'

'So my granny died again, so what? But back to what I was going to say . . . I came along here tonight to go out with you, and what do I find?'

Kitty shrugged.

'That you have turned into old Mrs Dickson.'

'What do you mean?'

'Look at you. You're seventeen and it is six o'clock at night. You've still got your hair wrapped up in dinky curlers and swathed in a turban. And for heaven's sake, take off that bloody awful cross-over overall and dump it. It does nothing for you.'

'And I suppose you think that because you've been working in Coventry that you're up sides with Ginger Rogers.'

Laura started to dance herself about the room. 'Well I do like the dancing. Have you been lately?'

'To a dance hall? Good heavens, no. The Polish refugees are here now – you know them that get the name of being the world's best lovers . . .' Kitty now sucked in her lips to give the impression of being kissed sensuously.

'Well they'll sure as hell beat the Scottish men hands down. Especially the like of wee plooky Shug McKenzie!' Laura laughed in reply.

'Oh, Laura, forget Shug and listen to what Sally Day told me.' Kitty stopped to savour the moment then quickly blurted out, 'She went to the Palais dance hall up in Fountainbridge just last week and one of them Polish refugee blokes asked to walk her home.'

'And I hope she said no.'

'No, Laura, she didn't. And see when they got to London Road Gardens he guided her on to the wooded path and then he tried . . .' Kitty gulped. 'You're never going to believe this . . . but he actually tried to . . . well, you know what. And Sally, like us, is still pure, so she got such a fright!'

'Sally Day got a fright?' Laura exclaimed with a wry chuckle. 'Come off it, Kitty. Everybody, except you, kens she's as pure as the driven slush. Besides, men trying it on is par for the course nowadays.'

Kitty gasped. 'Laura, please don't tell me that it's happened to you too.'

'Maybe aye or maybe no . . . but that's for me to know and you to wonder. But one thing's for sure, Kitty, I don't want to end up like your Aunty Kate.'

'What are you going on about? My Aunty Kate has never ever even had a boyfriend.'

'That's what I mean – when she dies they'll pin a note to her chest saying, "Returned unopened"!'

Before the girls could continue with their banter, the door opened and old Mrs Dickson hobbled in shouting, 'Nothing to worry about. It's no the White Warden – it's only me.'

'Who in the name of heaven is the White Warden?'

'He's a man who dresses up in an off-white Mackintosh raincoat before he goes stalking around Craigmillar – scares the very life out of all the young women over there, so he does.'

'Don't think a white raincoat would put the frighteners on me,' chuckled Laura.

'Laura, what frightens everybody is that he suddenly jumps out of stair doors and attempts to . . .' Kitty gulped before adding, 'Well, you know what.'

'Oh, well at least there seems to be someone trying to lift old Edinburgh out of the doldrums.'

Ignoring Laura's comment Kitty started to get herself ready. Whilst taking out her curlers and brushing her hair she tentatively began to speak to Mrs Dickson. 'I made up Rosebud's bottle, Mrs Dickson. So if she wakens, and I'm sure she won't, just let her have a sook on it. We won't be late and as there have been no air raids these last few nights I'm sure there won't be any tonight either. If there is, don't panic because no matter what, even if I'm blown to smithereens, I'll still come straight home.'

Kitty was now dressed to go out and it was then that Laura noted that she was wearing a black band on the right arm of her coat. 'Oh, Kitty,' she blurted, 'please don't tell me that your brother Bobby . . .'

'No. He's in the Merchant Navy, right enough. A Fourth Engineer now would you believe . . .' Kitty stopped chattering to lovingly stroke the band on her coat sleeve. 'But this band's for my granddad.'

'Sorry, I forgot that he was . . . and how is your granny doing?'

'It will be some time before she gets over it. You see . . . it was just so horrible. These blasted German bombers were to blame and they don't give a damn.'

'You're right there, Kitty, they don't,' Laura quietly replied.

'And see their continual air raids on the docks since they killed my granddad . . . well, they make me so nervous and frightened . . . I just couldn't bear it if anything was to happen to my brothers, Jack and Davy.' She stopped to grimace before adding, 'Or even my dad.'

Kitty's thoughts were back in November of the previous year. It was true that before then there had been some heavy air raids on Leith, and in particular the dock and shipyard areas. For a long time, she knew, everybody would remember the date 18 July 1940 when, at eight o'clock at night, two 250lb bombs and six 50lb bombs had rained down on the Victoria Docks at Portland Place. The Gerries had also plastered the surrounding areas including the coal depot and railway line at Newhaven. Kitty and her entire family however would never forget the raid of the previous week. It started at six in the morning of a bright 11 July day, when a 1,000lb bomb, the heaviest to be used against the entire city of Edinburgh, was landed beside the Albert Dock.

Her grandfather, Donald, and his lifelong friend Dodd Brown, were just coming off their Home Guard stint and were heading home when the bomb dropped. The blast blew old Dodd off his feet and he landed in the high-tide polluted water of the docks. He had only a few seconds to call out to Donald that he was being sucked under because of his army greatcoat. The heavy coat became weightier and weightier by the second as it greedily sucked in the salt water. Common sense, which had always been Donald's byword, eluded him that morning because even although Dodd had disappeared beneath the waves, Donald, without taking off his own cumbersome coat, jumped into the swirling brine in an effort to try to save his friend.

When the tide ebbed, both bodies were found within a couple of feet of each other. Everyone expected Jenny to be devastated and they were amazed and surprised when instead she said, 'I'm so pleased that they've gone on their last journey together. All their lives they've been the best of pals and helped each other through thick and thin. So . . . as much as I'm grieved to lose my Donald . . . I do understand why my darling husband tried to save his friend Dodd.'

Neither Kate, Johnny, nor Kitty were so understanding. They felt it had been foolhardy of Donald to jump in when there was no hope of even *finding* Dodd in the murky water, never mind saving him.

Three weeks after Donald and Dodd's funerals, Jenny had a sort of breakdown. She'd been so brave up until then and had urged her family to get on with their lives. 'Sad it is that your dad has gone,' she would say, 'but it's not tragic. He and Dodd had good lives and knew so many joys with their families. Tragic,' she went on, 'is the slaughter of all our young people in this blasted war.' That was all she ever said but she did ask herself, *Why, oh why, did the people of Germany put their trust in a mad man like Hitler? Why, oh why, did they blindly follow him?*

The breakdown saw Jenny retreating into herself and

she gave up everything. She even stopped trying to assist Kitty with her burdens that became heavier as each day passed.

Kitty, for her part, felt it had been bad enough to live without her mother, but now that she had also lost the support of her grandparents, life was becoming intolerable. To add to all her worries she felt that her inexperience in the art of cooking was adding to her problems. How was she going to satisfy her ravenous brothers and father out of the paltry rations that were being allocated? It was a nightmare. However, if Kitty was being truthful, which she was reluctant to be, her Aunty Kate was the one who was most affected by the sad events that had recently befallen the family.

On the morning of her dad's accident, Kate had been jolted awake by the wails of the sirens. 'Not another blooming air raid,' she hollered, jumping out of her camp bed in the department store.

'You say something, Kate?' Gladys asked, stifling a yawn.

'Yes, Gladys, it sounds as if we're under attack and I don't mean from our male colleagues who always expect us to be up before them and making their tea and toast.'

'Germans? Don't be daft, Kate, it's just coming up six o'clock in the morning!'

'Maybe so but these wails you hear are us being told to get to our fire stations.'

An hour later, after they had listened to the docks being bombed and blasted, they sighed with relief. The department store had not been subjected to a direct hit by any bombs or incendiaries.

By eight o'clock all had gone quiet and the fire duty team got themselves out of the store; they were heading home when one of the dock area policemen called out to Kate.

The constable had begun by saying how sorry he was but it looked as if her father had been drowned. Whatever he said after that failed to register with her. All she had taken in was that her beloved father, the only man in her life since Hugh, was now deceased. The manner in which he had been killed was of no importance to her. All that mattered to her was that he was dead. Her darling daddy was no more.

Through her daze she knew she must pull herself together because she was the one who would need to break the news to her mother. It had only been after the last air raid, when people were killed or injured, that Jenny had said how lucky the family had been – not one of them had received as much as a scratch. Kate's thoughts now became fully consumed by her mother and father. She had always thought that if Hugh had survived and they had wed, their marriage would have been like her mum and dad's. It wasn't that they never quarrelled – they did, and how – but they never went to sleep without kissing each other goodnight.

Kate had been amazed when Jenny took the news about the death of Donald, her husband, in her stride. She appeared so strong and, at first, it was she who held the family together. This mystified Kate because her own grief was such that she was unable to hold up anyone, even herself. She also noted that her brother, Red Johnny, hadn't crumbled the way she had. Perhaps with their dad's demise coming so soon after Sandra's, Johnny was now past caring.

The night after her dad's accident, Kate was due to be on fire duty again. Her first response was to ignore this commitment but Jenny insisted that the family had to go on and do their duty. 'There is no other way, Kate,' she had emphasised. 'Dad wouldn't want us to let others down. Fires may have to be put out. Women, and more importantly, bairns rescued.'

When she entered the locked-up building by the back door a man who she reckoned was ages with herself came forward and offered her his hand.

'Sorry, very sorry about your father, Miss Anderson,' he said in broken English.

Holding back surging tears, Kate nodded as she recognised the man as Hans Busek, who had come to work as a porter in the store six months before. All she knew about him was that he was Polish. According to the shop gossip he had been a native of Warsaw. It was also said that he had escaped the German occupation of his homeland by stowing away in a Port of Gdansk fishing boat.

'Can I do anything for you?'

Kate shook her head but she did manage to mumble, 'Thank you so much, Mr Busek.'

Quite suddenly Kate found herself then thinking that there was a refinement about Hans. She also acknowledged that he was very polite and worked very hard, but always he kept his distance from staff and customers alike. Giving further thought to Hans, she also admitted that he appeared to live in a world of his own which he did not wish to share with anyone. This being the case, it was such a surprise to Kate that he had hung about waiting for her to come into the building that first evening after her dad's accident. Reluctantly she admitted to herself that until tonight she hadn't even given the man a second thought, and yet he was concerned enough about her to offer his condolences.

Being the senior employee on duty, it was Kate's responsibility to inspect and ensure that all was ready in case of an attack. She had just finished checking that all doors and passageways were free from obstructions and that all the pails were filled with either water or sand when she once again came upon Hans filling a kettle in the staff-room.

Wearily dropping herself down on a dining chair, she decided that she had to speak to someone, it didn't matter who. What did matter was that they would engage her in a conversation that had nothing at all to do with the war or the untimely death of her father.

'You're making some tea, Mr Busek?'

Hans turned, and for the first time that she could remember, he smiled at her – a radiant smile that completely changed his expressionless face, turning it into a warm and friendly, caring countenance.

Kate's elbows were now resting on the staff dining table and Hans set down a cup of hot weak tea in front of her. 'Thank you, Mr Busek,' she managed to mumble.

'No trouble, Miss Anderson,' he replied, holding out his hand to her. 'And it would please me if you would call me Hans.'

Gripping his outstretched hand she nodded. 'Nonetheless' – she swallowed and paused before adding – 'when others are about in the store we must address each other formally. You see,' she hesitated again before whispering, 'Hans, this superior Leith Provident Department Store has its standards and we must be seen to be keeping them – especially as this blasted war is changing everything.'

He nodded, stepped back and withdrew quickly into himself again.

Kate knew she had offended him and she wished she could take back her words but he had lifted up his cup of tea and left the staffroom. All she heard was the adjacent door of the cubbyhole open. She knew he would now be sitting on an upturned packing case in the large windowless cupboard where the manual staff took their breaks.

The shipyard where Johnny worked was owned and run by the Robb family. It was a compound of mismatched buildings situated in the docks area of Leith and was encircled by the tidal waters of the Firth of Forth.

To enter the yard at the Portland Place entrance, one of the two larger access portals, you had to be admitted by a police constable. The constabulary's job was to ensure that no unauthorised person gained entrance to the yards and dock area. This task at the start and finish of the shifts was a sheer impossibility. Thousands of men, who were employed on an hourly basis, would stampede at the start of their shift to get to the 'clocking-in' area on time. If they were as little as a minute or two late then they could see their wages docked by a quarter of an hour – and most men needed every penny to support either their families, the street bookies or their drinking habits.

The Dock Police Officers, who operated out of a good-sized wooden shed, would, if it was in their interest, turn a blind eye to a privileged few of the dockers and stevedores who always seemed to be snaffling out food and alcohol that had 'accidentally' fallen off the back of lorries. It wasn't really an uncontrollable black-market affair. In the main it was just that some of the men couldn't resist the temptation to make life easier for their families – and really what else can you do with an accidentally torn sack of sugar and a couple of bashed tins of New Zealand butter other than to divide it up amongst the men unloading the ship?

On the morning of the raid that cost Donald his life, Johnny was on the early shift, starting at seven o'clock. At 6.55 a.m. precisely he and a group of about twenty other trotting mates approached the entrance gates to the docks and were about to push past the police box when the elderly cop called out to Johnny.

'Sorry, Hamish,' Johnny blustered, 'but I'm in a hurry. It's nearly clocking-in time. But I promise that I'll catch you later, mate.'

'Aye, son, it is nearly seven,' Hamish replied, 'but clocking in is no your priority the day.' Hamish now beckoned to Johnny before adding, 'Come in here, Johnny lad, I need to . . .'

'Surely you're no going to inspect my piece box? You did that last week when I was going out and all you found was a crumb of cheese that wouldn't have satisfied a wee moose.'

By now Hamish was out of his police office, and when he pulled on Johnny's coat sleeve Johnny drew up abruptly.

'What is it? I mean the all-clear has just sounded so I just have to get into our workshop and see that all's well.'

'You're right there, Johnny lad, but . . .' Hamish now ushered Johnny into the shed, and as he pushed him down onto a stool Johnny knew something was amiss.

Everyone, including Hamish, the police officer who imparted the dreadful news to Johnny about his dad's demise, was surprised at how well Johnny coped. Johnny and Donald had had a good relationship, and Johnny knew that a lot of the important things he knew about life, and living it well, he had learned from his dad. Johnny accepted that not having his dad's tuition and advice on tap would be a great loss to him. He was truly sorry about Donald's death, but when the worst thing in life has already happened to you, as it had to Johnny when Sandra had passed over, everything else, in time, becomes bearable.

A week after Donald's funeral, the yard manager, Frank Tonner, who felt he was being driven to distraction by Johnny and his outrageous demands, began to think about ways of controlling Johnny. The wily old fox, who had years of experience of the yard's politics, started to consider just what he could do to rein Johnny in. Whilst he was deliberating this problem, Johnny, out of the blue, called another stoppage over demarcation. This situation called for management and union representatives to meet as a matter of urgency.

Now one of the deputy managers was a man called Jock Weldon, whose grandparents had come to settle in Leith at the time of the Irish potato disaster. Like Johnny, Jock wished to see the lot of the working man improved. Nevertheless, unlike Johnny, he always put the interests of his family first. In all his industrial-relations dealings he would support reasonable deals for the men on the shop floor. But, if it came to head-to-head confrontation between the trade unions and the management, he would shy away. He just wasn't into wildcat strikes that ended up with less or no pay at the end of the week for the men on the shop floor, nor was he into union bashing.

At the start of the present pressing negotiations Frank decided to sit back and allow Jock to put across the management's point of view. As always, the management's chief spokesman, in this case Jock, pointed out that there was a war on and the common enemy was Germany – not, as in this case, some silly wee apprentice painter mucking about in the turner's shop in the dinner break. Johnny conceded with a nod. Frank began to relax. What he was seeing was that Jock, a trade unionist but also management, was a man who could do business with Johnny Anderson. He decided there and then to give Jock the opportunity to go further in playing the management role. He knew that this was a gamble, as Jock was a member of a trade union and it might be against his socialist principles to completely abandon his fellow trade unionists.

What Frank wished to happen was that the shop stewards, especially Johnny, would feel that in Jock they had a man in management whom they could work with and trust. The other bonus was that management would also have an appointed representative in Jock who would work hard in their interests too.

Within fifteen minutes, Jock had managed to do a miracle in 'shop-floor bargaining', with Johnny agreeing to call off the strike. Subtle Jock knew that Johnny had to keep face by taking something back to the men. This something turned out to be that if Johnny did agree to call off the strike, Jock would promise to have consideration given to the management getting the shipwrights to knock up cubicle lavatory facilities with lockable doors. Up until that moment all the men had were places in the open air behind their work stations. To add to the indignity the lavatory facilities were long wooden planks with six 'bum' holes drilled into them. This meant six men, with pressing engagements, could be sitting in a row chatting to each other as they communed with nature and allowed their excess wind to break free.

The morning after the deal was struck, Jock was surprised when he was invited up into the boardroom. As he sat drinking tea from a china cup and nibbling a Rich Tea biscuit, he accepted that he had not been summoned to be sacked – far from it. Instead it seemed Frank, the yard manager, had managed to convince the board that from now on Jock was the one who should be delegated to deal with all industrial-relations matters that arose within the yard – especially if Johnny Anderson, a man Jock respected and admired, was the mouthpiece.

*

Kitty was still recounting the reminiscences of what had happened to the family in the aftermath of her grandfather's death to Laura when the bus they were travelling on turned off Great Junction Street and into Bonnington Road. Immediately both girls jumped up and alighted from the bus as soon as it drew up at the official stop. They then literally sprinted back along Great Junction Street. This haste was not because there were bombs falling from the sky on top of them, nor was there a fire anywhere. No, it was so that they could catch the start of the big picture being shown in the State cinema.

'You are sure,' Laura gasped, 'that it is *The Private Life of Henry VIII* that's showing tonight? My mum says it was on a year ago.'

'That's right, but it is so good they are showing it again. And if Connie is to be believed Charles Laughton is just wonderful in the part of the king.'

The lassies were fully engrossed in the film, which had just got to the part where Anne Boleyn was about to have her head parted from her neck, when the dreaded wail of the sirens sounded.

'W-w-w-what will we do?' Laura stuttered.

Suddenly a voice boomed out from the front of the auditorium. 'As there is now an air raid being carried out, anyone wishing to leave the cinema should do so quietly as those remaining do not wish to have their attention distracted.'

Suddenly Laura found herself being yanked out of her seat. 'Come on,' hissed Kitty. 'Let's go. Old Mrs Dickson and Rosebud . . . what I mean is they'll be trapped up the stair. Oh dear, they won't be able to get themselves out and down into the shelter.' As she scurried off, Kitty wailed, 'How the devil will I live with myself if Rosebud is blown to bits?'

The two girls were now racing along Great Junction Street when through gasps Laura managed to splutter, 'Why are we doing a Powderhall sprint for someone you say you hate?'

Kitty drew up abruptly, for she now needed to cross over Constitution Street and a racing fire engine was about to block the path in front of her.

'What now?' asked Laura.

Snorting and gasping, Kitty replied, 'We'll have to run all the way home because the buses stop when bombs are falling. You just have no idea how bad things are here in Edinburgh. Never know when the planes are coming and what they are going to drop on you. Honestly, Laura, people have been killed here . . . and not just my granddad.'

Laura let out a derisive cackle. 'Kitty, believe me, you're living in a protected zone here compared to Coventry!'

'Aye, that'll be right.'

Kitty had just finished speaking when Laura grabbed hold of her arm and pulled her around to face her full-on.

'Oh, Kitty, I couldn't take it any more. I thought I was living on borrowed time. Every night we had to endure wave after wave of bombers. Deafening noises – not only of the bombs exploding, buildings collapsing, glass shattering, fire engines howling, and ambulances speeding, but of people weeping and wailing, buried in rubble, yet still crying out for help. It got so bad that I spent my time just waiting to be pulverised. And so . . . last week I decided that if I was going to be blown to smithereens I wanted it to happen at home beside my ain folk.'

'You're home for good?' Kitty almost sang. Laura nodded. Kitty, somewhat bewildered, went on, 'But what about you wanting to work in a munitions factory to help the war effort?'

Laura nodded. 'Well, with my experience, and now that there is a munitions factory at Craigmillar, I can get a job there.'

The road in front of them was now clear so Kitty burst into a trot again and as Laura came alongside her she said, 'I know you won't understand, Kitty, because you have such an easy life here compared with what I had down in Coventry . . .'

'Easy life!' Kitty exploded. 'Right enough. I mean I get a long lie in bed until the back of five o'clock every morning and sometimes I'm still on my feet until ten at night. In that time I've shopped, cleaned, cooked and looked after Rosebud. It is true that I get an afternoon to myself on a Wednesday when Mrs Dickson looks after Rosebud and all I have to do in order to get that is take Mrs Dickson's and everybody else's turn of scrubbing the main entry and passageway. And see when you were saying that you thought I really hated Rosebud . . . Well now she's out of nappies it's not quite hate, just a sort of plain resentment. Believe me, she sure changed everything for me. But as I promised my dying mum that I would look after her, and I can't break that promise, I just have to get on with being saddled with her.'

Two dogfighting aircraft began to buzz above their heads and the girls jumped with fright. Kitty was the first to recover. Propelling Laura forward, she mumbled, 'And knowing my mum, I just wouldn't dare to have Rosebud join her in pieces so let's forget the aeroplanes and just keep running.'

An hour later, after Kitty had helped Mrs Dickson downstairs and into her own house, Laura and Kitty were sitting opposite each other at the kitchen table. 'Laura,' Kitty tentatively began, 'I'm pleased you've come home. I've missed you so. I need a pal. I'm surrounded here by old married women – not one of them is under twenty-seven.' Kitty was now looking down sadly at her work-worn hands.

'Are you saying, Kitty, that the silver lining your granny always talks about is that with me coming home from Coventry you and I can be young and carefree again?'

'Don't know about carefree,' Kitty replied dolefully as she slipped her hand towards Laura, who covered it with hers, 'but if we are going to go out of this life early, we most certainly will go out singing and dancing. Welcome home, Laura.' Kitty then inhaled and hunched her shoulders, before leaning into Laura and whispering, 'But do tell me about . . . what I mean is, see when you were going on about . . . well, you know what . . . was all that just bluster . . . What I am trying to ask is are you still able to be married in white?'

Laura started to giggle. 'Well, mainly white with maybe a couple of very tiny blue bows on the side.'

Both girls suddenly jumped apart when they heard the outside door open and someone call, 'Cooee, it's only me.'

Laura made a grab for Kitty's hand. 'Who's me?'

Before Kitty could answer Connie entered with a covered bowl in her hand. On seeing Laura she swiftly about-turned and was about to leave when Kitty called out, 'It's fine, Connie. It's just my pal Laura who's done a runner from Coventry.'

Connie turned back and squinted at Laura. Grinning, she laid the bowl down on the table. 'Sorry about that, Laura love, but I have to be so careful.'

'About what?'

Kitty had now stretched over and lifted the bowl and when she took the cover off she squealed with delight. 'Oh, it's full of butter. Quick, Laura, get the bread out of the bin and start toasting it. Oh, there's nothing in the world that tastes as good as hot buttered toast when you're hungry.'

'Maybe so,' said Laura. 'But that bowl is holding at least two months' ration for your entire family! And where exactly did it come from?'

Closing the door, Connie looked about the kitchen. She seemed to be checking that there was no one else in the room. Satisfied that they were not being spied upon, she whispered to Laura, 'It came from New Zealand and it should have made its way to the cold store in Tower Place, but it couldn't find its way there in the blackout. Luckily my Uncle Hamish – he's the policeman on the dock gate – found it, and as he quite rightly says, we must waste nothing now we are at war, so he sneaked it to me on my way out.'

Looking directly at Kitty with an accusing scowl Laura announced, 'That's dealing in the black market.'

'No it's no,' responded Connie. 'No money changed hands and if Uncle Hamish hadn't rescued that tin and its pal they would have been washed into the water. And would that not have been a shocking waste?'

The tea was now made, the three slices of bread toasted and Kitty was already slapping them with lashings of butter when Connie pulled out a chair and pushed Laura down on it. 'Here, Laura, just eat and drink, and if your conscience is bothering you that much, turn Roman Catholic and confess it! But right now let's just enjoy ourselves.'

The aroma of the hot toast was now circulating the kitchen and as it wafted up Laura's nose she replied hesitantly, 'All right, but just a little slice then. And I'm only relenting because I don't wish to appear to be holier than you two.'

3

JANUARY 1942

Johnny Anderson and Jock Weldon had decided to have a New Year pint together and in a pub that wasn't a favourite of the men from the shipyards. Everybody knew that Johnny and Jock now had a good working relationship but, as they were supposed to be representing opposite sides when negotiating the yards' industrial relationships, it wasn't in Johnny's interest, as he thought, to be seen to be in the management's pocket.

The Links Tavern, a men-only bar, situated next to Noble's the Chemist at the foot of Restalrig Road, was their secret choice of venue. This pub was mainly frequented by white-collar and artisan workers, which meant you could have an uninterrupted, discreet discussion in peace and quiet – just what Johnny and Jock needed.

Once they were seated in a booth, Jock was the first to lift his pint and, as he winked and cocked his head towards Johnny, he said, 'Here's tae us, Johnny lad.'

'Aye,' replied Johnny, lifting his glass to take a gulp. 'Here's wishing you all the best for 1942, Jock. And I'm damned sure now that America's in the war we might get the victory we need – quicker.'

Jock nodded. 'Talking of America, Johnny, we still have to refit four of our share of the fifty Great War destroyers they gave us.'

'Gave us?' exploded Johnny. 'Naw. Naw, they gave us bugger all – they're only on "lease lend". See when the blasted war is over we'll hae to pay for them.' A derisive

76

chuckle escaped Johnny before he continued. 'Can you actually believe that our government has agreed to pay them – stump up good money – for ships that they would have had to send to the breaker yards?'

'Aye, but admit it, Johnny, getting them sorted out and action-ready has helped the sea battles and' – Jock now stopped to wipe the beer froth from his mouth – 'kept quite a few of your men in overtime.'

'True, but don't forget that the most important work has been the building and launching of the new ships like the prefabricated frigates, the cheap and quick-to-build nasty corvettes . . .'

Jock nodded before butting in with, 'And we couldn't have built so many if we'd not had the structural steelwork done by engineering firms all over the country. A real British team effort it has been.'

'Aye, and it's the team effort of us all paying the extortionate higher income tax on our wages that is helping finance the blooming conflict.'

'True, Johnny, but you get your wee certificate to say that they will pay you back with interest after it's all over.'

'Interest when it's all over? Try telling that to my Kitty, who is forever begging for a rise in the housekeeping. See since that Laura came back . . .'

As the glow emanating from the fire lessened, Laura was finding it difficult to see the pages of the Littlewoods Home catalogue. 'Look, Kitty, if you want me to buy something from this book then you're going to have to light the gaslight.'

'I will once I've drawn the blackouts. My dad will go daft if I get another warning from the air-raid wardens.'

'Honestly, Kitty, I think that young warden keeps coming up here to say there's a light showing because he fancies you.'

'That right? Well he's in for a dizzy. Here, Laura,' Kitty said, 'Connie was saying I should ask you to take the catalogue into the factory as I might get some orders from the lassies you work with.'

'Could do, but you'd have to sell them some clothing coupons first.'

'Talking of selling coupons, what's the going rate?'

'Shilling each. And, Kitty, I wish I had a hundred.'

'And what would you do with a hundred?'

'Sell some, and with the money I make I'd get myself all toshed up for the Yanks coming.'

'Connie was telling me that she'd heard they'll be here next week.' Kitty made a loud slurping sound before adding, 'And she also said that they are overpaid, over-sexed and God help some stupid lassies when they get over here.' She paused. 'Mind you, none of that will make any difference to me.'

'Why not? You'll soon be eighteen.'

'Aye and I'm still saddled with a snotty-nosed three-year-old, who's going on ninety, dragging at my skirts. Besides, my dad would go apoplectic if I was to walk off with a GI.'

'Kitty, you have to tell him that you're entitled to a life of your own.'

'Can't do that – unless of course I want to end that life of my own.'

'Talking of ending a life – wait till I tell you about what has happened at my work.'

The curtains were now drawn and Kitty had added some railway sleeper logs to the fire. Sitting down she pulled Rosebud on to her knee before she said, 'Right, we're all blacked out and these "found" logs might stink but they'll at least keep us warm. Right, Laura, it's time to dish the dirt.'

'Well,' Laura began slowly as she savoured the moment, 'it seems, no it is a fact, that a young lassie was going round the doors in Craigmillar asking questions about what was going on in the munitions factory.'

'Scots lassie?'

'No, she had an Irish accent or so they say. But back to the story . . . Anyway one of the things they are good at in Craigmillar is sticking the gither. You know, no rising to the bait and certainly no giving anybody sneaking about any information. Anyway, one old ex-army smart alec phoned the polis and the lassie was arrested.'

'Arrested for asking questions?'

'Aye, turns out she was a German spy – and you know how we've been told that loose talk costs lives. Anyway she's gone and she'll never be heard of again because they put her up against a wall and shot her.'

'Shot her – without her being found guilty at a trial?'

'Seems that if you're a spy you're not entitled to appear in court and have your say. Mind you they didn't shoot her quick enough because she obviously got some news about the factory through to the Germans.'

'She did?'

'Kitty, surely you've worked it out that that was why they pasted Craigmillar last week. Folk were killed and injured.' Laura sighed before adding, 'But thank God they missed the factory so it's on with the war work.'

Before Laura could expand on her story any further, Connie came in. 'Any chance of a cuppa?'

'Aye,' replied Kitty, going through to the kitchen.

'And I don't suppose you've any of your homemade shortbread left?'

'Connie, get real. I know you gave me half a tin of lost New Zealand butter to make it but you're forgetting I have two brothers and a dad that are forever famished and . . .'

'It was delicious,' Connie purred. 'Look, as I've still got some butter left, tell me again how you made it.'

'I just went into Brown's the victuals dealer and asked him for two pounds of his shortbread mixture. He makes it up himself with plain flour and something else like semolina or cornflour, then all you have to do is just rub in some strayed butter, stir in some mislaid sugar and bake it in a slow oven.'

'See this war and all the rationing . . . it's no joke,' Connie huffed. 'Three days ago I queued for two hours at the offal butcher in the Kirkgate and by the time I got served there was no liver left. Had to settle for a sheep's tongue, so I did.'

'Aye, Connie, but you do so much better than most of us.'

'What makes you think that, Kitty?' Connie snorted before lighting up a cigarette.

'Well it's a funny week that you don't get a share of something that has miraculously fallen, once again, off the back of a lorry in the docks.'

Connie was about to respond that Kitty also did very well out of the docks as she always shared the spoils with her. However, she decided not to have a confrontation with Kitty so she changed the subject and cooed, 'But things might be looking up with the Americans joining the war. Surely they will be able to help us sort out these heartless German submarines.' She shrugged. 'If not we'll be starved into surrendering.'

'Here, Connie,' Laura began, 'see before you came in we

were just saying that when the Americans come they will be loaded up with . . .'

Before the ladies' conversation could continue, Jack, David and Johnny came into the room.

'Kitty, I'm starving, what's for tea?'

'Davy, you're always hungry,' replied Kitty.

'So he is,' Jack laughed as he ruffled Davy's hair.

'Well if you have to know it's the hough shop's ham ribs. Delicious they are and you're getting big dollops of mashed tatties and savoy cabbage to go with them.'

By now Connie had sidled over to Johnny. 'Sobered up, are you?' she crooned.

'What do you mean, sobered up? I never drink myself under the table.'

'That right? Well let me tell you, you might not have landed under the table on Hogmanay, but you did land—'

Before Connie could go on Johnny slapped his hand over her mouth and he hoarsely whispered in her ear, 'Don't say another word, Connie. What I mean is don't push your luck.'

Whilst Kitty busied herself with dishing up the tea, Johnny escorted Connie to the front door and as he closed it firmly on her his thoughts went back to Hogmanay.

Grudgingly he admitted he had been what you would call 'merry' when he came home from the Learig pub on Hogmanay, but he was in no way out of control. It was only when Connie offered him what he thought was a glass of sherry that things started to go . . . He swallowed hard. He really didn't want to think about what happened after he had quickly downed three double twelve-year-old whiskies – and contraband whisky at that, which, he later learned, was part of a consignment that should have ended up in

America. How it somehow managed to get itself lost in Leith Docks would always be a mystery to him. And what was even more confusing was how that bottle he had imbibed from, and two others, ended up under Connie's sink.

Reluctantly he recalled that he had just swallowed the third glass and was looking for a fourth when Connie had said that if he would chum her across the landing and into her house she would fish out another bottle for him that was bunked behind the soap powder.

What happened next he was not sure about but what he did know was he had passed out and on awakening in the early hours of the morning, not only was he in Connie's double bed, but so was she! Johnny gulped again as he admitted that it was not being in Connie's bed that had unnerved him, because he knew he was so drunk he was incapable of doing anything. The real problem was that he remembered just how much he wanted to lie there and cuddle in like he used to do with Sandra. The bed felt so cosy and it smelled so fresh and as he looked over at Connie he began to see her in a different light . . . She really was quite lovely and, as her hair tumbled around her head, he had a desire to stroke it, to bury his nose in it, to allow the scent of her shampoo to intoxicate him. These desires were quickly extinguished when a sense of guilt and indecency overwhelmed him and he slunk out of the bed, picked up his trousers and shirt off the floor and fled back to his own home. He had just got safely back into his own house when he accepted that the deathbed promises he had made to Sandra were starting to . . .

Johnny was rudely brought back into the present when Kitty screamed. 'Dad, Dad, listen, there's the siren and I can hear the drone of the planes already. Quick, you grab Rosebud and I'll follow you once I've filled the Thermos flask for you and made up a jam piece for her.'

Although dazed, Johnny began to organise things. Firstly he called out to Davy and Jack to follow him down the stairs. When he reached the bottom landing he banged on Mrs Dickson's door before turning the key and entering the house. The old buddy, who was profoundly deaf, was sitting by the fire drinking tea, blissfully unaware of the drama unfolding outdoors. The boys, who knew the drill, assisted their dad in hauckling the old women out of her house and into one of the two Anderson shelters on the back green.

Connie had dashed back into the house to assist Kitty with preparing the air-raid picnic and as the two of them started to flee the house they could hear explosions reverberating all around the outside area. 'That was close,' Kitty mumbled.

'Too bloody close,' was Connie's angry retort.

They had just arrived on the ground floor when Kitty turned to Connie and gasped. 'Oh, Connie, that new woman who has just come to stay opposite Mrs Dickson – will she know where to take her two lassies and herself?'

'Don't know. But let's knock her up.'

Kitty and Connie frantically banged on the door. Eventually they heard a chair being dragged along the hall and then slowly the lock turned and a wee voice cried, 'My mummy isn't well. She's lying on the floor and she's crying.'

Connie swallowed hard before saying, 'What's your name, little girl?'

'Ina and my wee sister's called Dolly.'

'Right, Ina, climb down off the chair and pull it back

from the door so that Kitty and I can come in and help your mummy.'

It seemed a long time before the chair was dragged along the floor again to allow Kitty and Connie access to the house.

They were running along the hallway when the sound of close overhead machine-gun fire startled them. Ina and Dolly immediately began to scream in unison. Connie grabbed hold of Ina and Kitty took Dolly, and they got them into the living room. Both women suddenly let go of the children and gasped when they were confronted by the children's mother lying on the bare linoleum floor in obvious distress. Alarmed, Kitty looked at Connie in the hope that she would tell her what they needed to do.

Connie, who always appeared to be so self-assured, seemed to be in an even greater panic than Kitty. Gazing down on the woman, who was obviously in need of urgent medical attention, all she could do was mumble, 'Oh. Oh. Oh.'

'Mrs . . . I don't know your name but I'm Kitty and this is Connie,' Kitty stuttered whilst grabbing hold of Connie's hand to make sure she didn't run away and leave her. 'We both live upstairs. Are you able to tell us what is wrong with you?'

'I'm not due for another month . . .' The woman gasped. 'My man, Sergeant Fred Ferguson, is in the Air Force over in Pitreavie. No due leave until the weekend.'

'And what's your name?' Kitty pleaded.

'D-o-o-o-r-a . . .' was the whimpered, stuttered reply.

Overwhelmed by anxiety, Connie gulped before wriggling free from Kitty's grip. Leaning backwards she then murmured, 'Kitty, I don't . . . No, I just don't . . .'

'Don't what?' Kitty hissed through gritted teeth.

'Know how babies get themselves . . . born.'

'But you must have some experience.'

'No, I haven't. You see, the only birth I was ever at was my own!'

Kitty's instinct was now to rise up off the floor and flee down Restalrig Road and get a midwife to come up and deliver the baby. But just then the tenement was shaken violently by more bombs exploding. These noises were still reverberating and terrifying everybody in the room, especially the children, when directly above them pandemonium in the form of several dogfighting aeroplanes added to everybody's anxiety.

Kitty reluctantly concluded that the only thing that should be done right now was for her to grab the children and flee to the probable safety of the shelters. She was just about to carry out her plan when a shriek from Dora stopped her dead in her tracks. It was then Kitty heard Connie say, 'Come on, Kitty, we can't leave her so we will just have to roll up our sleeves and do what we can.'

All Kitty could say in reply was to mumble, 'B-b-b-b-b-b,' until Connie slapped her hard on the back. 'Your mother had children so you must have an idea of how they get themselves into this world. And I'm told that, nowadays, you get a lesson on it before you leave school.'

'A lesson on it before you leave school, Connie?' Kitty sniggered. 'Well let me tell you, the dried-up old spinster of a teacher who took the lesson began by saying, "When you bath a baby the two things that you must have are a bath and a baby!" And as to her knowing anything about the facts of life . . . it was all a mystery to her and always would be!'

'Oh,' was all Connie could say as Dora let out another howl.

Kitty's eyes were now bulging and her head was rocking slowly from side to side. She wanted to shout that the only birth she had anything to do with, forby her own, was Rosebud's. Then a supposedly fully trained midwife had made such a mess of bringing her into the world that her mother had bled to death. Thinking of her mother and how she had been so badly let down had Kitty resolve there and then that, ignorant as she was, she could not leave this woman and therefore she would have to offer her any assistance she could.

Springing immediately into action, Kitty firstly ordered Connie to get the kettle and pots filled with water and then to put them on the stove to boil. Kitty wasn't sure why she would need hot water but it seemed that was one of the most important things you must have when someone was in labour. She then helped Dora to get up off the floor, and with the assistance of Connie, they placed her into a big easy chair.

Dora Ferguson turned out to be a model patient but when Kitty had to kneel down in front of Dora to look between her legs she nearly fainted. There in front of her was a huge gaping hole like that of a large fish's head. Like a fish it appeared to be gulping, dilating, contracting, and then, out of the blue, the hole was filled by a round hairy ball. How on earth, she wondered, did a woman's vagina stretch to such a size, and what was the obstruction that was now filling the hole? Was it the baby's head? A long and agonising series of moans from Dora abruptly brought Kitty back from her stupefaction.

The yells had just abated when Dora gasped, 'Can you see the head?'

'Well,' replied Kitty, 'there is something there now that wasn't there before, but in this flickering gaslight . . . I'm not quite sure what it is.' She quickly looked again and now she could see that it was a small round head and that it was free to below the nose. Within seconds the whole head and neck and the top of the shoulders were clear. Instinctively Kitty knew that if she hooked her fingers under the baby's oxters she would be able to pull it completely free.

Connie started to weep when she heard the baby slip and slither its way into the world. And when the all-clear was ringing out, Kitty smacked the baby gently to make it cry. Instinctively she knew that she must now sever the umbilical cord before handing the baby to Connie. However, Connie seemed reluctant to take hold of the child so Kitty forcibly said through clenched teeth, 'Get this wee soul washed and dressed, Connie.' Swiftly turning back to Dora she asked in the same impatient, commanding voice, 'You do have some clothes ready for the baby?'

'Aye, aye, I waste nothing,' Dora stammered, 'so Dolly's baby clothes are in the bottom drawer in that chest over there. They have all been washed and ironed. And as soon as you can, Connie, let me hold her.' Exhausted, Dora then collapsed back against the cushions and surprised Kitty when she announced with a smile, 'I'm going to call her after you . . . Kitty.'

Five minutes later Connie took the new baby to Dora and as she laid the bundle into her arms she chuckled. 'I don't think the name Kitty will suit this baby.'

'And why for no? Kitty's such a lovely name.'

'Right enough it is, Dora,' laughed Connie, 'and true I've not got any experience with babies, but this wee mite has an extra bit that your lassies don't have.'

'Are you saying I've got a son?' Dora exclaimed before opening up the shawl to check for herself. 'Oh you're right and won't him being a boy not half make my Fred so happy.'

The clamour of old Mrs Dickson being brought back into the safety of her home echoed throughout the stair. On hearing it Connie rushed to the door and called out, 'Johnny, we're in here. We need some help.'

Johnny immediately left the boys to attend to Mrs Dickson and he joined Kitty and Connie. He didn't know what he expected to find in the house he had just entered but it certainly wasn't his daughter Kitty smeared with blood. 'What on earth has happened here? Were you injured in the air raid?'

Kitty chuckled. 'No, Dad. Dora here was in labour and I—'

'We,' Connie quickly corrected.

'We brought the baby into the world.'

'That's right,' crooned Dora, 'and what a girl you have in Kitty. Don't know what I would have done without her.'

Johnny nodded, then he looked expectantly about the room, but all he could see, forby the three women, were Ina and Dolly huddled together on the floor and now fast asleep.

'Where's Rosebud?' he stammered.

'With you I hope,' Kitty replied. 'Remember I told you to go and get her and take her to the shelter.'

Johnny's face drained of colour. His bottom lip began to quiver and his breath was coming in short bursts. Quickly, followed by Kitty, he dashed out of the Ferguson household and, taking the steps three at a time, he bounded up to his own front door.

As he approached the closed door he felt the hair on the back of his neck rise. It rose even further when he heard from behind the door a tearful little voice sobbing, 'Kitty, Daddy, Jack, Davy where are you all? I'm scared of the bangs.'

Turning the key in the lock Johnny pushed the door open and there stood Rosebud as he had never seen her before. Her face was awash with tears and yellow mucus was dripping from her nostrils. Intuitively he reached out to draw the distressed child into his arms and was taken aback when she shied away from him. 'I hate you, Daddy, and you too, Kitty. You left me and I was frightened for the bangs and that's why I've messed my new pyjamas.'

Kitty had pushed past her father and as she trod in Rosebud's faeces she felt sick but her need to try and comfort the little girl pushed that feeling back down before she whispered, 'Come on, dear, we're sorry that you were overlooked.'

Rosebud sniffed and panted as she blubbered, 'No, you and Daddy are not sorry! You don't like me and I don't like you.' Without warning Rosebud lifted an excreta-covered foot and kicked Kitty in the shins.

Kitty's first reaction was to smack Rosebud but Johnny had jumped in between them and, as he held Rosebud close to him, he whispered in her ear, 'It is true that I have tried not to love you . . . but when I realised that you were all alone up here when the air raid was going on . . . I knew that if anything had happened to you I could not have lived with myself.' Johnny increased his hold on Rosebud. 'I was wrong, very wrong, to never say to you that I adore you. Believe me, sweetheart, I love you just as much, if not more, than my other children.' Johnny's head was now buried in Rosebud's hair and he was weeping profusely. 'Darling,' he panted through his sobs, 'from this night on I'll spend as much time as I can with you so you'll understand that you are one of us. You always have been and I was wrong to keep you at arm's length.'

Witnessing the emotional scene between Johnny and Rosebud was just too much for Kitty and she stole away into the kitchen. Without being aware of actually doing it, she began to run some hot water into the washtub. She wasn't going to start washing clothes right now. No, she was going to do the only thing that she could for Rosebud – sponge her clean.

Connie, who had followed the family into the house, gently began to rub Johnny's back. 'Come on, my bonnie lad,' she purred. 'Pull yourself together, and to help you do that I think I just might have a wee dram left in that bottle under the sink.'

Johnny didn't wish to hurt anyone else tonight and he had an urgent desire to reply to Connie and say, *No thanks, not just now. Not for a while yet. But do keep it because as life goes on . . . well you never know.* But instead he stayed mute and then got up and joined his sons at the fireside.

By this time Kitty had taken Rosebud away from her father and had laid her gently in the warm suds she had prepared. She wanted to say to Rosebud as she washed her clean that she did care for her. Unlike her father, however, Kitty could not completely let go of the price that had had to be paid for Rosebud to be born. Right now she 'cared' for Rosebud because it was a promise she'd made to her mother. Kitty sighed, wondering, *Will I ever truly and freely love Rosebud for herself?* Reluctantly she accepted that only time knew the answer to that conundrum.

Once Rosebud was in fresh nightclothes Jack lifted her

up to sit on his knees while Davy went to spread some jam on a piece of bread for her. Emotionally drained and physically exhausted, Kitty looked at the happy trio sitting in the firelight glow. Grudgingly she admitted to herself her brothers were better people than she was. Rosebud had from the day she was born been 'one of us' to them, whereas to Kitty, poor little Rosebud was a burden she resented, yes, even now.

The sound of the outside door clicking shut caused Kitty to turn and find that Connie had left without saying goodnight. What Kitty was unaware of was that Connie just so yearned to be one of them. Ever since they had arrived she had somehow longed to be accepted as the mother figure they had lost. She had fooled herself into thinking that this family would give her the proper and decent purpose in life that she prayed for every night.

CONNIE'S STORY

Connie had been born and bred in the coal mining town of Whitburn in West Lothian. Being the third daughter of a miner was not an easy life. Poverty and deprivation stalked all miners and their families.

Often Connie would reminisce about life in what were called the miners' rows. These were rows and rows of small terraced dwelling places that were owned by the limited coal mining company. The pit was called The Lady, but in reality she was in no way a lady – she was nothing more than an unfeeling bitch. Men, some so young you could have called them children, slaved in her deep underground. Day in and day out they banged away continually to drag out the black gold, the good-quality coal. And what was their reward? Wages that were hardly above subsistence level and, for some, their further recompense would be the black lung disease, pneumoconiosis, when their lungs became filled with choking coal dust. If the afflicted miner was lucky he would be able to stay in his 'rows' house, but most workers who became disabled, gasping for breath, would find their houses removed from them, and they had to rely on charity or the council to house them and their families.

Connie gave a derisive chuckle when she recalled how her mother always proclaimed that she was pleased that she never had a son – a son whose sole purpose in life would have been to spend his life like a mole in the dark bowels of the earth. Her mother, a firebrand if ever there was one, also hated to be beholden to the pit owners, and after years of badgering the council, she was awarded a two-bedroomed house in Whitburn's Armadale Road. The house even had a bathroom – so no longer did her dad have to endure the indignity of being scrubbed clean in a tin bath in front of the living-room fire while family life went on round about him.

The miners' resilience was something Connie tried to emulate. Fondly she remembered the gala days. So vivid was her recall that she always started to tap her feet when she remembered how the annual parade was led up Main Street by the colliery pipe band, followed by the award-winning brass band. Her dad had been a trumpeter and so it was only natural that when a young lad called Mark Sharp, not a miner but a trainee painter and decorator, joined the brass band, that she was drawn to him.

The first thing that Connie noticed about Mark Sharp was his fingers. They were long and elegant, like a surgeon's fingers. There was also an air about him that marked him as different and she admitted that it was true that she was the one who had pursued him.

Gentleman that he was, he did try at first to discourage her. Unfortunately this only added to her desire to pursue him. The result was that when he finished his apprenticeship the two of them were married. Connie had dreamt about how wonderful her wedding night would be, but Mark preferred to spend the night drinking with his lifelong friend, a blond, blue-eyed chap called Jamie Oman. Mark's friendship with Jamie was so close that when he decided to move through to Glasgow, it was a trio that set up house there.

Connie had led a sheltered life as far as sex and adult relationships were concerned and it came as a shock to her that the sexual encounters that took place in her home were between Mark and Jamie, not between husband and wife. She recalled with shame just how naive she had been until she came home early one day from work to find the two men in bed. Humiliation and disgust overwhelmed her and it was then she moved into Jamie's room and he moved into Mark's. That was not the only thing she did. No, from that day on she dyed her hair blonde and flirted indiscriminately. She really became quite coquettish and ended up being the talk of the town. This wanton image that Connie had thought would provoke people into asking what was amiss with Mark only served to have people pity him for having such a fast piece for a wife.

After ten years in Glasgow, Mark announced that he was arranging an exchange with a family in Edinburgh who needed to move to Glasgow. This was a bolt from the blue to Connie but she went along with it and then, surprise, surprise, the day before the move Mark arrived home to announce he would not be moving to Edinburgh with

Connie and Jamie because he had started up a relationship with a lad ten years younger than Jamie.

Connie had spent the night consoling Jamie, who continually kept asking, 'How can he do this to me? I love him. I trusted him. What will people think of me?' Connie felt for Jamie, but hadn't she been treated even worse by Mark?

The removal truck had just left and Connie and Jamie were boarding a train for Edinburgh when Jamie grabbed her hand and kissed it. 'Sorry, love,' he blubbed, 'but I can't live without him so I'm going back to put up a fight for him.'

Whether Mark and Jamie did get back together Connie didn't know or care. What she did know was that when she arrived in Restalrig Road she found that she had a three-bedroomed house all to herself. And indeed it was to her a silver lining, because she was happy living there with no one knowing about her past.

That past did not come back to haunt her until Johnny Anderson fell down drunk and incapable on to her bed. He looked so comfortable there that she undressed him down to his long johns and climbed in beside him. Snuggling into him she felt an overwhelming sadness engulf her as she accepted that even if Johnny did recover from losing Sandra, he could never be anything to her – she was a married woman and he was strict Church of Scotland and that meant he would consider it sinful to sleep with another man's wife!

*

Ever since Jenny had sunk down into her depression she had refused to go out into the air-raid shelters when the alarm sounded. On the night that all the commotion was going on around the Restalrig area she grabbed hold of Kate's hand and dragged her under the solid oak table.

Kate was of the opinion that hiding under the table was a bad idea because, should the house be hit and the table collapse, they would be killed by the sheer weight that would descend on them.

When a bomb – meant no doubt for the docks – landed close by the house it shook the building so violently that ornaments and clocks crashed to the floor. Once the all-clear sounded, Kate emerged from under the table and began to clear up the debris.

She wasn't in the least sorry that the Whistling Boy that had stood all its life looking out from the front-room window would whistle no more. Nor could she shed a tear for the smashed Royal Doulton china cups that no one had been allowed to drink from. But when she looked at her father's granddaughter clock lying smashed beyond repair, all the pent-up emotion that she had refused to release since he had died now erupted from her. Lying across the wooden frame she wept for all she had lost, not only in this war but also in the previous one.

Jenny knelt down to console Kate. It was then she realised that she had been so wrapped up in her own grief that she hadn't been aware of the needs of others. Why hadn't she realised that Kate and Johnny would also lament the passing of her Donald, their beloved father? Instinctively she attempted to lift Kate up into her arms, and drawing in a deep breath, she vowed there and then that from this day onwards she must become the matriarch again.

The morning after the air raid that had terrified the districts of Restalrig and Craigentinny, Kitty was busy washing Rosebud's soiled clothing when Jenny walked in.

'Oh no, Granny, please don't tell me that something awful happened to you or Aunty Kate last night.'

'Not quite awful. You see, the things that were smashed are replaceable, with the exception of your granddad's clock.'

'The clock he wound up every week with the key we were never allowed to touch?'

Jenny nodded. 'Anyway, last night I decided to stop licking my wounds so I'm here to see if there is anything I could be doing for you.'

Kitty lifted her hands out of the washing tub and as she dried them on her apron she gave a little giggle. 'Well, Granny, last night's raid, which was not one of the worst to happen here, sure shook our family up. Look' – Kitty pulled out a chair so that Jenny could sit down at the table – 'just sit down and I'll tell you all about . . .'

Rosebud had now come into the kitchen and when she saw her grandmother she squealed, 'Granny, Granny, have you come to smack bad Kitty for what she did to me last night?'

Jenny turned her head towards Kitty. Her fingers then began to tap, tap, tap on the table. Kitty took this strumming as an indication that her grandmother was waiting for an explanation.

Since she was a child Kitty had known that it was not a good idea to get into her grandmother's bad books. This being so, she swallowed hard before she submissively said, 'It was just that I was so busy delivering Mrs Ferguson's baby that I forgot to check that Dad had taken Rosebud to the shelter, so . . . Oh, Granny, we never meant to leave her here all alone.'

Normally Jenny would have read the riot act to Kitty about being so careless but she looked long and hard at her granddaughter. What she saw was an overburdened eighteen-year-old who had gallantly dealt with the responsibility of the household here while she herself had wallowed in her grief.

An extremely anxious Kitty waited expectantly for the verbal storm that she knew her grandmother would unleash on her. However, she was somewhat surprised when Jenny quietly said, 'Kitty, how about I keep Rosebud overnight on Friday night so that you and your pal Laura can go out to the pictures or the dancing?'

Laura and some of her workmates had been to the Palais dance hall since the Americans had arrived, but it was Kitty's first time. To say she was filled with excited anticipation was an understatement. When they arrived, to Kitty's annoyance, Laura dragged her firstly into the ladies' powder room. Never had Kitty seen so many mirrors and she was just so thankful that she was not the poor cleaner whose job it was to keep them crystal clear.

Nose properly powdered, lipstick refreshed and not a hair out of place, they eagerly emerged into the ballroom itself. A feeling of elation overtook Kitty as Glenn Miller's 'In the Mood' rang out and reverberated around the hall. Instinctively her feet, and even her hands, started jiving in time to the beat.

All of the dancers were, like herself, intoxicated by the rhythm, which resulted in them throwing decorum to the wind. Indeed she had never seen such a display of indecent dancing as was being performed on the floor just then. Young men smartly dressed in the uniform of American soldiers were literally throwing young women through their legs and over their shoulders with breathtaking ease.

Kitty was just about to turn to Laura to ask if all American soldiers were contortionists when she was grabbed by the arm and propelled on to the dance floor. Her first words of protest to the brash young man had just left her mouth when she found herself winging her way between his legs. The twisting and curling movements resulted in Kitty's skirt landing up over her head, and her knickers and suspenders could then be viewed by those standing on the fringes.

The indecent experience should have had Kitty running out of the hall but Laura was amazed to see Kitty jive, whoop and whirl herself off the sprung floor. Obviously she had thrown caution to the wind and no longer cared one whit who was able to see her underwear. Just as the bouncers started to speak to the dancers and warn them that that sort of jiving was not allowed, the tempo of the music changed to that of a foxtrot. The young man, however, instead of releasing Kitty hung on to her and they elegantly circled the floor.

The music finished when the bandstand's revolving stage started to turn and all that could be heard was the signature tune of the orchestra that was now taking over. When the music changed to 'We'll Meet Again', Kitty was keen to stay on the floor with the pleasant young man, who told her his name was Hank Rogers, but she felt a bit put out when he then bowed to her and thanked her for the dances.

Back on the fringe, where the women waited to be asked the all-important question – 'Are you dancing?' – Kitty was surprised when a young black, very handsome American soldier cocked his head towards her and said, 'May I have the pleasure?' Now the etiquette in the dance hall was that if you refused to dance with someone then that meant you could not partner anyone else for that particular dance. If you did the man whom you had rejected could ask the bouncers to evict you from the hall. Knowing this, Kitty smiled sweetly to the young man and they took to the floor. To say that her new dance partner was charming and polite would have been an understatement. As soon as the music stopped he tucked his hand under her elbow and escorted her back to the selection area. It was then that she was accosted by Hank Rogers, the first young man she had danced with.

'You've made a fool of me,' he hissed. 'Where I come from no decent young white woman would suffer the advances of a black man.'

Kitty was incensed. 'Well, you see, I come from Leith,' she replied, 'and we accept all people and we do not judge them by their religion, nationality or colour of their skin. Believe me, we are only concerned as to whether they are decent human beings and indeed if they have good manners.' Kitty gave an exaggerated sigh before adding, 'Unfortunately, sir, because of your attitude you would certainly not be welcome where I come from.' She then pointed to the young black soldier and added, 'But he would!'

The response from Hank was not what Kitty expected and it certainly was not the gift of nylons or chocolate: it was a rather hard slap across her face. As she reeled backwards she became aware that someone had come to her rescue and that he had landed a hard punch on Hank's face. At first she thought it was the young black man who had decided to defend her but she was astonished to find her champion was none other than her brother Jack.

Before anyone could do or say anything else the bouncers

summoned the American Military Police, who were on duty at the Palais dance hall, and they soon had both the young white man and young black man in custody and very quickly they were whisked out of the hall.

'What in the name of heaven are you doing here? And why did you interfere?' Kitty demanded of Jack.

'Look, we don't live in America so we don't know what their racial tensions are about. Now get your coat on. You're leaving.'

'But I'm enjoying myself.'

'That right? Well until you are more streetwise could I suggest you just keep going to the YMCA dances in Fire Brigade Street.'

'Fire Brigade Street?'

'Aye you know, Junction Place, where there are no GIs and certainly no fights. Take a look about you, Kitty. Look at all the bottle blondes who are hoping to marry a GI and get a better life over in America. You don't need to go after that; you have a good life here – a very good life.'

Kitty was about to challenge Jack and his views when a bouncer came up. 'I trust, sir,' he said, emphasising the 'sir' to let Jack know that in no way was he suggesting that he considered Jack to be a gentleman, 'that you will be escorting the young lady out of the hall.'

'Too true I will,' was Jack's explosive reply before propelling Kitty towards the exit. Then before leaving he decided to shout back to the bouncer, 'Believe me, she's far too good for this den of iniquity.'

Kitty could only sigh. It had been some week. Firstly she was held responsible for Rosebud being abandoned, then she thought she'd done a first-class job delivering Mrs Ferguson's baby only to be told by the midwife, Joan Fowler, when she arrived the next day, that the umbilical cord had not been tied off properly. And now she was being dragged home because it would appear she was going to be blamed for a further deterioration in America's race relations.

Two hours later a fuming Kitty was sitting in an easy chair. The night that she thought was going to be just so magical had turned into a nightmare, ending as it did with her being shoved on to a bus and told by an officious Jack to go straight home. He, of course, was not going to have his Friday night capers curtailed. The last Kitty saw of Jack was him, accompanied by three mates, heading towards the Royal Mile. No doubt they would be going down Niddry Street to St Cecelia's Halls, better known as the Excelsior Ballroom. This little backwater off the Royal Mile wasn't as well known as the main dance hall in Edinburgh – the Palais – and therefore fewer American servicemen strayed there. So, to the delight of the locals, no chocolate-waving GI would be waltzing all the best-looking ladies around the dance floor.

Kitty felt completely humiliated at being treated like a naughty child by her brother. After all, Jack was only a year older than herself, and in her opinion less mature. As her vexation grew she inhaled deeply to calm her chagrin but when the outside door opened she shouted, 'I hope that is you, Davy?'

Light footsteps sounded in the hall before a female voice called, 'Sorry to disappoint you, Kitty, but I'm not Davy. And I'm surprised to find you here. I thought you were going to be out on the tiles until the wee small hours.'

'Well, Connie, it would appear that Jack was told to watch out for me. And being overzealous in carrying out his duties, he ended up with me being evicted – evicted, mind you – from the Palais.'

Connie's bawdy laughter echoed around the room. 'You've got to be joking,' she spluttered.

'Unfortunately no!' Kitty spat. 'And I would like to know who it was that put that rabid guard dog on to me.'

'Are you talking about Jack?'

'Yes. Brother Jack.'

'It was your dad. I heard him telling Jack to follow you to wherever you went and to make sure you got on a bus back home by ten thirty.'

The cushion that had been behind Kitty's back was suddenly hurtling through the air. 'Just because my dad has decided to live a monastic life doesn't mean that I should become a nun.'

'Och, get real, Kitty. Your dad is only trying to protect you.'

'Protect me? Surely you mean that he wants to make sure I will continue to be his unpaid housekeeper.'

Shaking her head, Connie responded, 'Kitty, you are lucky, very lucky, to be loved and wanted.'

No response was forthcoming from Kitty but her attention was now fully on Connie. *Funny,* she thought, *in all the time I've known her I've never heard her talk about her past life.* Kitty knew, because Connie wore an engagement and wedding ring, that at one time she must have had a husband. But where was he now? Had he died or perhaps deserted her because of her continual flirting with other men? Kitty wanted to ask Connie what had happened to her marriage but she felt in doing so she might damage her relationship with Connie – a relationship that had become so important to her.

Sensing Kitty's curiosity, Connie slowly said, 'Kitty, my dear, life can be shit. But when it is you can do one of two things – wallow in its stench or brush it off your feet and get on with your life as best as you can.'

Kitty look perplexed. 'What exactly do you mean?'

'I'm just trying to say to you that the only person who can make you happy is yourself. Believe me, Kitty, no one can make your life worth living other than yourself.'

'Did something awful happen to you?'

Connie nodded. 'It did, and when I accepted there was only me who could put it right, I did – and I've never regretted having moved in to this place with no hang-ups.'

4

OCTOBER 1943

Kitty was sitting at the table writing her weekly letter to Bobby and, as she dipped her pen into the ink bottle, she began to think about how the war had dramatically changed the lives of all those related to her and in particular the womenfolk, who were especially anxious and afraid for the men doing the actual battling.

She knew it was true that Scotland, because of her vital industries – factories, engineering, coal mines and shipbuilding – was always a target for German bombers. She grimaced as she conceded that Edinburgh, however, was not, with the exception of the dock and shipbuilding areas where her menfolk worked, as badly affected as Glasgow, Clydebank, Coventry and London. With a wry smile she also conceded that the recent air raids were now being concentrated on the cities of Glasgow, Coventry, Liverpool, Manchester and London in the vain hope that the people would be bombed into submission. This meant that Edinburgh, although still a major target in her beloved Leith area, could enjoy some nights without a bombardment.

Her musing, however, was brought to an end when Rosebud impatiently wailed, 'What are you doing?'

'Just writing a note to Bobby to say that we are all missing him and that we all hope that he will get some home leave soon.'

'Does he write back to you?'

Reluctantly, Kitty laid the pen down. She was about to

say to Rosebud that it didn't matter that Bobby very rarely wrote back to her, or anyone for that matter, but what was important was that he got letters from home, to keep his spirits up. But just then the doorbell rang.

On opening the door Kitty was alarmed when she was confronted by a telegraph boy. Thrusting the yellow envelope into Kitty's outstretched hand the young lad quickly about-turned and fled. Gazing down at the ominous telegram, Kitty experienced her thoughts tumbling into free fall. Her first instinct was to rip open the envelope to read the message. But as it was addressed to her father she could not – and dared not – open it. She was sure that the message was to say that Bobby . . .

'Oh no!' Kitty howled out aloud.

'What's wrong, Kitty? Are we in trouble?' Rosebud asked as she tugged at Kitty's skirt.

Tucking the envelope into her pocket Kitty then grabbed Rosebud's hand, before opening the door and fleeing downstairs.

Banging on the Fergusons' bottom-flat door Kitty shouted, 'Dora, Dora, I need you to look after Rosebud.'

Kitty was somewhat taken aback when the Fergusons' door opened and, instead of being confronted with her understanding friend Dora, there stood Dora's husband, Fred. 'Calm yourself, lassie,' he began. 'What a state you're in. And what is wrong exactly?'

'That's the trouble, I don't blooming know!' Fishing in her pocket Kitty dragged out the envelope. 'This came for my dad and I'm sure it's bad news about my brother Bobby. He's in the Merchant Navy on the Atlantic convoys. So you see, Mr Ferguson,' she babbled on, 'I just have to get down to Dad, so he can tell me . . . I wish I could open the blooming thing but I just can't open anything that's addressed to my father.'

Fred nodded, and by this time Dora too had come to the door. 'Off you go, Kitty, and I've told you before to bring Rosebud down here to me at any time. Sure she should be mixing and playing with other children.' Dora paused. 'Honestly, Kitty, I think her being constantly with adults is the reason that she's so lippy.'

'I am not lippy, Mummy Ferguson,' Rosebud snorted before pushing past Dora. 'And I am here to play with Ina and Dolly and not with you.'

Kitty didn't realise how fit she was until she raced from Restalrig Road to the shipyards without once having to stop to ease her laboured breathing.

On arrival at the dock gates she ignored Hamish, the duty constable, who had stuck out his arms to prevent her from entering the dock area. 'Whoa. Whoa!' he shouted. 'Where do you think you're going? And where's the fire?'

Kitty did not respond. She was completely unaware of anything going on around her, even Hamish's extended arms, which resulted in her colliding into him. She then lost her balance and crashed down on to the ground. 'Good grief, man, why did you knock me over?' she whimpered pulling herself up into a sitting position. 'Look, I just have to get to my dad, Johnny Anderson.' Slipping her hand into her pocket she brought out the envelope that was terrifying her every thought.

Hamish, who knew Kitty through Connie, bent down and picked her up. 'There, there now,' he soothed. 'Come into my office and I'll . . .' It was just then Hamish saw that one of the young apprentice lads was about to go out to the shops and he called out to him, 'Over here, son. I want you to go back into the platers' shop and get Johnny Anderson to come here to me – and *tout de suite* at that.' The boy nodded.

When Johnny took hold of the telegram, his first inclination was to throw it away. That way he wouldn't need to read what he knew would break his heart. It was Kitty's distraught pleading – 'Dad, Dad, please, please, I just have to know' – that made him realise he had no other option than to tear open the envelope.

Pulse racing, eyes brimming, Johnny swallowed hard before ripping the telegram apart. However, before he could unfold the note, Kitty tore it from his grasp. 'Dad,' she exclaimed through laboured breathing, 'it just says his ship was torpedoed in the Atlantic last week and he's missing. But we have hope because it doesn't say that he is . . .'

Collapsing down on to a chair, Johnny knew that he should say to Kitty that shipwrecked sailors could face worse fates than being killed instantly. But had he the right to terrify her so? Could he really say to her that being flung into the wild freezing waters of the Atlantic Ocean, or finding yourself adrift in a lifeboat in the open, where death stole up on you slowly, were destinies far worse? Johnny's thoughts then went to the many, too many, repaired and refitted ships that the yard had dealt with during this bloody awful war. In particular, he thought of the recent repairs they had carried out on HMS *Fame*. She had sustained unspeakable near-miss bomb damage to her side and, regrettably, a number of her young officers, who were unfortunate enough to be in the wardroom at the time, lost their lives. Young men like Bobby, with so much to live for, so much promise. *Why,* he asked himself, *are the ordinary people not able to say, 'No, our sons are no longer cannon fodder?' Why is someone in Germany not pulling the rug from under Hitler? Surely,* he continued to argue with himself, *the hearts of the mothers in Germany are as sore wrung as ours when the telegrams arrive?*

A long, long week passed ever so slowly for the family. All were in mourning for the loss of Bobby, except Kitty, who was adamant that she knew he had survived. *Somehow,* she convinced herself. *I just know that he and I are so close that if ever he was to pass from this world he would get a message to me.*

The following Monday morning found Kate in the staff-room for her tea break. However, she was not drinking her tea; she just sat staring into space whilst continually turning and twisting a key in her hand. Gently yet firmly a hand covered hers and this action brought her back to reality.

'Sorry, Mr Busek,' she managed to stammer through her tears. 'Was there something you wished to ask me?'

'Yes,' Hans replied, whilst he expertly plucked the key from her hand. 'What is this key and why do you keep rolling it through your fingers?'

'It's the key for a granddaughter clock.'

'I already know that. And I have also noted that you have never let go of it since the—'

'Air raid, when my father's clock, his pride and joy that he wound up and dusted every Sunday, was smashed to pieces when a bomb exploded on the Links.' Kate paused to compose herself. 'You see, Mr Busek, the reverberation of the blast shook our house so violently that the clock . . . crashed to the floor.'

Gushing tears were now running down Kate's face, and

Hans, handkerchief in hand, bent forward and tenderly wiped some of them away. 'Now, now,' he crooned, 'why didn't you have the clock repaired?'

'Don't be stupid, man,' Kate blurted.

Embarrassed by Kate's strident rebuke, Hans stepped back from her.

Ignorant of the distress that she had caused Hans she went on, 'I would have had it restored but it was irreparable – do you hear – irreparable! Oh, why can't you understand that all I could do was to pick up the bits and pieces and roll them all together in a bed sheet?'

'That bad, was it?' Hans replied pensively, before quickly adding, 'but somehow I think that you kept all of the parts?'

Kate nodded. 'Couldn't part with them – no – I just couldn't. So I stored them in a large suitcase under my bed.'

'Good,' Hans enthused. 'Now if you will permit me I will come over to your house and look at the clock. It just might be that I will be able to do something with it.'

'You?' Kate rudely exclaimed. 'And what would you know about repairing clocks?'

'Everything,' was Hans's emphatic reply. 'You see, Miss Anderson, back in Poland I was a master watch- and clockmaker. Then ...' Hans drew himself further away from Kate before he continued: 'The war came, and in an air raid, I lost everything dear to me.' Hans was now the one who was lost in a world of his own as he admitted to himself that, yes, it was all gone – smashed to smithereens – never to be put back together again ...

Ghostly silence filled the room and a few minutes ticked slowly by whilst Hans was lost in his memories. Memories that were so painful to him that he wished he could suppress them forever.

Without warning Hans eventually clapped his hands and said, 'Right, we have had enough of the sadness today. The past is past and we must work and prepare for a better future. Never give up hope about that, Miss Anderson. No. You see I know that no matter how black and thick the clouds are the sun always manages to struggle back through again – it has for me and I pray that it will do so for you too.'

Kate sniffed before she allowed a smile to lighten her face. 'Hans,' she whispered as she hoped that the smile signalled to him that she now valued him as a friend, 'you are so like my niece, Kitty. She is the one who is so sure that my nephew, Bobby, will somehow have survived.'

Hans grinned before nodding a salute to her, then very quickly he lifted up his mug of steaming tea and slunk off to his cupboard under the stairs.

The news about Bobby's ship had cast a gloom over Johnny Anderson's household. Even Kitty, who refused to be anything but hopeful, was affected by the report and she had fallen behind with her household chores.

Looking out from the kitchen window, Kitty could see that the sun was shining brightly and a light breeze was blowing. It was, as her grandmother Jenny would say, 'A fine drying day.' Kitty noted that Mrs Dickson had seen the advantages of the weather. Already the old woman had washing hung up and dancing on the ropes in the back green. This sight spurred Kitty into action and an hour later she had a basket full of freshly laundered clothes ready for the outside clothes line.

Balancing the full wash basket on her right hip, and keeping hold of a truculent Rosebud with the other hand, she had just struggled down the stair and was turning to go out of the back door when the front door opened. Sensing the draught, Kitty turned to see who had come in. Immediately she let go of Rosebud's hand and, without realising it, she allowed the wash basket to tumble from her grip.

The horror that had unnerved her was the sight of a telegraph boy who was squinting at the nameplate on the Fergusons' door.

'Oh no!' Kitty screamed as she rushed forward to speak to the boy. 'Please tell me that you haven't brought a telegram for Dora Ferguson?'

'I haven't,' was the lad's quick retort.

'Then for who?'

'A Mr John Anderson!'

Before the lad could do anything Kitty had wrenched the telegram from his hand. And as her father was in Glasgow for the day, Kitty felt she was therefore entitled to open his mail and quickly ripped the envelope apart.

'Look, look,' she screamed, waving the telegram in the boy's face, 'he's been found. He's in a hospital but he's alive!' Kitty was now slumped at the boy's feet and through her hysterics he could hear her say, 'He's alive, alive. Oh, Bobby, darling, Bobby, somehow I knew Mum would be looking out for you and she would send you back to us.' Her voice stilled. Calm entered her soul as she accepted that to have lost him forever – never to be able to look on his face again, speak to him again – was beyond her contemplation.

Kitty's cries had alerted Dora Ferguson, who emerged from her house and immediately asked, 'What's wrong? What's going on?'

'Dora,' Kitty began, 'my brother is alive. Alive, do you hear? And I must go to him.'

'But where is he?'

Brandishing the telegram, Kitty sobbed, 'In a small cottage hospital close to Liverpool.'

'Will your dad be going with you?'

'Dad . . .' Kitty hesitated. 'Isn't it just like the blooming thing for him to be through in Glasgow helping with the signing up of the thousands of workers who are now joining the union?'

'When will he be back, Kitty?'

'Not till late, Dora.'

It was past ten o'clock in the evening when Johnny finally arrived home. From the pavement he could see that the house, and indeed the whole tenement, was correctly shrouded in darkness. But from the street he felt he could feel a sense of desertion emanating from his flat.

Ominous silence seemed to be echoing all around him. He shuddered as a feeling of pending gloom unnerved him. He tried to argue with himself that all was well within his home but the image of the bombed-out, now deserted buildings, and the misery that had been inflicted on the hard-working people of Glasgow, was still affecting him. Somehow as he lifted the latch and walked into the stairway he sensed that there was no welcoming life within his home.

Bounding up the stairs he was further overcome by a feeling of dread. The times they were living through were so violent, challenging and changeable that your own survival, or that of your loved ones, was not assured. Hadn't the loss of Bobby brought him face to face with the fact that no one was promised tomorrow? And now with sheer panic swamping him he conceded that if there had been a raid tonight and he had lost any more of his children, he knew he would have been unable to face tomorrow.

Forcefully flinging open the door he yelled, 'Kitty, Kitty, where are you?' Only a deafening silence responded.

'Johnny, Johnny,' a familiar voice from behind him called.

He turned to be faced with Connie. 'Where are my children?' he demanded as he grasped her by the shoulders.

'Rosebud and Davy are with your mother and—'

'Has something happened to Jack or worse still Kitty?'

'Jack – well, he might think something has happened to him at the rate Kitty dragged him away to catch a bus.'

'A bus?'

'Aye, they needed to catch a Corporation bus so that the two of them could catch the Liverpool express train from Princes Street station.'

'Are you saying they are away to Liverpool by train?' When Connie nodded, Johnny went on, 'Has Kitty gone mad? Liverpool is getting plastered worse than we are!'

'Aye, that's true, Johnny, but when Kitty found out that Bobby was in a hospital there, well, wild horses wouldn't have stopped her from getting to him.'

Johnny grabbed Connie's head in his hands. 'Are you saying my Bobby's been found?' he spluttered.

'Aye,' Connie replied through chattering teeth, 'but before you think you can get to Liverpool tonight, the last train has gone. So, my bonnie lad, you'll just have to content yourself until the morning.'

Johnny slumped. Unconsciously his hands then began to massage Connie's cheeks.

Not wishing to break the magic of the moment she placed her hands over his. 'But,' she simpered sensuously, 'if you're nice to me I'll heat you up some rabbit stew.' Before she could go on Johnny seemed to come to his senses. His hands dropped to his sides and he stood back from her. Confused, she quickly added, 'I would have offered you a bacon roll, but I know it's against your principles to let a piece of black-market bacon pass over your lips.'

Johnny shrugged. 'Rabbit stew's more than fine.'

'Right you are, I'll be back over with it in two shakes of a lamb's tail.'

Connie had just left when Johnny checked that the blackout curtains were correctly closed before lighting the gaslight. Wearily, he sank down on his favourite big armchair and gave a long sigh. Wasn't it just like the thing for the word to come about Bobby, for whom he had never stopped praying, when he was caught up in Glasgow! He had been so pleased with the way things were working out for the unions there. And indeed it was a measure of the esteem in which he was held that he had been asked to go through and do a bit of shop-steward training. Johnny really believed that at last the hoi polloi was gaining the courage to speak up in one voice and demand the better standard of living that was justly their due.

He laughed to himself as he acknowledged that trade union membership had grown to close on three million since the start of the war. Johnny believed this was in some measure due to the spread of recognition agreements in the vital industries. Other contributing factors were that the government did not wish the vital war work to be held up, so it openly denied contracts to firms who did not conform to the minimum standards demanded by the various trade unions. It also helped that Bevin was anxious to avoid the labour unrest experienced in the Great War and therefore he sought to promote conciliation rather than conflict – and these were words that anybody with anything to do with industrial relations in Leith knew were the bywords of Johnny and Jock. Strikes did occur but they were mainly in support of wage demands or better working conditions on the factory floors. As those who worked in both management and unions at the shipyards were anxious not to disrupt the crucial war effort, strikes were normally settled within hours. In other areas like coal mining and engineering some strikes became bitter and prolonged and ended up with mass prosecutions.

Connie startled Johnny by shouting from the kitchen, 'Come on, bonnie lad.' He had been so caught up in his thoughts that he hadn't heard her come back into the house. Going through to the kitchen he drew out a chair, and as he sat down at the table the aroma that was wafting up from the rabbit stew reminded him that he was hungry – in fact he was ravenous. That was no surprise because he had been so engrossed in union duties that he hadn't had time to eat properly all day.

Whilst he devoured the delicious food, Connie busied herself tidying up the kitchen. Once Johnny was finished she lifted his plate and washed it. 'Right, Johnny, everything is shipshape, so as tomorrow will be a long and emotional day for you I think you should get yourself off to bed now and I'll get off to mine.'

Connie had just closed her outside door behind her and was halfway up the hall when Johnny pushed the door open again. 'Connie,' he croaked hoarsely. 'I can't do it. I just can't do it!'

'Do what?'

'Stay in my house on my own. The silence is echoing off the walls and it's screaming at me. Connie, none of my children are asleep in their own beds!'

'No, they're not. But they will be asleep somewhere,' an exasperated Connie retorted.

Although she could not clearly see Johnny's face in her torchlight she knew he was pleading to her with his eyes – those soulful eyes that had always beguiled her. What, she wondered, could she say to him? Nonetheless she surprised herself when she patiently replied, 'Look, I'm not going to come and sleep in your house but you are welcome to bunk in with me.'

Johnny needed no further invitation. Before she could have second thoughts he was heading towards her living room.

Both Kitty and Jack knew that it would be difficult to find seats on the Liverpool train. They were becoming increasingly despondent when they finally came upon a six-seat carriage with one space vacant.

Four of the seats were occupied by servicemen but it was only the American airman who suggested that Jack should sit down on the available chair and that he would be more than happy to accommodate Kitty on his knee. Naturally the offer was declined and Kitty sat down on a seat whilst Jack was reduced to sitting on the floor with his back to the door.

It wasn't a pleasant or comfortable journey for either Kitty or Jack. What added to their chagrin was that they expected to arrive at eight o'clock in the evening but the train did not in fact pull in to the Liverpool terminus until after ten.

'Blast,' was Kitty's reaction to their late arrival. 'You know what us being this late means, Jack?'

'No. What?'

'That as Bobby is not on the danger list we won't be able to visit him until tomorrow morning.'

'Right enough.'

'So what do you think we should do?'

Rubbing his numb backside Jack wearily replied, 'Firstly we must find a chippie and eat. Then as I'm so blinking tired we'll go and find a bed and breakfast where I can get my head down.'

Jenny had been ecstatic when a breathless Kitty had asked her if she would look after her sixteen-year-old grandson Davy, who was a plumber's apprentice, and her precocious and gossipy soon-to-be four-year-old precious grand-daughter Rosebud.

She had always felt that somehow she and Kate should have taken Rosebud when Sandra had died giving birth to her. But how they would ever have got her away from Kitty and Johnny she just didn't know. The trouble, as she saw it, was that both of them had sworn to Sandra, in the vain hope of easing her passing, that they would always care for Rosebud. Jenny realised then and now that no way would she and Kate ever have been given custody of Rosebud.

By the time Kate had got home from work Jenny already had Rosebud washed and ready for bed.

'My!' exclaimed Kate. 'I didn't know that we were going to have our darling Rosebud staying overnight.'

'Well you are,' chimed Rosebud, 'and you've just missed Davy, who is also staying here.'

'What has happened to Kitty and Johnny?'

'Johnny's in Glasgow on blooming union business,' Jenny replied, rolling her eyes up to the ceiling, 'and Kate, wait till I tell you, Kitty's away to Liverpool . . .'

'Surely not on her own ... and why would she go there?'

'Not on her own. Oh no, Jack insisted on going with her. You see, Kate . . .' Jenny stopped to sniff and rub under her nose. 'My gracious God, whom you doubt, has listened to my prayers and our Bobby has survived. Survived, do you hear? But now he's in hospital.'

Kate slumped down on a chair and began to sob.

'Why is Aunty Kate crying? Is it because you're going to send her away to the evacuation as soon as she's old enough?' babbled Rosebud.

Jenny ignored Kate's crying and turned to face Rosebud before asking, 'Who is going to be sent to the evacuation?'

'Me,' chanted Rosebud, who loved being the centre of attention. 'Every day, Granny, after I've been a wee bit, a very wee bit, naughty . . .'

'Naughty?'

'Yes, Granny.' Rosebud sucked in her lips, obviously thinking of the naughtiest act she had committed. 'Like . . . like . . . asking Mrs Dickson if she has any spare sweetie coupons or sitting on Kit Ferguson when he falls over. Kitty then says to me that just as soon as I'm old enough she's going to put me on the bus to Lasswade.'

'Lasswade?' shrieked Jenny.

'You know, where all the evacuees go so they can learn to be good. And,' Rosebud emphasised, 'nobody visits them until they are.'

Jenny quickly changed the subject by asking Kate if she was happy to have ham and eggs for her tea. Nonetheless she vowed, as the egg sizzled in the pan, that she was going to have more than a few choice words with Kitty when she got back home.

* * *

An uneasy, eerie silence had fallen in Connie's house as both she and Johnny undressed down to their underwear. Nightclothes for them were still luxuries that even now, if they could afford them, they could not justify spending precious clothing coupons on. Besides, if there was an air raid it was so much easier just to pull on your jumper and skirt or trousers.

'I'm sorry, Johnny,' Connie gulped, 'the only room in the house that has a bed in it is mine. So you either can bunk on the sofa,' she tittered, 'or if you are in need of a cuddle get in beside me.'

'I am an honourable man, Connie, so the sofa it is.'

Johnny heaved himself on to the couch. For a full ten minutes he tossed and turned. 'Connie, I'm too long for this couch,' he loudly protested. 'And I can't get comfortable. What do you think I should do?'

Connie chortled. 'One of three things.'

'And what are they?'

'Firstly, you could try cutting cut off your feet; secondly, and probably the least drastic measure, take yourself back through to your own bed; or finally throw caution to the wind and . . . cuddle in with me.'

Next thing Connie heard was Johnny rolling himself off the sofa. Then the slip-slapping of his bare feet on the linoleum floor caused her to emit a girlish giggle, which turned into full-blown laughter when he mumbled, 'To hell with it. And as I have such high standards and therefore nothing is . . .' He paused. 'See when I come to think of it . . . who would blooming know or care . . . especially if they were getting bombed to hell?'

Being a lady, Connie pulled back the covers so Johnny

could get in beside her. He had just got himself settled in the bed when she chuckled. 'Now, Johnny dear, if I put the bolster pillow in between us would that be enough for your high standards?'

Johnny humped and turned his back on her. That was until he was overcome once again by that lonely, desolate feeling. Without saying a word he turned back and drew her into his arms.

Drumming her fingers on his chest, she murmured, 'Johnny, just in case things get . . . well . . . you know they might get . . . So I think you should know that when I married Mark I didn't know that he was . . . What I'm trying to say is that he was . . . is . . . a nancy boy.'

Johnny could only grunt, 'A what?'

'A nancy boy,' Connie quickly confirmed. 'So that meant he brought his then lover, Jamie, with us on . . .' She hesitated and kept pounding her fingers on Johnny's chest before adding, 'Or to be correct, he took me along with them on their honeymoon.'

Silent minutes slowly ticked by before Johnny drawled, 'Well, if that little story is not a damper on any passion that might have arisen – and I'm not saying that any has – then I don't know what else is.'

'You're just like Mark,' Connie blubbed through heart-rending sobs. 'You led me on to think . . . that you liked me as a de . . . sir . . . able . . . woman . . . and just like him you promised me so much a few minutes ago and now you are rejecting me.'

'Rejecting you? No I'm not. It's just that I'm wondering . . .' Johnny halted and sat bolt upright in the bed. 'If your husband is still alive would he . . . ?'

'Well as far as I know, he is alive and kicking.'

120

'That's what I mean – he could burst in here any minute now and justly kick the living daylights out of me.'

'Don't be daft, Johnny. In the ten years I've lived here he's never as much as put a foot over the door.'

Relief swept over Johnny. He snuggled down in the bed again. 'All right, Connie,' he drawled, 'tonight I'll share your bed but . . . well, it's against my religion to . . . with a woman who is not free . . .'

Connie started to howl again.

'What's wrong with you now?' Johnny huffed.

'It's just that I'm going to be like your sister Kate and die a virgin.'

'Virgin!' Johnny was bolt upright in the bed again. 'Now let's get this straight. Are you saying that you're still a virgin?'

Connie sniffed. Her nodding head bounced off his chest.

'How old are you?'

'I turned thirty-eight but just last week.'

'Well, if this is not a first for Leith, I don't know what is.'

'What do you mean?'

'That you, a sassy bottle blonde, are still a virgin at thirty-eight!'

'But your sister Kate is born and bred Leith and at forty-three she's still . . .'

'Aye,' Johnny replied coldly, 'but she's not sassy. She's like the Little Sisters of the Poor married to frigidity.'

Connie snuffled. Profuse tears spilled over. Johnny felt guilty. *Nothing else for it then,* he argued with himself. So reaching over he drew her into his arms again. 'There, there,' he cooed. 'It's all right, Connie. Now come on, stop crying, and I promise you that I won't tell anyone your secret. Nobody will know but me that you're a . . .' He blew out his lips as temptation began to raise its ugly head.

And so it was true that when Connie Sharp allowed Johnny Anderson to share her bed that night she was a thirty-eight-year-old virgin. But long before dawn broke she might still have been thirty-eight years old but she was most certainly no longer a virgin!

Jack had put his hand forward to run it over the plaster cast that was covering Bobby's left arm. 'Does it hurt, Bobby?' he asked tentatively.

'Not as much as it did . . .' Bobby's thoughts were racing back to the night his ship was torpedoed.

Twenty-six merchant ships loaded up with food and vital supplies left North America bound for Liverpool. The spaced-out fleet was flanked at the front, sides and rear by an escort fleet of destroyers, frigates, corvettes and fighting planes.

Bobby remembered he had just congratulated himself again for not only having survived the disastrous runs of 1942 – when nearly six thousand men lost their lives and around 450 ships were torpedoed by the U-boats – but also having got almost safely home again this trip.

He then recalled that he had volunteered to become one of the gallant band of merchant seamen who were risking their lives to make sure Britain was not starved into submission. He and his fellow shipmates had become buoyed up with great expectations when they were assured that in 1943, life in the Atlantic would be so much safer for them. Convoys, at last, would enjoy the protection of escort planes that could fly as far as the infamous Atlantic Gap.

This black pit had in the past been favoured by the German U-boats because no escort planes could cover the convoy at that distance – meaning ships were like sitting ducks and thousands were consigned to a watery grave.

Bobby huffed as he thought, *Aye, things should have been better on my last trip. But as all us Scots ken, the best-laid schemes 'gang aft agley'.* He became pensive as he reluctantly remembered that strict blackout was still the order of the day and the convoy had endured the added menace of being engulfed in a silent pea-souper fog. No one on board his ship had voiced their concerns but they all knew that they were now at even greater risk.

To be truthful it was the tanker in front of them being torpedoed that was the start of the problems. Then he admitted to himself that the ship that he was travelling on was not really seaworthy. Had it not been for the fact that Britain was so short of vessels, his ship would now be a pile of junk in the breakers' yard. The ship only caught a glancing blow from the torpedo that was aimed at it, but as it exploded, it did enough damage for the captain to know that he had to abandon ship – and speedily at that.

Luckily they had stayed afloat long enough to get two lifeboats launched, and through what Bobby considered the captain and the chief engineer's courage, fortitude and determination, all but five of the crew were housed in the two boats. Bobby, however, was unfortunate enough to be racing through the ship to get to the lifeboats when a door banged shut on his arm. Luckily the captain and the chief engineer, who were going to be last to get into the lifeboats, grabbed hold of him and they got him safely aboard.

After four hours of drifting, luckily in the right direction, the fog lifted and then they had to contend with biting-cold, swollen seas. Another two hours slowly and painfully passed before they were picked up by another merchant ship bound for Liverpool. The injured Bobby was then transferred to a small cottage hospital.

Kitty and Jack had been standing beside Bobby's bed as these thoughts and memories raced through his mind: her asking, 'Has he said anything, Jack?' and Jack responding 'No' as Bobby opened his eyes.

'I've not been asleep. I've just been thinking,' he protested. 'Oh, Kitty, pretty Kitty, I am so glad to see you. You see . . .' He stopped as uncontrollable sobs overtook him.

Kicking off her shoes, Kitty jumped up on the bed and drew Bobby up into her arms. Rocking him backwards and forwards she whispered, 'Sssh, my love, it's all right now. And I've just spoken to the Sister and she says if we wait another two days we can take you home with us.'

'Sure, Bobby,' Jack encouraged, 'we're all so proud of you. And because Britain is an island and we have to import so much we know that if it had not been for you and your brave Merchant Navy brothers we would have lost this war. And yes, the Germans only allow a third of what we need to get through but that vital third keeps us going.'

Bobby's sobs were just subsiding when a pert brunette arrived at his bedside. 'What's going on here, Bobby? And why are you allowing this woman to molest you?'

'I am his sister, Kitty, and what I would like to know is what are you doing here?' Kitty sharply responded. 'And I trust that you are aware that only next of kin are allowed to visit outwith visiting hours?'

The young woman did not answer but she did raise her hand to display a diamond solitaire engagement ring.

'Kitty, this here is Harriet Wales. She hails from Wales and she and I are engaged.'

Jack and Kitty looked at each other before Kitty offered a rather begrudging, 'Congratulations.'

It had been Johnny's intention to go to Liverpool to visit Bobby but Kitty had sent a telegram saying that she was bringing Bobby home in two days' time. He then decided that he would therefore just stay put.

With time on his hands he thought that he had better call in on his mother, Jenny, to check on how Rosebud and Davy were getting on. As expected, both were being overindulged by Jenny and Kate – so much so that Rosebud announced that she was going to stay with 'her' granny forever.

Johnny at first ignored Rosebud's remarks but when Jenny said that when Kitty returned home she was going to have a word with her about the things she was saying to Rosebud, he began to grow wary.

'What do you mean, Mum?' Johnny said ever so quietly.

'Just,' Jenny replied with vigour, 'that she appears to be saying threatening things to Rosebud. Come on now, Johnny, the wee darling is only going on four and I don't think she should be living in fear.'

Johnny, who was eating a meal, allowed his fork to drop loudly on to his plate. 'And you have decided all this on the word of Rosebud? Rosebud who I love but who I also know drives people to distraction when they are left to look after her.'

'Maybe so, Johnny, but as I seem to be able to handle her better than Kitty I think she should now come and live here with Kate and me.'

The response from Johnny was not what his mother

expected. Indeed, when he pushed back his chair with such force that it toppled over, she flinched. Without another word to her he turned and addressed Davy and Rosebud. 'Right,' he began, rolling the 'r', 'you two gather your things together.'

Davy just gaped at him but Rosebud hollered, 'But why, Daddy?'

'Because, lady, you're both coming home with me – and right now at that.'

'But, Johnny,' Jenny protested, 'you can't do that. What I mean is, who is going to look after Rosebud when you are at work?'

'Well tonight I'll get Connie to look after her whilst I'm on Home Guard duty and tomorrow she'll be with Dora Ferguson and her kids. And that is the best place for her, where she will be just another bairn and not be pandered to by a group of over-indulgent adults.'

'Please, Johnny, don't do this. Let's sit down and talk about it. Rosebud would be better with me, and next year when she is five she could just hop across the road and be in Links Place Primary School within minutes.'

Johnny had no desire to have a full-blown row with his mother but Rosebud was his child and she would be living with him. Gathering up all of Rosebud's belongings, he grabbed the child by the hand and started for the door. Rosebud immediately threw one of her famous outrageous tantrums. This time not only did she kick the furniture but she also started to strike out at Johnny with her right foot.

'I hate you, Daddy,' she hissed. 'I want to stay with Granny. She lets me have cola and sweets whenever I want them. So I don't want to go home with you . . . ever again.'

A stern Johnny looked accusingly at Jenny. She could

only shrug and plead silently with her eyes. Rosebud now foolishly decided to bite into the calf of her father's leg. When the pain gripped him Johnny lifted his hand and it met her bottom with such force that she tumbled straight out of the outside door, which Davy had opened so they could leave.

Jenny was aghast. 'Johnny,' she cried, 'that was a cruel thing to do. Sure children should be chastised, but not brutally treated.'

'That right, Mum? Well how come I still remember the weals that rose up on my legs and backside when you beat me with a besom – and what exactly was the heinous crime that brought about such barbaric treatment?'

Jenny's head now sank down on to her chest. 'You spent a penny of the money I gave you for the church collection on sweets.'

'Sweets!' exclaimed Johnny. 'And the rest of my punishment was to be denied so much as a caramel for a whole month. So what do you think I should do with Rosebud?'

'Nothing,' a defiant Rosebud screamed in response.

'And nothing is what you will get except an early bed. Now get up the road,' Johnny expounded as he jerked his thumb.

Rosebud looked as if she was going to face her father up but she thought the better of it and, rubbing her tingling backside, she began the slow trek home.

Connie was looking from her living-room window when she saw Johnny come into view. Her heart soared. In addition to her preparing a liver and onion dish for him she had also given herself a quick wash, changed her blouse, donned her only pair of pure silk stockings, and had added the mandatory dab of Four Seven Eleven exotic perfume behind her ears. This was all because she knew that after he ate he would be going to bed so that he would be alert for his Home Guard duties. She giggled like a star-struck teenager as she imagined and hoped that he would invite her to join him for a couple of hours . . . just cuddling and, well, who knows what between the sheets.

Giving a quick pat to her hair she looked beyond Johnny and utter disappointment caused her jaw to drop. There in tow behind Johnny were Davy and Rosebud. *Well,* she thought, *Davy will probably be going out with his pals but as sure as hell darling Rosebud will still be on the floor with everyone dancing attendance on her when Johnny leaves at nine thirty for his Home Guard duties.*

Connie was further disenchanted when Johnny told her that he had already eaten at his mother's. Davy, who was never anything but a famished young lad, said that he too had just had some corn beef hash but as he preferred liver and onions, which he didn't get very often, it would be a shame to waste such a treat so he would eat them.

Within an hour Davy was away to meet up with his pals at the football training and a bewildered Rosebud had found herself packed off to bed in Connie's bedroom. Connie and Johnny were alone at last and it was then that he took the opportunity to say, 'Connie, I can't thank you enough for agreeing to look after Rosebud tonight. It was just when I was at my mum's that I realised that I have to do something about her.'

'Something about her?'

'Aye, you see, most of the time she's sweet and lovely . . .' Johnny hesitated. 'But there are times she is positively . . .'

'Horrid?'

'Aye, and I have to sort her out because I don't want people to dislike her.'

'I think you're being a bit unfair. The wee lass has never had a mother. And Kitty has done a good job on her but she's not her mother – I mean she was a fifteen-year-old lassie when she was landed with Rosebud and now she's nineteen and she still doesn't have a carefree life of her own.'

Johnny nodded before sinking down on to a chair. An uneasy silence then engulfed the room and the only movement, forby the ticking of the clock, was when Johnny leant forward to support his head in his hands. Perplexed, Connie was at a loss as to what she should do.

Slowly raising his head Johnny sought for Connie's hand. Hope slowly flowed into her. Kissing the back of her hand Johnny began, 'Connie, last night reminded me just how sweet and good life can be and it would be easy to just go on like that . . .'

Connie drew back a bit and she began slowly patting her chest with her left hand. There was something in his tone and words . . .

'But – and it is a big but,' Johnny continued, 'I have responsibilities. I see clearly now how selfish I have been where my two girls are concerned. I just bundled Rosebud on to Kitty and I didn't see, or wish to see, that Kitty and Rosebud had needs that neither could fill for each other.'

'Johnny,' Connie interrupted sharply, 'you've got me confused. Could you spit out what you're trying to say.'

'It is just that I do like you, and I fancy you, but both of us have other commitments. What I mean is, going on like we did last night would cause grief for others. I am a widower with a young family and my wants and desires must come second to their needs. Now if we could marry, people may, given time, get used to that, but we can't. You are married and you haven't even a clue as to where to find your husband.'

'You are so like your mother,' Connie hissed. 'You worry too much about what the people you pray beside on a Sunday think. Well I don't give a damn what anybody thinks. I have only been really attracted to two men in my life. The first I married and it was a real slap in the face when I found out he was homosexual and I was therefore rejected even before my marriage vows had been made. Now I thought in you I had found a decent, honourable man who thought me attractive and desirable and now you say . . .' Connie was now weeping bitterly.

Johnny got to his feet. He shrugged, indicating that his mind was made up. Last night had been wonderful but the reality was that a happy liaison with Connie was nothing more than a pipe dream.

He put on his army great coat and when she heard her outside door click shut she knew it had closed forever on all her dreams.

In Liverpool, Harriet and Kitty had got off to a bad start. Both young women thought that they should be the one to look after Bobby in his convalescence. Bobby valued both of them and wished he didn't have to choose between going with Kitty back to Restalrig, or with Harriet back to Wales.

In the end his desire to feel the safety of his own home about him was the overriding factor. In addition to this, he had an overwhelming need to go and kneel at his mother's graveside and tell her that he was safe and back home. He was as sure as he could be that when he became numb with cold, and hope was ebbing from him, her presence came to him in the lifeboat – especially when he had truly thought that there was no way that he, and the others, would be rescued in time. She had consumed his every thought and he knew he had heard her say, 'You must hold on, son. You are going to make it.' Maybe it was delirium but it was so real to him that he would never forget her urging him not to give up on life.

The news of Bobby opting to go home to Restalrig caused Harriet to become incensed and noisily she began to tap her foot on the hard hospital floor. 'All right, Bobby, I see clearly that I wasted my time coming all the way from Cardiff to here. But I hope when you get back to Scotland you think about all of the plans we made for you continuing at sea and becoming a chief engineer. Being a chief would mean that when this war is over I could travel with you on your voyages. And could I also remind you how we vowed that eventually we would build a home for ourselves in Cardiff? A home big enough to house any children we might have or . . .' She stopped and snorted before adding, 'Or accommodate any of your relatives who may wish to visit us.'

'That still stands, Harriet. I do love you but I have been through a lot and I just want to go back to Edinburgh to see my dad and my home again.' He would have liked to have added, *And also speak to my mum*, but he didn't want anyone to know that he thought – no, knew – she had been with him in the lifeboat.

After updating Kate on why Rosebud and Davy were no longer being looked after by herself, Jenny donned her coat and set off for the servicemen's welcoming station. She had indicated to the management that she would be unable to do her shift there because she was needed to look after her grandchildren. But since the scrap with Johnny, who had then decided to make other arrangements for his children, she was at a loose end. This being the case, and the fact that there were never enough volunteers to assist the servicemen and -women 'en route to somewhere' who called in at the station, she decided that the most useful thing she could do was go there.

Jenny had been gone an hour when Kate heard a soft rap on the outside door. Making sure that there would be no shaft of light to alert enemy aircraft she slightly opened the door.

'Sorry to bother you, Miss Anderson,' said Hans Busek's distinct European-influenced voice.

Kate then fully opened the door. 'Oh, Mr Busek, what can I do for you?'

'Just that you said you still had the parts of your father's granddaughter clock and I thought that as I now have time I could be looking at it to see if I could repair it.'

'Of course. I do remember that you said you would look in. It's upstairs under my bed.'

Hans had just stepped inside the hallway when Kate laughed, 'No it's not under my bed. I remember now that I put it out in the shed because I thought it would be easier to get at when you did come.'

Hans and Kate were busy rummaging through the articles in the shed when Kate gulped as she thought, *I do so hope my mother has not put it out in the rubbish collection*. Relief seeped into her when she found the package under an old rag rug, but this feeling was short lived as the ominous wail of the siren warning blasted out.

'Quick, Hans,' she shouted, 'let's get back into the safety of the house.'

Hans firstly grabbed the cumbersome bundle away from Kate and then he turned and they both began to run towards the house. 'Surely,' he said through gasps, 'we should be going towards the shelters in Leith Links.'

'No,' replied Kate as they arrived in the living room, 'my mother says we are safer under this solid table. So put the clock down and dive under it with me.'

Once Hans was under the table beside Kate she realised how close they were lying together. So close that she could feel the heat of his body and the beat of his heart, which in itself was causing her heart to pound. Her discomfort was then compounded when a sudden burst of gunfire and the drone of aeroplanes above the house frightened her so much that she began to tremble.

Instinctively Hans started to rub her arm in an effort to calm her. She swallowed hard before stammering, 'Thank you, Mr . . . Hans . . . And do you know I have never heard you speak very much about where you once lived and what brought you here?'

Hans's immediate response was to stop rubbing Kate's arm. Then, speaking very quietly, he gripped her right hand and his thumb gently stroked the inside of her palm and fingers. 'You, Miss Anderson, think that the air raid raging outside is just awful. But I tell you this: Warsaw, the city where I was born, was reduced to rubble by continual and callous bombardments. I also say with conviction that no matter how many blitzes there are here in Britain or were in France, Holland or anywhere, they will never ever meet the intensity and total destruction that Warsaw endured. Merciless it was, and everything I held dear perished in the ruins.'

Kate wanted to say something to comfort Hans, but what? Unaware of her dilemma he continued, 'And what, you will be wondering, was the fate of my family? Ah well, my gentle, loving and faithful wife, my two sons with so much promise, my doting parents and siblings – all perished on the same night. Wiped out completely in the fury that was unleashed on us . . . innocent unprotected civilians. I only survived that night because . . . To be truthful I don't know why I survived, and at the time, I truly wished I hadn't. Believe me it was more difficult then to go on living than it was to die. All that kept me going was my desire for vengeance. The next day I made my way to link up with a cousin at Gdansk and we made our escape by a fishing boat. Now I wait because I do know that somehow my God will assist me to come to terms with what has happened to Poland and He will make sure that she rises from the ashes. But now, Miss—'

'Please, Hans, I am your friend, so call me Kate.'

'Kate it is then, and as I was saying, now I will remain here and try to make a new life for myself.'

Another blast made Kate shriek in terror before she buried her head in Hans's shoulder. Drawing her closer into him, Hans gently purred, 'There, there.' These words of comfort had a relaxing effect on Kate. No longer did she feel, in any way, that he was invading her privacy. Indeed she was pleased, very pleased, that he was now so close to her that she could smell his manliness. It was a pleasing odour that awakened longings within her – tempting longings that she thought she would never experience again.

When Bobby was escorted home by Kitty and Jack to his old home at Restalrig, he was surprised to find when they entered the house that it was standing-room only. It turned out that Davy, who hero-worshipped Bobby, had thought that his 'big brave brother' should be welcomed home with a Hogmanay-type party.

Unfortunately the over-long and tedious journey from Liverpool had completely exhausted not only Bobby, but Kitty and Jack as well. All that the trio wished to do, as Bobby declared, was have a plate of good old Scottish broth, a quick wash and then collapse down on a bed. Thanks to Kitty, who was not afraid to speak her mind, within an hour everybody, with the exception of Granny Jenny and Aunty Kate, got the message and they left, promising to return within the next few days when Bobby would be feeling more in a party mood.

It was then that Kitty decided she was going to bed to get some rest. She was just about to leave when she looked around the room. Something wasn't quite right. Someone who should have been in the house when she arrived home was not. That someone was Connie. Turning around she looked directly at her father and asked, 'Why was Connie not invited to the party? She isn't ill or anything?'

Johnny bowed his head and he had the grace to blush before saying, 'She's fine. It's just that now that Robb's are taking on women as apprentices . . .'

'Are you that short of boys?' Bobby chuckled.

'Yeah we are. So Connie has decided to advance herself and she starts her apprenticeship tomorrow.'

'Which trade is she going to train for?' queried a derisory Jenny, who felt that life was changing too fast and women becoming tradesmen was further proof of that.

'Plumbing!'

'Plumbing, Dad?' Kitty exclaimed. 'But she likes to

135

smell nice. What I mean is, she always smells like Jenners' perfume counter, so how will she cope with . . . Oh no, it doesn't bear thinking of!'

When Kitty got into bed she firstly pushed Rosebud further over so that she could stretch herself out. Sleep should have come immediately but there was something bothering her about her father and Connie. As she tossed and turned she wondered why her dad was so eager to say that Connie hadn't turned up at the party because she was going to be on early duty in the morning. Early starts had never stopped Connie in the past from being the life and soul of any get-together.

Once Johnny, Jack and Davy were up and away to work the next morning, Kitty thought she would look in on Bobby to see if there was anything he needed. Or more importantly she couldn't wait to hear the full and true story from him about how he had managed to get himself engaged to Harriet Wales, who in Kitty's opinion was an intimidating and dominating Welsh lassie.

Pushing open the door as quietly as she could, Kitty was dumbfounded to see that Bobby was up and about. She breathed in deeply and grimaced when she witnessed how difficult it was for him to get himself dressed.

'Bobby, why are you out of bed? And what on earth are you doing?'

'Firstly, who in our family has ever been for lying in bed? Secondly, and more importantly, I want to go out and speak to Mum.'

'Mum?' Kitty exclaimed. She was sure without suggesting it to him that he was suffering from some sort of delayed concussion.

'What I mean is, I want to visit her grave and just speak to her.'

Kitty gasped. Her eyes rolled.

Bobby continued. 'Try and understand,' he explained, 'that before I left to join the Merchant Navy I went to Seafield cemetery to speak to Mum and tell her what I was doing and why. But I couldn't, because you were there blubbering and bawling like a bad-tempered baby.'

Kitty snorted. 'I go there to speak to Mum every week and tell her of any problems that I think she should know about. And if you must know, that day you saw me there I was just letting her know that you, who could have stayed in the shipyards as they are exempt employment, had decided to ignore Dad's advice and my pleas to stay at home. My blubbering, as you put it, Bobby, was for you because I knew what a dangerous job you had taken on.'

'Okay. But it's hardly what you could call a protected zone here.'

'I'll give you that but it's not fraught with danger the way the convoys are. And before you say anything, I know that Dad can take the occasional bucket and is in danger of getting knocked down – but he never ends up drifting rudderless in a tin-pan boat out in the North Sea.'

'Is this going to be the start of you begging me to leave the Merchant Navy and get my job back in Robb's?'

'You could do worse.'

'No. I have to be where I'm able to be the most useful.'

'Useful? And where do you think this country would be if it wasn't for all the ships that we are building and repairing – and before you answer that I'll tell you – under Hitler's jackboot!'

Bobby blew out his lips before starting to make loud

clicking sounds with his tongue. He accepted that there was nothing to be gained from arguing with Kitty. The best thing he could do was change the subject. With a disarming smile he wheedled, 'Any chance of a wee bite of breakfast before we go and see Mum?'

Before Kitty could answer Rosebud hollered, 'Kitty, where are you? I'm starving.'

'Hungry maybe, Rosebud, but starving . . . never,' was Kitty's trite reply.

Two hours later Kitty and Bobby were kneeling at Sandra's grave while Rosebud was running amok around the cemetery.

Whatever it was that Kitty wished to tell her mother she did so in silent prayer. This unspoken chat, however, was brought to an abrupt halt when she became aware of Bobby speaking aloud to their mother.

'Mum,' she heard him utter though deep sobs, 'I'm just here today to thank you for being with me when I was lost and adrift in the Atlantic.' Kitty was astounded. Up until then she thought she was the only one whom Sandra was still there for and talking to. But here was Bobby saying that she was still real to him too. That his ordeal in the lifeboat had been made bearable because he had believed that she – and who could argue that she hadn't – had arrived to soothe and comfort him.

An hour later Kitty and Bobby were taking it in turns to hold on to Rosebud's hand as she walked along the sea wall at Seafield. It was one of those magical mornings when the cool winter sun danced on the incoming tide and the rush of its buoyancy and energy filled you anew with hope and determination. Bobby and Kitty looked at each other and both knew what each other was thinking as they walked on in comfortable silence. Both were now thinking back to the days of fish-paste sandwiches, red cola, Mum and Dad – many happy childhood days on 'Porty' beach.

Eventually they had walked along the prom until they reached Demarco's coffee shop. 'Changed days,' Bobby chuckled as he put his arm around Kitty. 'Sorry I don't have any sodden sandwiches or broken biscuits but I could take you inside here and treat you to a coffee.'

Before Kate could respond Rosebud demanded, 'And can I get a cone with raspberry stuff running off it?'

'Why not,' replied Bobby, who had now linked arms with Kitty. 'And just think in eight weeks' time it will be a new year. And who knows – 1944 could finally see the end of the war.'

As they entered the café and took a seat, Kitty thought that the war being over next year was a dream too far, but she did think that it would soon be all over and Bobby would come home to Leith for good. She hesitated before adding silently, *Or make his land base in Cardiff.*

'Bobby,' she began when her curiosity was beginning to choke her, 'when the war is over what are your plans?'

'Simple – make a career for myself in the Merchant Navy. I know it will mean me going to the Nautical College from time to time but that's what I'm going to do.' He winked and leant over and squeezed Kitty's hand. 'How do you fancy being the sister of a chief engineer?'

'Is it only the captain's and chief engineers' wives that are allowed to go on voyages with them?'

Bobby nodded and chuckled before saying, 'I think being able to sail the seven seas is the main attraction for Harriet.'

'You're joking?'

'Of course I am. I hope she loves me for who I am and not the uniform and' – he stopped and winked again at Kitty before adding – 'the cruises around the world.'

'Hmmm,' was all Kitty offered in reply.

'Look out there, Kitty, what do you see?'

Kitty stared long and hard out of the café window. All she could see were mountainous waves crashing on the shore while seagulls soared, dived and whooped. Her attention then strayed to the brilliant blood-red sun that coloured the sand, sea and spray as it glinted and shone on them. At that moment she became mesmerised by the beauty and the energy of it all. She earnestly wished then she could paint and capture this picture so that she could keep it beside her for the rest of her life.

Bobby brought her back to the present by saying, 'I'm still waiting, Kitty, for you to tell me what you see.'

'I see a turbulent sea doing what it pleases and tossing the rubbish where it belongs, out of its way. A winter sun determined to shine brighter than in the summer and making the best of the time that it has.'

'Exactly,' enthused Bobby. 'And that is what I intend to do. Make my life anywhere that it suits me and aim for the sky. As to you, Kitty, you were dealt from the bottom of the deck but you are just nineteen and you still could make a good life for yourself.'

'And how will I do that?' She chuckled before searching in her pocket for a handkerchief to wipe melted ice cream off Rosebud's face, hands and finally shoes.

'Yeah, at present you have Rosebud to look after but she will grow up and already she is showing signs of doing her own thing. Eventually she will leave you and then, Kitty, do you still intend to be scrubbing stairs, washing boiler suits and being at everybody's beck and call – surely not!'

'And what do you propose I do about it?'

'Start now. Enrol in night school and demand that someone else cares for Rosie Buddy here on those nights.' Bobby was now tickling Rosebud and she was chortling.

'You mean you can see me serving my time like Connie – as a plumber.'

Bobby's uproarious laughter echoed around the shop. 'Good heavens, no – I expect you to have ambition, drive. Come on, Kitty, you are intelligent and pretty with it. So take your time but as soon as possible make up your mind what it is you are going to do with your life and then get on with it.'

'And what about Dad?'

'I have a feeling that when the war is over the shipyards won't be enough for him. He's clever too, Kitty, and wily. Never had the chance . . . or more correctly never took it.' Bobby stopped to grin and chuckle. 'And I hope that somehow, after the war, he gets the opportunity to show everybody exactly what he is capable of.'

'You've become quite the philosopher.'

He chuckled. His gaze was out at sea again. Without really addressing Kitty or anyone else he put his thoughts into words. 'See, when I was drifting aimlessly in the Atlantic and the pain in my arm was unbearable and I had to distract myself from the agony – I thought deeply about life and I now know that you only get one shot to be who you really are. What I'm saying is that you shouldn't be hanging about until the dark clouds roll away – no – it's all about learning to sing and tap dance in the rain.'

*　*　*

Going to work as an apprentice, especially for a mature woman, was a daunting experience. Connie knew all the pitfalls that she mustn't fall into – like being sent for a long stand or a tin of tartan paint. That was all fine but what she had not taken into consideration was that if she had been male she would have had to share the men's lavatories and even although they had doors and locks on them now she decided to stay constipated – even wait until dinner time, when she would be able to use the women's facilities in the main administrative block.

Everybody had told her she would be nauseated at the start of her plumbing apprenticeship, because the trainees got all the foul-smelling jobs to practise on, but she wasn't. In fact she was the best of the new starts that day and more than able to cope with not only the foul odours and the clearing out of the unsightly gunge but also with the relentless teasing from the men.

5

JANUARY 1944

The New Year did not come in with a bang . . . more of a damp squib. Well, it would after the amazing events of December 1943.

On the night of Christmas Eve, Kate had congratulated herself on the fact that she had managed to wriggle out of fire duty. Whilst looking into the fire burning brightly in the grate she gave out an impromptu burst of laughter. *Poor Santa*, she thought, *no way will you get down our chimney without getting your whiskers singed.*

An alarming noise – not so much as a knock but more of a thump and a kick on the outside door – put an end to her musing.

Making sure to draw the living-room blackout curtain securely over the door she then warily unlocked and opened up the entrance to the house. Peering into the black forbidding gloom she was startled when a heavy object fell against her.

'What in the name of heaven is going on?' she gasped before beginning to dance with the load.

'Nothing to worry about, Miss . . . No, we are not at work so it is . . . Kate,' Hans said in muffled reply. Lifting his face clear of the package he went on, 'I have just brought your clock back.'

'In bits?' Kate tittered as she continued to waltz with Hans and the stack.

Once they had got the load into the living room Kate shut the door and Hans balanced the clock against the wall.

Immediately Kate pounced forward to drag the covering off the timepiece, but Hans restrained her. 'No. No. No. No,' he chastised. 'We must not waste. Let me unpack the clock and I will keep the corrugated cardboard and paper for future use.'

Standing with her hands tightly covering her mouth, Kate started to pant. *Has he,* she wondered, *managed to salvage it for me?*

When all of the considerable packing was stripped away, she uttered a short cry. There standing in front of her was a sight to behold: it was her father's granddaughter clock. The antique timepiece had not only been repaired but it was now more beautiful than she remembered it had ever been. Being a craftsman, Hans had not only restored the mechanical workings of the clock but he had also repaired the casing – the casing that had then been finished off with a long overdue French polish.

Kate at first was so overcome that she stood mute and motionless. Then, as if in a dream, she gently reached out to stroke the shining coffer. Lifting her eyes to the clock's face she then lovingly ran her hands over it. She still had her hands on the glass when it seemed to her that her father joined her. His presence was even more evident when the clock began to sweetly chime out the evening hour of eight.

Minutes passed with nothing being heard but the rhythmic ticking of the clock. Hans would have liked to say something to Kate but he knew it was only right that he allow her time to enjoy the clock that was so dear to her.

Eventually, she held out a hand to him and he raised it to his lips and passionately kissed it. Through scalding tears she mumbled, 'Thank you so much, Hans. You are a master. This clock means so much to me and I feel that you have not only skilfully restored it but you did it with love and devotion. Love that is now living within this clock, and all who look at it will see and feel it.'

She wished now that she had bought him a Christmas present, but she knew from the frequent outings they had recently been on that the one thing he wished for could not be purchased.

Tenderly taking his hand in hers, she slowly began to guide him to the stairs and as they mounted the step Hans whispered, 'Are you sure?'

She hesitated. It was a big step. Nonetheless, she knew from their several intimate conversations that he was an honourable man. It was more than evident that he wished to bed her, but only if she would agree to become his wife. Her hesitation to grant his wish had been because he was a penniless Polish refugee. She was afraid that people would think that because she was now perceived to be over the hill, he was all that she could attract. Truth was there was not one man in Leith, or indeed Edinburgh, that she would favour in front of him, so all she said was, 'My darling Hans, believe me, I am more than sure.'

'Your mother?'

'No need to worry about my mother right now. Tonight she's babysitting Rosebud up at my brother's house and tomorrow I will . . .' She didn't finish what she was about to say because her bedroom door was open and the bed was beckoning.

Always when Jenny arrived up at Johnny's house she would have 'goodies' in her message bag. Being Christmas Eve things were no different except that she came in over-laden.

'Oh, Granny,' screamed Rosebud, dragging the cover

from the shopping bag so she could rummage through it, 'please say that you've brought me sweeties to keep me going until Santa comes.'

Jenny ignored Rosebud. Her attention was on Kitty, who was all togged up for a night on the town. She beamed a broad smile and nodded when Kitty did a little twirl so she could see the full effect of the renovated dress.

Kitty slowly stopped pirouetting. 'You know, Granny,' she said, looking directly at Jenny, 'I am just so grateful to you for offering to look after Rosebud so that I can go out dancing with Laura and Jack.'

Wrestling a poke of sweeties from Rosebud's hand, Jenny replied, 'I'm not so sure that I've done the right thing in offering. I mean how did she get as high as she is?'

'Oh, everyone going on and on about Santa Claus and what he is going to bring her. And if you try threatening her that if she does not behave herself then she can forget about getting a doll and pram, that only seems to make her worse.'

'What time is your dad due home?'

'Any time now. He has finished his work but he went for a pint or . . .'

'Three or four?'

'No, Granny, when he says a pint or two now it is never more than two.'

The dancing trio were just about to run to catch the bus to the Eldorado Ballroom in Leith when Connie stumbled into their pathway.

'Are you ill, Connie?' a concerned Kitty asked.

'Just feel a bit light-headed. Honestly I was doing so well with my plumbing training. Then today when I was confronted with some dead rats in a water cistern in a ship that's in for repair I just felt like vomiting. Have felt green ever since and see when I got off the bus . . .' She stopped to put her hand over her mouth as she retched. 'The smell from the chip shop just made me want to oh . . . puke . . .'

'Look,' Kitty replied warily, 'do you want me to come back and look after you?'

'Don't be ridiculous. You're young and it's Christmas Eve so off you go and enjoy yourself. Is your granny looking after Rosebud?'

'Yes,' chorused the three. 'But,' Kitty went on, 'don't expect any help from her. Honestly, our Rosebud, who I'm positive is one of Hitler's secret undercover agents, is enough for her to contend with. So come on now, Connie, best thing we can do is to tap on Dora's door.'

'No. No. You just go.'

'And do you think I could jitterbug if I didn't know someone was caring for you?'

Kitty had just left and Dora was now boiling the kettle to make Connie some tea. Suddenly Connie clamped her hand over her mouth and started to heave. She then attempted to stand up, and as she did so she seemed to sway from side to side. Luckily the quick-witted Dora managed to grab her before she hit the floor. Lowering her down on to the chair again Dora began to wipe the clammy sweat from Connie's brow.

'I know that with the rationing it's easy not to have enough to eat. So what I'm wondering is, have you had a good meal today?'

Connie shook her head. 'To be truthful I just can't face food right now. The minute I look at it or even smell it I just want to be sick, sick, sick. Oh, Dora, I am just thinking that if I can't cope with the plumbing I might have to eat humble pie and go back to the parts depot.'

'But would that be such a bad thing? The work there's not as heavy as I imagine plumbing is.'

'You don't understand, Dora. I just have to stick it out because I made such a fuss about being able to do my time as an apprenticed plumber when they took on Peggy Duncan. And what's galling is that she was the one who was vomiting at the start but now she takes it all in her stride.'

'Aye, but she's not married so she's . . .'

'What's being married got to do with her not being sick any more?'

'Nothing, but it has everything to do with you being so scunnered.'

'What do you mean?'

'Oh, come on, Connie, you can't fool me. I've been pregnant three times and every time the first three months was a nightmare.' Dora sighed and grimaced. 'Honestly these endless bouts of sickness, especially in the morning, and falling down all over the place could put you past having any more bairns.'

'Are you trying to say that I'm . . . ?'

'Well, I know your husband is in Glasgow but you must have been . . . well, you know . . . with him lately.'

'I haven't seen him for years.'

'Oh well, Connie,' Dora exclaimed with a series of puffs, 'you'd better see who you have been seeing . . . and pronto at that.'

'But I just can't be,' Connie insisted.

'That right?' Dora retorted. 'Well all I've got to say is that I know it's Christmas Eve and weird and wonderful things happen at this time of year. But please, dear, don't insult my intelligence by claiming another immaculate conception!'

A while later, Dora had just seen Connie safely into her house and she was about to turn and navigate herself down the dark steps with the aid of her torch when Jenny opened the Andersons' door.

'Is there a problem?' Jenny asked, flashing her torch light into Dora's eyes.

'There will be if you don't stop blinding me with that light.'

'Sorry,' said Jenny, lowering the torch. 'But what are you doing up here? Should you not be downstairs with your bairns? There might be a raid.'

'Just chummed Connie up to her house – she's a wee bit under the weather.'

'Under the weather?' exclaimed Jenny. 'I hope that's not a nice way of saying she's the worse for drink?'

'Oh, if it was just drink I'd be happy because she'd be sober in the morning.'

Dora's answer alerted Jenny, who sensed there could be a good bit of gossip coming her way. 'And what do you think is amiss? And you do know that anything you tell me won't go any further. No. No. I'm the soul of discretion.'

'Jenny, would you believe,' Dora confided in a loud whisper, 'that she's trying to tell me that she's not got a bun in the oven.'

'What?' Jenny exclaimed.

'And that's not all – she's adamant that she's not been with her own man nor anybody else's!'

A loud hiss escaped from Jenny but before she could reply, the bottom door opened and Johnny shouted up, 'Is everything all right up there? And it beats me how you still have dirt to dig at this time of night. Besides it's freezing cold and time you were all inside your own homes.'

Naturally Jenny couldn't divulge to Johnny exactly what Dora had imparted to her, but she did wish to warn him that Connie was probably a fast piece – a very fast piece. So, as she dished up his supper, she tentatively said, 'You know, son, I don't think Connie is all that she pretends to be.'

Johnny didn't reply. But he did give the sausage that he had just stabbed with his fork a great deal of attention – so much attention that anyone observing him would have thought that he'd never ever seen a sausage before.

'What I am trying to say is that I don't think she's a good influence on our Kitty.'

'That right? Well, Mum, I just don't know how Kitty would have coped when you were having your breakdown if Connie hadn't been here to shore her up.'

The atmosphere between mother and son was now so thick that you could have cut it with a knife. It was therefore no surprise to Johnny that Jenny lifted her coat and bag and left without wishing him a Merry Christmas.

When she first started out on her steep trek down Restalrig Road Jenny did not feel cold because her wrath was keeping her warm. Her hot indignation did not solely come from her resentment about the way Johnny had spoken to her, though. Her main concern was about the way that standards were changing – and in her view, dropping.

Turning at the foot of the road and into Summerside that would take her up to Industrial Road and then on to her colony house at Parkvale Place, she gave an involuntary shudder. The cold was beginning to seep into her bones now and all she wanted to do was to get home – to firmly close her door on a world that was becoming alien to her.

Once she had locked the outside door behind her she was surprised by the silence that greeted her. She expected to be deafened by the blaring noise from the Bakelite radio that Kate was forever listening to. Surely, she argued with herself, Tommy Handley on *ITMA* (*It's That Man Again*) or Mrs Mopp asking, 'Can I do you now, sir?' should have been entertaining Kate as she got on with the ironing.

Switching on the light, Jenny was concerned to see the pile of ironing just lying as she had left it. Then her eyes spied the granddaughter clock. Her mouth gaped. It was restored – better then new! She wanted to cry – to tell someone that Donald's clock was working again. Instinctively she dashed up the stairs and immediately switched on the light in Kate's bedroom.

The sight that greeted her of her sleeping daughter and Hans lying entwined under the blush-pink eiderdown caused her to cry out. 'Kate, Kate, what is that man doing in your bed?'

Kate sat bolt upright. She then looked down at slumbering Hans's contented face and she smiled sweetly before replying, 'Sleeping, Mum. Just sleeping.'

'I can bloody well see that he is sleeping, Kate. But has he done anything else but shut his eyes since you let him into your . . . bed?'

Kate giggled. 'Mum, next week it will be 1944 and I am forty-three and as we all might not see tomorrow, Hans and I have decided to be together.'

'Be together? He's . . . he's . . . he's a Polish refugee and worse still he's only a lowly porter.'

Kate was now out of bed and Hans was wide awake. 'Hans dear, I'm just going downstairs to talk to my mum. Now you get dressed, at your leisure, and I will have some tea and toast ready for you when you come down.'

'Tea and toast!' Jenny exploded. 'I would have thought with what he has had in here tonight he wouldn't be requiring anything else but forgiveness. Fornication, Kate, in case you have forgotten, is a sin!'

Kate and Jenny were now back down in the living room and Kate could not resist giving the clock another loving pat. 'You were saying, Mum, that he is only a porter. Think you might be wrong there. I mean, how many lowly porters do you know that are as skilled as my Hans?'

Time slowly ticked by. Jenny tried to think of an appropriate answer to Kate. None was forthcoming. 'This has been some night,' she eventually sulked. 'Sodom and Gomorrah is what Leith has become.'

Kate dissolved into laughter. 'Sodom and Gomorrah! And how do you come to that conclusion?'

'Unlike you, I don't think any of what I found out tonight . . . to be funny.'

'Like what?'

'Connie not being what she seems.' Jenny was quite animated now. 'And she could be . . . Worse still I then came home to find you, my daughter, shacked up with a Pole.' She paused to take in a breath. 'And when I think back to last September, which I really don't wish to do, and all that was going on in Leith Links, I am convinced that . . .' Jenny now drew herself up before whimpering, 'Kate, with all this . . . this . . . God-forbidding sex going on I honestly believe that everybody now thinks that the continuation of the human race depends on it!'

* * *

Times were hard. Everything from food and clothes to coal and even adequate housing were scarce, yet somehow Santa Claus managed to still get through with presents for the children.

At five o'clock on Christmas morning the Anderson household was awakened by Rosebud shouting, 'Dad, Kitty, Jack, Davy, Bobby, he's been! I've got a doll and a pram to push it in. There's also an apple . . . a rosy apple and a Mars Bar!'

Johnny groaned and rolled over in his bed. He was tempted to fall back into enjoying a long-overdue restful lie-in – that was until he remembered he was Rosebud's daddy and he should be up and spending time with her.

On the other hand it took Rosebud hauling the bedcovers off Kitty to get her to rouse.

Sleepy Kitty squinted at her old grey metal alarm clock. 'Oooh,' she groaned, 'it's not even six o'clock, my usual time for getting up. Rosebud,' she continued, 'don't you remember that I said to you that we were all supposed to have a long lie-in this morning?'

Kitty's plea to Rosebud was ignored. For the next half hour Rosebud pushed and shoved the second-hand refurbished pram up and down the hallway – at least twenty times. Whilst she was doing that she also dangled the doll by the arm, leg or upside down . . . anyway at all except how you would expect to see a precious baby handled. Its clothes also had been on and off so often that they now required washing. Naturally the Mars Bar had been scoffed but when it came to eating her porridge, which Kitty had got out of her bed to make, Rosebud wasn't hungry. It was then she said, 'I wonder if Connie is up and if she would like a shot of my pram?'

Kitty glanced at the clock; it was now just past six. 'Well, Connie will be up because she's on an early shift this morning so let's you and I go over and give her a peek at your new doll.'

The pram had been banged into Connie's door at least three times but there was no response from the house. Kitty became wary because Connie had been so sick and upset yesterday. She decided then to go back to her own flat and get Connie's house key.

Opening up the door Kitty shouted, 'Connie, Connie, nothing to worry about, it's only me, Kitty.'

There was no response. In fact it appeared to Kitty that there was a creeping feeling of unease in the house. Firstly she told Rosebud to go back and get Johnny, then she went from room to room looking for Connie but there was no one at home. Going back into the living room her apprehension mounted. Connie's work clothes were hung on a chair by the fireside. This meant that wherever Connie was she was not at home, nor was she going out to work.

When Johnny joined Kitty he asked, 'Where is she?'

Kitty shrugged. 'She was a bit queasy yesterday but that wouldn't explain where she has got to now. In an hour or so if she hasn't come back I'll ask Dora or Mrs Dickson . . . That's it – Mrs Dickson will know where she is.'

Bounding down the stairs Kitty then rattled Mrs Dickson's door handle before going into the house. She knew the old lady would be awake but not out of her bed yet. 'Mrs Dickson,' she called into the bedroom, 'it's me, Kitty. I'm just wondering if you know where Connie is.'

'No,' replied the old woman as she struggled up to a

sitting position in the bed. 'Something funny happened last night but I can't remember what it was now. Think I'm getting the old folks' disease. But ask Dora, she knows everything. Honestly if I sneeze twice she's in here with a hanky.'

Kitty decided that it was too early to knock up Dora and she was just about to go back upstairs when she heard whoops of joy coming out of Dora's house. Chapping the door she called, 'Dora, Dora, can I ask you something?'

Eventually the door was slowly opened by Dora who was dressed in a voluminous nightgown that Kitty was sure must have at one time belonged to Queen Victoria. 'Is there a problem, hen?'

'Not really a problem, Dora. It's just that I can't find Connie. Do you have any idea where she might be?'

Dora scowled. 'Not really, but a queer thing happened last night. You see I had just got all the Santa stuff sorted out and was getting into bed when I heard the stair door shut then a car or a taxi take off. Now that is unusual for around here.'

'You think so?' replied Kitty, who was deep in thought.

'Aye, hen, I do. You see there are plenty of bikes and a few number thirteen buses that go up and down the outside road, but cars . . . well they're for toffs and that's no any of us, is it?' Dora shook her head from side to side as the mystery of what had happened to Connie got to her too.

After Christmas, the next six days leading up to Hogmanay were spent with everybody wondering what had become of Connie.

Thankfully, on 31 December Kitty got a letter with a Whitburn, West Lothian, postmark. Ripping open the envelope, she was surprised to find it was from Connie. In the short communication, Connie briefly pointed out that she had had to go urgently to Glasgow to deal with an unexpected matter. Once she had got things sorted out in Glasgow she had then transferred herself to Whitburn where she had been born and raised. She then indicated that it was important, very important, that what had taken place in Glasgow should be laid to rest in Whitburn. When this was done she would then come home. In the meantime, could Kitty get her dad to speak to the managers at Robb's and explain she had been called away suddenly but that she would be back to take up her duties again on 5 January. She closed by wishing everybody a very happy New Year.

Kitty, who had felt all week that Dora knew something about Connie that she did not, was even more put out when, after reading Connie's letter, Dora said, 'Aye, it all figures. Poor lassie. What a thing to have on your conscience.'

Hogmanay was a hard day for Kitty. She knew, because her mother and granny had drummed it into her, that if a house was not spick and span, coal burning brightly in the hearth and food and drink available when the bells rang and the tall, dark and handsome man 'first foot' arrived, then bad luck would follow the household for the whole year. Terrified of inviting this curse into her home, Kitty had spent the whole day cleaning the house from top to bottom and cooking. By eleven o'clock at night all she still had to do was put the glowing hot ashes from the louping fire into the outside ashcan before the bells.

She heaved a deep sigh as she remembered the problems she had had with the food. This was because the days of the mandatory red salmon sandwiches for New Year visitors were long gone. Unfortunately, they would not return until after the war when shipments of the tinned fish would start to come in again from Canada. Another problem, one that she had not anticipated, was that with Connie still at large there was no black-market butter to make scrumptious shortbread. Kitty had tried her best with Stork unsalted margarine but, when she sampled it, she knew it lacked the luxury flavour that butter would have given it. On the bright side she had managed to get a large tub of Cairn the butcher's potted meat for the sandwiches. This delicacy, in everybody's opinion – in Restalrig anyway – was to die for. Kitty herself just couldn't believe how Mr Cairns got it to taste like roast beef.

All the shipyards in Leith had closed a couple of hours early on Hogmanay because there now was a growing belief that the war would soon be over and that the allies would emerge victorious.

Johnny and Jock were sitting nursing their second pint in their favourite watering hole when Johnny wiped the froth from his mouth with the back of his hand before announcing, 'Aye, next year is going to be some year, Jock.'

Jock nodded and replied, 'Aye, I think so too, son.'

'Mind you, the main obstacle will be the invasion of Europe.'

'You're right there.'

'Don't suppose you have any idea of when, where and with what they will do it?'

Jock shook his head. 'Your guess is as good as mine. Mind you, I don't think wee Monty, who don't forget sorted out Rommel's hash in . . .' Jock hesitated as he tried to remember the exact date and place.

'October 1942, Jock, at El Alamein, it was.'

'Aye, that's right, Johnny lad, and do you know that was when the tide in this war turned. But that will make no difference, you mark my words. Oh aye, that Eisenhower, the big American bloke with the even bigger ego, will get overall command when the big push does come in Europe.'

'Talking of the push, will they big concrete things, that seem to get bigger every day, have anything to do with the invasion?'

'Big concrete things?' Jock mused.

'Aye, the massive ugly building-like things that are standing in the water at western corner . . .'

'Do you mean they big prefabricated sections that are sitting in the big launching lagoon?'

'Aye.'

'Dinnae ken what they're for . . . just ken they're top secret. And, before you ask again, I really don't know. I was only told that they are vital to the war effort and that we had to give priority to building these sections because they will eventually be married up with other bits being built on the Clyde.'

'Hmmm,' was all Johnny replied.

'But what I do know,' Jock whispered, leaning forward towards Johnny, 'is that you shouldn't be asking all these questions. Sure you go on too much about things that are no for eating. Honestly I am beginning to think that you're some sort of double agent.'

'Look, I only asked what they prefabricated buildings that we've spent so much time banging the gither are for.'

'Best finish our pints and get ourselves home.'

'Aye, but if we want to walk in on the first chime of the

New Year how about we go and have a sit-in fish tea in the chippie up the road?'

'See, is that no what I've just been saying that when you talk about food you keep yourself out of trouble.'

By the time Johnny got himself home his sons Jack and Davy, along with their pals – and thankfully Colin, Jack's best mate, who was tall and dark – had been the house's first foot.

Johnny immediately took himself into the kitchen where Kitty was making a pot of tea just in case any guests were teetotal. 'Happy New Year, darling,' Johnny chuckled before hugging Kitty tightly. 'And I hope it is a good one for you.'

Extricating herself from her father's embrace and lifting her sherry glass, Kitty sighed, 'You know, Dad, I do so miss Connie. So how about you get yourself a dram from off the table there and we toast her good health.' Both now had their glasses raised and Kitty continued, 'Here's to you, Connie, and thank you for helping me get through these last few years and whatever it is that took you away I hope you've got it sorted out now and you're getting yourself back to us.'

Johnny nodded. 'Aye, and I also say hurry back, lassie, because not only do Kitty and Rosebud miss you, but so do I.'

The SMT bus had just revved up and then sped out of Whitburn on Sunday 4 January 1944 when Connie accepted that she had to pass an hour before it would drop her off in St Andrew Square.

They were barely away from Whitburn's Cross when the conductress relieved her of a bob for a single to Edinburgh.

It was then that Connie snuggled down in her seat and for the first fifteen minutes, as they had called in at Blackburn, the old Livingston village, then on to the Calders, she tried hard not to think about anything except these places that had been so important to her in her childhood. Mid Calder was receding from view and she could do nothing other than go over the events of the last ten days.

These happenings she knew could alter her whole life and the very way she looked at it. To be truthful, it had been such an earth-shattering shock for her to accept the fate that had befallen her. As Sighthill loomed over the horizon she inhaled deeply, trying to convince herself that the decisions she had come to and what she had done, and would do, were the right things to do. Some would say that she should have heeded the teachings of the Bible. She shrugged. They could say that, but they didn't have to live with her conscience; she did.

By the time she finally reached Restalrig it was seven o'clock in the evening. She shrunk down into herself. Grateful she was for the dirty, black fog that added to the blackness of the night. Yes, she was just so pleased to have this shroud to conceal her.

Tiptoeing into the stair she felt her way along the passage and was relieved when her right hand grabbed for the stair banister. She had scaled the steps up to the first landing and was just about to turn towards her own door when the Andersons' door opened and Johnny, torch in hand, came out.

'Is that you, Connie?' he barked, shining the flashlight into her face.

Connie nodded. 'The last time I looked in the mirror that was who I was, right enough.'

'Very funny. Don't you realise that I've been worried sick about you? Where the hell have you been and why did you do a runner?'

A deep intake of breath through her nose was necessary before Connie plucked up her courage to say, 'Johnny, if you have a minute or two to come into my house . . . I will try and explain to you . . . bring you up to date with some happenings . . .'

'Tell me here on the landing.'

'No. What I have to say is private and confidential and not for discussion like a stairheid rammy.'

'Phoo oo oo,' Johnny puffed. 'Look, I was just going downstairs to our shed to get a couple of briquettes to keep the fire going through the night. I mean it's just so Baltic right now that you just have to try to keep some heat going. But once I've done that I'll come over. Mind you, I'll probably have Kitty and Rosebud in tow.'

Connie leant forward and grabbed Johnny's right arm. 'No, Johnny, what I have to say is for your ears only.'

Half an hour passed before Johnny's light tap came on Connie's outside door. On hearing it, the apprehensive Connie had the desire to ignore it. She wondered if he would be able to cope with what she was about to confide to him and would he understand her reasons for not doing what seemed proper?

On opening up the door, Connie deliberately did not switch on the light. She really felt that what she had to say to Johnny was best said by the light of the fire, which, thanks to a Neill's firelighter, was now aglow.

When Johnny followed her into the living room she indicated to him that he should sit down. Watching her pour two liberal glasses of whisky, Johnny concluded that she was preparing him for a shock.

Sitting herself down on a chair opposite him Connie swallowed hard before she slowly began. 'Johnny, there are two things that happened to me that I have to tell you about.'

'Uh huh,' Johnny responded as the amber liquid warmed his throat.

'But I think I should start with the second one first and then I'll go on to the first thing that is what really concerns you and yours.'

'Fine.'

'Now the day that I left I had been so sick and dizzy all day that I just wanted to crawl into my bed and die there. Within an hour I was awakened by someone knocking on my door. Reluctantly I got up and there on the doorstep was a ghost from my past.'

'A ghost?'

'Well he looked like a ghost. He was so pale and drawn. Immediately I asked him in.'

'Your husband, what's his name?'

'Mark Sharp. No it wasn't him.'

'Then who?'

'None other than Jamie Oman, my husband's lover, and the poor soul was completely bereft. You see it turns out Mark was knocked down and killed in the blackout.'

Johnny made to butt in but he was silenced when Connie put up a restraining hand.

'Poor Jamie, who had stood by Mark through all the years and affairs,' she continued, 'thought he had nothing else to do but get Mark buried.' Connie sniffed back her tears. 'You know people who are . . . well . . . like Mark and Jamie have no rights. They are treated like scum. I was so sorry for Jamie; he truly loved Mark. So much so he forgave him everything and all he wanted was to get him laid to rest respectfully.'

'So what was the problem then?'

'As I've already said – Jamie had no rights so it had to be Mark's next of kin who would see to his disposal . . . and that unfortunately was me. So you see, what else could I do but go through to Glasgow with Jamie and sort things out? We did that and then we decided to take Mark to Whitburn and lay him to rest in the old churchyard cemetery beside his grandparents. I should add there was a bank book so even after we paid Brownlees, the undertaker at Whitburn, there was a four-figure sum left. The bank would only pay it to me and I know you will think that I am daft but I did not want Mark's money. So,' she grimaced, 'I just took fifty pounds to cover my expenses and loss of wages and I handed the rest to Jamie.'

'I take it he didn't want it.'

'Not at first. But I persuaded the poor soul that it was only right that he take the money. And before you say anything, I truly believe that it was Jamie's right. Whatever else, he and Mark had spent their lives like a married couple and therefore he should inherit what Mark left.'

'So that was it then?'

Connie shook her head. Getting to her feet she then went over to her handbag and from it she fished out an official-looking document which she pushed into Johnny's hand.

After quickly scanning the paper Johnny commented, 'It's Mark's death certificate, but why would you want that?'

'Well, I will now have to go up to the Edinburgh Corporation and ask for the rental deeds for this flat to be changed into my name and they may, and quite rightly so, decide that I, as a widow with no dependent . . .' She hesitated and he could see her face was now afire before she elaborated. 'I have no children, so I may be transferred to a one-bedroomed house on the other side of the road.'

'Is your probable flitting the second issue you want to speak to me about?'

Connie was now gnawing on her right index finger and Johnny rose up and grabbed her hand. 'Biting your finger isn't going to tell me what's worrying you. So come on, let's both sit on the settee and you can tell me there.'

No sooner had Connie sat down next to Johnny than she was convulsed with tears and sobbing. 'Johnny,' she tentatively began, 'I know you will be angry and please believe me I never thought it could happen, but on the day I ran away to Glasgow, I was happy to scamper because I realised that I was . . . Oh, Johnny . . . Pregnant!'

'What?' he exclaimed before jumping up and running his hands through his hair. 'You don't mean . . . You just can't . . . I mean, how old are you again?'

'Thirty-eight.'

'Good grief! I know that life begins at forty for most and I was hoping it would for me too, but . . . a baby!'

Connie was weeping quietly now. 'Thank you, Johnny. Thank you. Thank you.'

'For what?'

'Not trying to say that the mess I am in . . . I mean that . . . you would not have denied that the baby was yours. Oh, Johnny, that is so good of you.'

'What else could I do because I know for sure that you were a virgin . . .' He gulped and shook his head. He did not say to Connie but his thoughts were now on his mother's warnings to him when he was just a teenager and they were as binding today as they were then. 'Johnny,' she would warn, 'remember if you get a lassie into trouble you have to do the right thing by her and marry her. No child should go through life without the protection of their father's name. It is so degrading to be labelled a bastard and therefore second class.'

His reminiscences were interrupted when he heard Connie say, 'So you see, Johnny, when I went through to Glasgow I was desperate. Completely out of my mind with worry, I was. I just couldn't think of anything other than finding a solution and quick at that . . . so I . . .'

Johnny was now backing away from Connie. 'No. Please don't tell me that you went to one of these places up an alley or somewhere as sordid and . . .'

'What are you talking about?'

'You aborting our child!'

Connie at first cackled and then, going over and striking Johnny on the shoulder, she hollered, 'All my life I have wished to be a mother. That is why I took on your brood. Do you ever think of how much time I put in with Kitty, Davy and Rosebud? Abort?' Connie was now lovingly rubbing her hand over her stomach. 'Me, abort? Oh no, do you think so little of me that you think I could do that?'

'Then what was the solution you came to?'

'Well, now Mark has died, and I spoke to Jamie and he says he will corroborate my story, I will claim that Mark was the father of my precious bundle. So that means, Johnny, you don't have to . . .'

'No. I don't have to . . . But I bloody well will. Mark dying changes everything. You are now free to marry me and I am free to marry you.'

Utter relief seeped into Connie, causing her to collapse

down on to the couch. 'You mean you will marry me, and soon at that?'

'Precisely . . . and in the meantime, because I lost one wife who was a bit on the old side to be having a baby, away you go through to your bedroom and get your things and move into my house.'

'Move into your house right now?'

'Aye. You will be properly looked after there.'

'Don't be silly, Johnny. Once I'm your wife I will move into your house because I will have the right to do so. But at this present time it would not only cause upset and tongues to wag but—'

'Let them wag. I don't care.'

'You wouldn't, but Kitty, Jack and Davy would. Besides, by waiting the six weeks it will give Kitty time to accept that there will be two women in the Anderson household.'

'Look, as far as I'm concerned we have made a child together so technically we are married and in six weeks we will also be churched so . . .'

'As I have already said I don't think your family, especially your holier-than-thou mother, would find me sharing your bed . . .' – Connie gulped – 'easy right now. And, Johnny, neither would I.' She hesitated before quietly adding, 'And what is also important to me is . . . Johnny, do you . . . do you love me?'

'To be honest I missed you so much when you went away that I realised that I have grown very fond of you . . . but to love you like I loved Sandra . . . well, in time, who can tell? Right now what I'm offering you is . . . to work very hard to provide for you and our child and my name as protection . . . is that enough to be going on with?'

If she was disappointed she hid it well but she did accept his terms. After all, if she was being truthful she loved him so much that any terms he laid down would have been acceptable to her.

Everyone thought that Connie and Johnny getting married would be welcomed by Kitty. After all, was this not her way of escaping and being able to lead her own life? But Kitty was a young romantic and she still thought that Johnny's love for her mum, Sandra, should endure, even beyond the grave.

The morning after what Kitty had thought was the worst Sunday night of her life, she found herself kneeling down by her mother's grave. 'Mum,' she began as she patted the snow-covered mound, 'I thought you should know that Dad, who should be remaining loyal to you, is going to marry . . . marry Connie Sharp. He says it's got nothing to do with how he felt about you – and still feels about you. It's because he's lonely and as he's a relatively young man it is only natural that he wishes to share his life with someone.' Sniffing and blubbering, Kitty continued, 'Mind you I don't think it will be . . . well, you know . . . a proper marriage. I think he just wants a pal – especially as he knows I want to go out and get a job. Anyway, what do you think?'

'Not quite sure what to think,' a disembodied voice replied.

Kitty jumped and quickly looked about until her eyes landed on the figure of one of the gravediggers. 'What do mean?' demanded Kitty. 'And you shouldn't be listening in to people's private conversations.'

'That so?' the man huffily replied. 'Well if you want to keep it private you should just talk to yourself. Anyway what I think is that your dad should get married again and you, Miss, should take the opportunity to do something with your life.'

'What do you mean?'

'Just that it is about time you and your brothers and the rest of them should stop coming here and pestering this poor woman with all your problems.'

'Pestering her? I'm only trying to give her all the family news.'

'Aye, and then ask her what she thinks.' The man now turned to point at the large Italian memorial stone and added, 'See there at the top of that memorial stone it says RIP. Well that means "Rest in Peace", and how your mother ever gets to rest in peace I sure don't know. Not a week goes by without someone coming in here and telling her something that she doesn't want to know or can't do anything about.'

Kitty grunted, before deciding to leave the cemetery, there and then. Going out of the gates she decided to go and tell Jenny the news about Johnny and Connie. Hoping she was that she would get the right answer from her grandmother – the one she wished to hear.

Jenny's response, however, was not what Kitty expected. But then someone saying, 'Well he could do a lot worse and look at the advantages for you,' wasn't quite music to Kitty's ears.

'What advantages?' shrieked Kitty.

'Well as history tells us there is nothing but war when two women share a kitchen. And I have always thought it was a shame that you were tied down when your mum died. So grab the chance. Away and look for a job.'

'A job?'

'Aye, find yourself some work that pays well. And by the way, I think since there is the rationing to contend with, that your dad and Kate should get married on the same day and then I will only have one wedding tea to beg, borrow and cook for!'

'Aunt Kate is getting married too?' Kitty asked.

'Aye.' Jenny sniffed long and hard before adding, 'To that Polish fellow.'

All Kitty could respond with was a large gulp.

Kitty was still fuming when she left her grandmother's house. To be truthful she was in a sort of smouldering daze. Just as she was passing the midwife's house, halfway up Restalrig Road, she jumped when a voice called out, 'Hello there, Kitty, is this you on your way home after delivering another baby?' When no reply was forthcoming from Kitty, the midwife, who had attended after Kitty had delivered Dora's baby, said, 'You look upset. As they say, Kitty, a trouble shared is a trouble halved, so why don't you come in and have a cup of tea and tell me all about it?'

An hour later Kitty was on her way home and whatever advice Joan Fowler had given her it put a spring in her step. Indeed, as she purposefully strode out, she seemed to have regained her positive attitude to life.

A couple of days passed before Kitty managed to get Jack to herself. 'Jack,' she began confidentially, 'what do you think of dad getting married again and what difference do you think it will make to us?'

Jack, for the next few minutes, blew his lips in and out in a series of small puffs. Kate could see that ever-cautious

169

Jack was going to measure every word before he uttered a syllable. Eventually he drawled, 'Have a feeling, Kitty, and it is just a feeling, that there is more to this than meets the eye. I mean, the peal of wedding bells came out of the blue. And if they knew they were going to be a couple why did she disappear over Christmas?'

'I'm uneasy too but it is just . . . Oh, Jack, I have run the house here since Mum died and . . . well, do you think Connie will be happy to let me carry on?'

'No. And I feel the two of us won't feel at home when Connie does take over.'

Kitty nodded.

'Look, Jack, it's not that I don't like her as a person it is just that she's . . .'

'Not Mum and in my book never will be.'

'Do you think it will be a . . . ?'

'No. And thankfully if it ever goes that way she is too old to present us with another Rosebud. So I think that you and me . . . and we have six weeks . . . have to think about how best we survive.' He paused. 'I think we may have to leave home.'

'Leave home! But where would we go?'

'I've finished my apprenticeship.'

'So what has you being a fully qualified engineer got to do with leaving home?'

'Well I'm now capable of being a fifth engineer on merchant ships. So I've applied to the shipping companies for a job . . .'

'No. No. Not on the Atlantic or Russian convoys, Jack, they are so . . . dangerous!'

'No. To keep you from worrying I have said on my application that I would prefer to sail in the Mediterranean.'

Kitty, who had been standing, now flopped down on to the couch. Placing her hand over her mouth she began to heave and sigh. 'Jack,' she whimpered, 'it is bad enough me being out of my mind with worry for Bobby, who is dicing with death in the Atlantic, without you going to the Med. They get torpedoed there too, you know, and they're sitting ducks for the Luftwaffe.'

'Aye, but Malta and North Africa can give us air cover.'

'And if you go and I am left . . . how will I cope?'

'That's what I am trying to get through to you. You just have to leave home and get a job where you get board and lodgings.'

'You mean in the Navy?'

'Well not necessarily the Navy; you could also try the Army or Air Force – anywhere that you will get digs thrown in.'

If Jack thought that his solution was going to quieten Kitty's apprehension, it only added to it. Especially as she realised that he would be away in the Navy before the wedding. She, however, would have to stay until after Connie became Mrs Johnny Anderson. Also, and just as importantly, her promise to her mother about Rosebud had to be honoured until, at least, there was another 'mother' in place. That was the one thing that Kitty *was* sure of. Yes, knowing Connie, she knew that when she did marry her dad she would willingly take on his responsibilities in the form of Rosebud and Davy.

The euphoria Kate felt at the upcoming prospect of becoming Mrs Busek was tempered by the knowledge that Hans was a porter in the store where she was looked upon as senior management.

Two weeks later, when dawdling to work on a bright Monday morning, Kate drew up abruptly. There, displayed in the jeweller's shop, just at the side of the Palace Picture House, was an advert which read: 'Due to family bereavement we require an experienced watchmaker to run this shop. All enquiries welcomed. Good wages and conditions.'

'That's just what my Hans needs,' she cried. 'A job where he can use his skills.' Looking at the opening hours, which were the same as the department store she worked in, she silently mouthed, *Blast*. No way could she hang on until the shop opened because if she did then that would mean she would be late for her own job.

As she scurried along Great Junction Street it was as if she had wings on her feet. Once she got herself inside the department store she didn't even wait to take her coat off before going in search of Hans.

She easily found him, cleaning out the gents' lavatory. This humiliating sight added to her determination that he must be found a job where he could use his talents.

'Hans,' she said, grabbing him by the arm, 'I must talk to you, and now at that.'

'You have changed your mind about . . .'

'No. And don't be silly. I love you and that's why I want what is best for us. And the two of us working together in here isn't that. Now do you know the small jeweller's shop on the end of Duke Street?'

'Yes. I looked in their window last week as I wished to go in to purchase a nice ring for you but it was all locked up.'

'Precisely. Now listen.'

Ten minutes later Kate was pushing Hans out of the back door and pointing him in the direction of Duke Street. She

172

smiled as she thought how smart his retreating figure looked dressed in the borrowed lounge suit, naturally taken out on the approval system, from Men's Outfitting.

By the afternoon Kate was making out a receipt for Hans for the smart single-breasted navy-blue suit complete with waistcoat. Now it was not as had happened frequently in the past, when customers took clothes out on 'appro' and had then worn the garments to a function and the clothing had become damaged so they had no other option but to pay for them. No. Hans Busek was now the newly appointed manager of the watchmaker and jeweller's shop in Duke Street. This meant he required to be appropriately dressed and therefore the suit was a necessary purchase.

Within three weeks Jack was sailing in the moderately warm waters of the Mediterranean and he acknowledged that his grandmother had been correct when she had advised him to always look hard into every situation and find the silver lining. He now knew that the silver lining for him, when his dad had announced he was to remarry, was that he was forced to go out into the big bad world and make it on his own. Up till then he had liked the comfort and security of being part of the family – being provided with a safe, accommodating shelter had been so important to him. This being true, he also admitted that since his mum's premature demise he had felt responsible for Kitty and Davy, and to a lesser degree Rosebud. Now he accepted that they, like him, would eventually have to cut the ties from the household home and make a life and family for themselves. After all, hadn't Bobby shown, by example, that that was what they should be doing?

* * *

The wedding day for both Johnny and Kate was Saturday, 26 February and even although it was at the end of February, it still had, for Kate and Connie anyway, some of the romance of St Valentine's Day two weeks before.

Two telegrams were delivered on the morning of the wedding. Kitty took possession of them. When she opened the first she was surprised and pleased that Bobby had sent his congratulations to his father and Connie. He also wished them a long and happy marriage. She was just about to open the second, which she was sure was congratulations from Jack to their father, when Rosebud screamed, 'Kitty, where are you? I'm very hungry and so is my baby doll.' Before she sped from the room Kitty tucked both telegrams into her handbag. She intended to hand both over to her father after the ceremony.

Both couples had favoured a registry office marriage but this decision had absolutely horrified Jenny. She even said that she would not attend either of the services. The reason given was that if her God was not being asked to bless the unions then she could not add to the slight to Him by attending.

After prolonged negotiations, both couples relented and agreed to be married in the vestry of South Leith Parish Church. For three of the group this was not too big a climb-down as they were all members of that church but, for Hans, it was a major step as he was not, nor did he intend to become, a member of the Church of Scotland. Nonetheless, as his most desired wish was to be legally married to his darling Kate, he vowed to keep faithful to her in sickness and in health, for better or for worse, for the rest of his natural life. These sacred vows were made in front of the South Leith church's ordained minister.

The brides both looked radiant and happy. Both were dressed in their very best, which, because of a shortage of clothing coupons, had been altered to suit the occasion. Kate, whom her mother had thought was starting to dress far too young for her age since she became engaged to Hans, wore a royal-blue suit with matching hat that Kate herself had decorated with ribbons and flowers. Connie, on the other hand, had chosen a voluminous red dress with a matching, thankfully moderately subdued, Carmen Miranda in *That Night in Rio*-style hat. Despite there being only artificial flowers and cherries available, it nevertheless took Connie three nights to produce an exotic Easter bonnet that brought smiles and titters to everybody who eyed it.

After getting her own way about having church blessed weddings, Jenny had thrown herself into providing a reception tea at her house in Parkvale Place. The spread in peacetime would have been remarked upon as extraordinarily lavish and even more so in times of severe rations and shortages.

Everything went according to plan except that Kitty, who had started crying in the church, seemed to be so forlorn that Jenny had to take her aside and say to her, 'I know it is difficult for you but this is your dad and Connie's big day so try to smile.' Kitty nodded but the tears still tumbled down.

At the end of the evening, Hans, who was eager to leave with Kate to spend their honeymoon night in a hotel, got up and thanked everyone, especially Jenny, for their lovely day.

It was now Johnny's turn to speak and, taking Connie's hand in his he began with, 'It has been a very special day for me and my lovely wife.' Everyone tittered. 'And,' Johnny paused to make sure he had everybody's attention before continuing, 'now we wish to share a wonderful secret with you.'

Connie blushed. 'No. Not here, Johnny.'

'Yes, here,' was Johnny's emphatic reply, while giving her stomach a loving pat. 'You see, my Connie is pregnant and our baby is due at the beginning of June!'

Jenny collapsed onto a chair. Kate gasped and Kitty thrust herself towards her father. Taking the two telegrams from her handbag she forcefully threw them at him. 'One,' she shrieked as she fell to the floor, 'is from Bobby wishing you well and the other . . . is to say . . . is to say . . . that my darling brother Jack's ship was torpedoed and he was . . . killed outright!'

Kate extracted herself from Hans's grip and she bent down to take Kitty into her arms. 'No. No. My darling,' she began. 'This cannot be. It must not be.'

'It is,' sobbed Kitty, 'and it is my dad's, and only my dad's fault. Jack, my darling brother, would not have signed up for the Merchant Navy except for our dad getting married again.'

Lifting her head she then surveyed all the guests before she added, 'He just couldn't bear to see our mum replaced but thank goodness he isn't alive, Dad, to know that you bedded Connie before you had a right to do so! Done what you dared all of us not to do for fear of giving you a red face. Well, Dad, look at my face, it's crimson with shame. Stinging red-hot because of the embarrassment I feel for our family. How could you, Dad?'

An uneasy silence filled the room and all eyes were on Johnny. They witnessed his face become bloodless as the horror of what Kitty had revealed sunk into his consciousness. Physically dropping down on to the floor his eyes sought Kitty's in an effort to plead for her forgiveness. Slipping his hand over towards her he tried to cover hers but she pulled away from him. 'I am so sorry, Kitty. Can't you see I was lonely and afraid the night you went to Liverpool? Connie, dear Connie, was the only one at home that I could turn to. She's not a bad person. All her adult life she too has felt forlorn and isolated and we thought . . .'

Kitty put up her hand to indicate to her father that she had something to say then in a voice full of emotion she muttered, 'That's the trouble, Dad, you didn't think. Both of you only thought of your own gratification and the result of that is my Jack, Mum's darling boy, her Jack Spratt, is now in a watery grave.'

'I admit I've done wrong and that I did not give you, my children, the support you needed when your mum . . .' He hesitated before whispering, 'When Sandra died, but if you will give us a chance . . .' He quickly held out his hand to Connie. 'We, Connie and I, will work hard to give you the home and support you all deserve.'

'Fine, Dad, but the other thing I was going to tell you when we got home tonight was that tomorrow I am moving out. You see I applied, and I have been accepted, to start my nurse's training in Leith Hospital on Monday. So what I had intended to do was spend the weekend with my supposedly supportive and loving family and then give you and Connie space.'

'We can still do that and mourn for Jack.'

'No, Dad, I will only be going back up to Restalrig to pack my bags.'

Kitty turned to face Jenny. 'Granny,' she pleaded, 'could I stay here with you until tomorrow night and then I will get out of everybody's way. Oh and Granny, before I can pack a suitcase do you have one that I could borrow?'

Jenny nodded. 'Of course you can stay. Hans and Kate also had something to tell everyone tonight and that is they will be making their home with me. Housing is so short and I too would by lonely without my Kate.' She said no more but the malevolent stare she gave Johnny spoke volumes.

The beginning of her married life with Johnny had not lived up to Connie's romantic expectations.

Kitty's news that Jack had been killed had completely devastated Johnny, and the feeling had only been aggravated by Kitty screaming that Jack had only signed up for the Merchant Navy as he did not wish to be around when Johnny replaced his darling mum, Sandra, with Connie.

The result of all this remorse was that when the family returned home from the wedding reception there was a melancholy air throughout the house.

Eventually Connie climbed into Johnny's bed. But instead of being welcomed by her husband, her partner for the night was none other than a very fractious Rosebud.

Inconsolable, Johnny spent his wedding night alone by the fireside. All he could do was plead with God. Over and over he asked Him through sobs and cries, 'Why, dear Father, did you decide to punish me yet again? I try to think what heinous crimes I have committed that make You test me so? And to take my Jack, who was just a devil-may-care slip of a lad. But he was a loyal son who deserved not to have his life stolen from him.' The other problem that was causing Johnny so much grief was that Jack wouldn't be buried in Seafield cemetery beside his mother, so the family could not go and pay their respects to him there. Instead

Jack's mortal remains were now in the depths of the Mediterranean Sea. It was just so difficult for Johnny to accept that all Jack would have in remembrance was his name on a plaque in South Leith church. The plaque would also register the names of the other young men in the congregation who had fallen in the present conflict.

Honeymooning with Connie was a prospect that Johnny just could not contemplate at this time of such overwhelming sorrow. Unfortunately this abstention was his way of doing penance, and never for a moment did he consider that it was wrong to inflict this punishment on innocent Connie.

Kate also had a problem with honeymooning. In her case it was not that she and Hans slept apart. No, they were very much together in every sense of being married. They had, however, not gone to a hotel for the wedding night as planned but had stayed at Parkville Place.

It was right that they had because Kate was awakened in the early hours with what at first she thought were the howls of a wounded animal. Going downstairs to investigate she found the wails were coming from Kitty, her heartbroken niece.

'Come on, darling,' she pleaded as she swept Kitty up into her arms. 'Jack is at peace and he would not wish you to be so distraught.'

'Aunty Kate,' sobbed Kitty, 'why?'

'Why did Jack have to die?'

'Yes, but also why did Dad and Connie . . . ?'

A few long sighs escaped Kate before she muttered, 'Don't be too hard on your dad or Connie. Can't you see they were just two lonely people who started to be attracted to each other? It is a natural thing for a man and woman to be drawn towards each other. Nature is clever. Her purpose is to get us to reproduce and it has made the union of a man and . . .' She was about to say wife but she hesitated before adding, 'a woman a desirable and beautiful experience.'

'It can't be as you say because I am always told it is wrong and dirty.'

Kate huffed. 'They say that to put you off. You see, my darling, no one would wish you to have a child out of marriage. It is just so important that a child is brought up in a home with a mum and dad.'

'Then why did God take my mum?'

Kate couldn't answer that question so all she said was, 'Monday is a new beginning for you. You are going out into the world and you will meet many people and be tempted so often to break the rules.' Kate paused. 'I know about temptation because I broke the rules twice and . . .'

'Did you ever regret breaking them?'

'To be truthful – no. And faced with what I was on those two occasions I would do exactly as I did then. But, my dear Kitty, one of them resulted in my having a miscarriage after an accident and that I do regret. Believe me, since then I have just yearned to be a mother. I am lucky in that your mum shared you and your brothers with me. That's fine but I have not had my own child to hold and I sorely regret having missed that.' Kitty made as if to interrupt but Kate silenced her by pressing two of her fingers over Kitty's mouth. 'Shush, dear, and listen. Your dad, my brother Johnny, is a good man. What I believe, and I most certainly do, is that Connie does care deeply for him. What I am saying is they are not bed-hoppers. They genuinely care for each other and they never meant to hurt anyone. Surely you won't punish two lonely . . .'

Kitty struggled free from Kate. 'Lonely? How could Dad or Connie be lonely when they had the family all around them?'

Drawing Kitty closely into herself again, Kate replied, 'Kitty, I know how lonely and isolated you can feel in a room full of people. There are different kinds of loneliness. Hans and I were lonely until we found each other.' Hoping that Kitty would in time mature and repair the broken relationship with her father, Kate reluctantly removed her arms from Kitty. Without saying another word Kate returned to her bedroom and sank gratefully into the comforting arms of her husband.

Monday saw Johnny up and dressed for work. The luxury of taking time to mourn was something that the war did not allow. He was just about to leave when Rosebud, dragging a doll with her, came into the kitchen. 'Dad,' she demanded, 'when is Kitty coming home? I don't like her bossing me about but I don't like this house without her.'

Johnny stopped to stoop down and take Rosebud into his arms and then in a voice laden with emotion he gently said, 'Kitty has gone away to a new job but I'm sure she'll come and see you on your day off. Now I will ask Connie to take you down to see Granny. Granny is very sad and seeing you will cheer her up.'

At the shipyards, a management and union meeting had been called and they all congregated in the boardroom at nine o'clock. 'What's the panic?' Johnny managed to ask Jock Weldon in a discreet whisper.

'Don't know but it's serious business.'

The chairman opened the meeting by thanking everyone

for coming. He then went on to say, 'Gentleman, I think that you are all aware that with the full mobilisation of Russia and America that the big push to liberate Europe will now be sooner rather than later. This means we will have to meet all of our obligations on time.

'Since the war began it has been evident that every man, woman and apprentice in our organisation has worked hard to assist in the winning of the war. What I am asking here today is that we continue to work in harmony to do all that we can to repair the damaged ships brought in and build the new ones – these new ones that are required for the forthcoming invasion.'

Jock put up his hand to indicate he wished to speak. The chairman nodded consent. 'Are we to be told the exact date that the invasion will take place?'

The chairman shook his head. 'That is top-secret information of which only top brass would be apprised. But hazarding a guess I think perhaps late spring. But now there is a triple consensus to be reached on the most advantageous date . . . well, who knows.'

Before the chairman could continue his secretary then came in and laid a note in front of him. He read the note and just nodded. 'Mr Anderson, Johnny,' he then continued, 'what I would like to say to you is . . .' He hesitated before adding, 'That just now I hope and trust that all industrial-relations matters that arise can be swiftly dealt with.'

Johnny just nodded. All the others around the table looked at each other in amazement. Why, they all wondered, was the verbose senior shop steward not replying verbally in the affirmative. They expected to hear him put an eloquent forceful argument for better conditions either by way of the pay packets or on the shop floor. After all, he had the ball at his foot, so why did he not kick it?

The chairman looked down at the note again and before he drew the meeting to a close he said, 'Johnny, the needs of the country are exceptional today but there is no one in this company, from the boardroom down to the man who cleans the lavatories, who would think anything other than that your place today is at home with your family.'

As everyone, with the exception of Johnny and Jock, filed out of the room they either nodded to Johnny or patted him on the shoulder. When there was only Johnny and Jock left sitting, Jock placed a hand over Johnny's. 'One of your laddies, son?'

Johnny managed to mumble, 'My boy Jack.'

'But the laddie just went away a few weeks . . .'

'Aye. This bloody war has shattered all my dreams. All I ever wanted was my bairns to thrive and have good lives. Live into their promised three score and ten. But Jack, my lad, who was one of the best young engineers to be trained here in Robb's, has been cut down in his prime.' He stopped to mop his tears. 'And then there's Bobby, who could have come ashore but decided to go back out on the Atlantic convoys to get the supplies in. And the Gerries, who know they are about to be paid back, will try even harder now to sink every ship that they can.'

'Aye, and that Polish guy that your sister, Kate, married will be anticipating what the next few months will bring too.'

Johnny nodded. 'The Poles, especially the ones that sought asylum here, have fought on. Most of them joined our forces and they are the bravest of the brave and the most reckless of any of the servicemen.'

Jock now wished to get Johnny either home or thinking about something else and he cautiously asked, 'How did your wedding go on Saturday?'

'Fine until Kitty threw the telegram about Jack in my face. Mind you, that was after I told them about . . . which ended up with neither Kitty nor my mother . . . how can I put it . . . well, Jock, they are certainly not looking forward to Connie becoming a mother in five months.'

Monday mornings usually meant women were up to their elbows in soap suds and they would be praying it would be a 'good drying day' so they could hang the washing out.

Connie knew that she should be trying to prove that she was as good a housewife as Kitty and hang the laundry out. The truth was that Connie had never wished to be known as housewife of the year. She really was more interested in people. This being the case she decided that as Jenny would be her mother-in-law for the rest of her life, she should go and try to broker a peace between them.

Not wishing to be left on the doorstep after the door was slammed in her face, Connie decided to take a peace offering in the form of Rosebud with her. She knew that Jenny would not pass up a chance to spend some time with the child.

When she arrived at Parkville Place Connie's courage began to wane and she was ready to do an about-turn when Rosebud wriggled out of her grasp and began banging on the door.

'Granny, Granny,' she screamed as her small hands pummelled the door. 'It's me and we've brought some of Moffatt's bran scones.'

Slowly the door opened and there was a dishevelled

Jenny still attired in a long cotton nightdress. Astounded, Connie's mouth gaped and she became anxious when Jenny leant forward and clung to the door for support.

'Are you ill?' Connie asked apprehensively.

'No,' Jenny gasped while attempting to straighten herself up. 'It's just . . .' She said no more because like a confused butterfly she began to flutter and slip towards the floor.

Before Connie could get to Jenny's aid a frightened Rosebud began to cry and reach out to Connie. 'In a minute, dear,' Connie replied. 'We just have to get Granny inside. Now you go in front of me and open the doors. And if there is anything on the couch, pull it off.'

By half carrying and half dragging Jenny, an over-anxious Connie managed to get her back into the living room and safely settled onto the settee.

'What's wrong? What can I do?' Connie implored as she stroked Jenny's forehead.

Struggling to sit up, Jenny put out a shaking hand towards Rosebud. The startled child pushed herself into Connie's side and she simpered, 'I don't like my granny like she is just now.'

Taking her hand off Jenny's brow, Connie turned to pull Rosebud on to her lap. 'There, there, precious,' she crooned. 'Granny is just a wee bit tired. Now you sit with her whilst I go and make us all a nice cup of tea.'

After a few sips of the warm beverage the colour began to rise in Jenny's cheeks again. Connie did earnestly wish to engage the old lady in conversation but she was frightened of upsetting her again so she stayed mute.

Fortunately Jenny broke the uneasy silence by saying, 'Connie, what I wish you to know is that I am not upset about you and Johnny's baby any more. To be truthful I did suspect from the start that you and my Johnny were . . . but on Saturday when it all came out . . . well I was worried about what the neighbours would say . . . But after two nights of tossing and turning I now realise that a baby is a miracle and it brings its own love with it when it comes into the world.' Jenny halted and Connie could see that her thoughts were far away and when she did continue she tearfully whispered, 'It is just the loss of . . . knowing that . . . please try and understand' – Jenny was now seeking for Connie's hand – 'that accepting that I will never see our boy Jack again in this life is so very hard to bear.'

Connie bent forward and covered Jenny's outstretched hand with hers. 'Jenny,' she falteringly began, 'we all feel like that. And for me thinking that if I had not got involved with your Johnny then Jack would not have run off to sea makes it worse. The thought that he just wouldn't have sailed out into that danger if Johnny and I hadn't . . .'

Scoffing, Jenny replied, 'Nonsense. Ever since Bobby left, Jack had been looking for an excuse to go too. It's only natural that the young wish to fly the nest and make lives for themselves. What kept Jack here was that he just felt that he could not leave Kitty with the whole burden of running the household and looking after . . .' She did not say Rosebud's name but she did smile towards the child.

Scalding tears that Connie had felt she had no right to shed for Jack were now cruising down her face. She was glad that she had come to visit Jenny this morning. Jenny, who had that invaluable insight that only comes with age, had managed to see the complete picture of what had happened in a different way. Saw it from the points of view of all the people involved.

Patting her stomach, Connie visibly relaxed. As the tension moved out of her she had the most wonderful feeling that she had ever felt in her life. The baby she was carrying, her very own child, started to kick within her. As the baby squirmed to let her know he was growing inside her she vowed there and then, to herself and to Jenny, that she would call him Jack when he made his debut.

Jenny nodded, knowing that the thought of a new baby would stop her from falling down into the deep depression that was about to engulf her again. All her life she had battled with that demon. In the past, Donald had supported her through the dark days and now as she looked at Connie, she thought that God, her God that she always turned to, had sent her another arm to lean on. An arm she wished she had been able to lean on last night . . .

When Kitty and Jenny had made their way over Leith Links towards Leith Hospital Nurses' Home on Sunday night, Jenny had earnestly tried to engage Kitty in conversation. Kitty's mind, however, was just so full of memories of Jack that she didn't hear a word her grandmother said. She was wondering why God had taken a young life like her brother's. Would it not have made more sense for Him to have answered old Mrs Dickson's daily plaintive plea: 'Why have You forgotten me, dear Lord? Don't You realise that people are talking and saying that You just don't want me up there beside You.'

All too soon they had gone up King Street and were at the entrance to the Nurses' Home. 'Kitty,' her grandmother had pleaded, 'is there nothing you would like to say to me before you . . .'

'Sorry, Granny,' Kitty had mumbled. 'Look, I just want

to get inside and away to bed. I start on the wards at seven thirty tomorrow morning. But I promise you that I'll come and see you on my day off. Don't know when that will be but what I do know is that I have to work fifty hours every week and for that I will be paid seven pounds a month.'

'Only seven pounds!' Jenny had expounded. 'But how will you manage on that? It will barely keep you in stockings.'

A sly laugh had then emitted from Kitty. 'Well I will just have to do as I did to get this nurses' Burberry coat and hat – either buy them second-hand or get Nurse Fowler's cast-offs. Don't worry, Granny, I'll survive.'

Before Jenny or Kitty could say another word a young woman with an oversized suitcase arrived at the door. 'I'm Dorothy Keane, but everybody calls me Dotty. I'm starting my nurse's training here tomorrow.'

'Good,' replied Kitty, 'I'm Katherine Anderson, but everybody calls me Kitty, and I'm pleased to meet you. How about we go in together?'

'Yes. And I'm sure that we all have a single room but perhaps we will be next door to each other.'

When the door closed on the girls Jenny had felt bereft. Her grandchildren were so important to her. She was beginning to think that somehow she was losing them. She knew she had to accept that Jack was gone never to return. She also feared that Bobby, even if he did not settle in Wales, would not make his home in Leith and now Kitty, Sandra's pretty Kitty . . . Tears welled up in her as she accepted Kitty would now become a career nurse and where that job would take her she didn't wish to guess or know.

* * *

Monday morning started with Kitty being startled by the clanging of a handbell being rung in the corridor outside her room by the Nurses' Home Sister. She glanced at her alarm clock which registered 7 a.m. 'Good grief,' she muttered as she leapt out of bed, 'I have to be up, dressed and breakfasted and report to Sister Burgess on Ward Two by seven thirty.'

She was just pinning on her white starched hat when her door opened and there stood Dotty. 'Not ready yet? I've been up since six. Just so want to get on to the wards and get started. Luckily I'm to be on Ward Two along with you. Don't know where the other ten who started with us are but we'll find out when we all have to meet the Virgin Mary at three this afternoon.'

'The Virgin Mary – who is she?' Kitty asked as she bent down to tie the laces in her plain black shoes.

'The Matron,' replied Dotty, opening the door and signalling with a jerk of her head that they should be on their way.

The minute Kitty and Dotty met Sister Burgess, who looked at the girls and then at her fob watch, which was pinned to her uniform dress, they knew she was a strict disciplinarian.

'You are?' her clipped voice asked while she surveyed them from top to toe.

'I'm Kitty and my friend here is Dotty,' an eager Kitty replied.

Sister Burgess sighed. 'On the wards when you are training you will be referred to as Anderson and Keane. Now, Anderson and Keane, we have wasted enough time. What is required of you is that you pull out all of the beds and sweep the whole ward floor. Then you will wash, with warm soapy water, all the lockers, give bedpans to those who require them and all this has to be done before you serve breakfast to the patients. Breakfast normally arrives punctually at' – she consulted her watch again before stressing – 'eight thirty.'

Dotty and Kitty just looked aghast. How on earth would they get all that done? They were still contemplating the problems when Sister Burgess added, 'Also you should note that Matron will be making her ward visit mid-morning and that you should stay in the background . . . Stand erect with your hands behind your back. You only speak to Matron if she deigns to speak to you. Now could I suggest that you both get a move on?'

At nine o'clock in the evening twelve very tired young women between the ages of eighteen and twenty-two arrived back at the Nurses' Home.

The three o'clock meeting with the Matron and Sister Tutor had been an eye-opener. The first half hour was spent with the Matron, Miss Mackay, an extraordinary and very slim woman who seemed to float about everywhere in her voluminous cape. Her welcoming talk commenced with her stating that the time spent at the meeting would be taken from the nurses' break time. She then went on to elaborate that they had joined a band of very intelligent, committed ladies and that there was no finer career available for dedicated women such as they would become. Sucking in her lips and sniffing loudly she paused before proclaiming in a sharp voice, 'Now it is best that you understand from the start that you will all require to meet the high standards of General Nurse Training, which will prepare you for State

Registration. That is your ultimate goal – to become a State Registered Nurse. Now I must advise you that in all my time here as Matron no one has failed their final exams! That is not to say that everyone who enters the portals of this magnificent hospital leaves as a State Registered Nurse. No. I, and especially Sister Tutor, usually know well before the final examination who is not fit to earn that illustrious title and we invite them to resign.'

Before Miss Mackay floated away to terrorise the ward sisters she said, 'And now I will hand you over to Sister Tutor, Miss Smart, and I advise you to follow all her advice to the letter.'

Miss Smart waited until the door closed on Matron before she smiled at the gathering. 'Now,' she began, 'you are all on the threshold of becoming fully qualified nurses. A qualification gained in this hospital will take you anywhere in the world that you wish to serve in. But getting there is a long, hard journey. Firstly you must be very disciplined in your approach, not only to your studying for examinations but most importantly to your patients too. Their welfare and well-being whilst they remain in hospital is your priority. Now just to the little things. You must always be punctual, polite and report for duty properly attired. No make-up is allowed whilst on duty, nor is the smoking of cigarettes. Please do not get engaged to be married whilst you are in training – any request for someone to be allowed to marry will be refused. Really, ladies, involvement with young men, I have always found, is detrimental to you achieving your goal of becoming a fully qualified nurse.'

Kitty had just opened the door to her room and had turned to wish Dotty goodnight when Dotty pushed past her.

Throwing herself down on the bed, Dotty snorted. 'Know something, Kitty? I didn't know that we'd joined a convent.'

After taking off her shoes Kitty flopped down on a chair. Gently she began to rub her tired right foot before dreamily uttering, 'Yeah, no make-up. No smoking. Mind you, that won't bother me as I don't smoke anyway. But . . . the next three years with no men in our lives as well . . .'

'That was what I was meaning. Believe me, we would have had an easier time of it if we'd signed up with the Little Sisters of the Poor. At least they get a rest when they pray on their knees for hours on end.' Dotty lay back on the bed and kicked her legs in the air before chortling. 'And just look how happy that would make my mum if we'd thrown our lot in with them!'

'Happy she would be – but why?'

'Because isn't my mum St Teresa of Avila incarnate.' Dotty now crossed herself before adding, 'Honestly, her giving birth to eight children was, as she saw it, her carrying out her duty as a good Catholic woman.' Dotty now clasped her hands in prayer and raised her eyes to the ceiling before adding, 'And when God calls her to kneel before Him she hopes to be able to say that it was her ambition to give birth to six sons who all became priests and six daughters who became nuns.'

'But you said you only have seven siblings.'

'That's right. But twelve good Catholic children were what my mother desired to have. She also prayed that any children she did have would be servants of her God.'

'And how many are in religious orders?'

'None.'

'Not one?'

Dotty was now sitting on the side of the bed but her legs

were still moving. 'That's right. Not one.' She gasped in feigned disbelief before mischievously twittering, 'She nearly had one success with my brother Paul but the devil stole the pattern. Lured him into the claws of Bernadette Shaw, he did.' Dotty sighed again. 'And believe it or not they don't take married men with triplets on the way into the seminary.'

Kitty chuckled. Already she knew that she liked Dotty and her even dottier sense of humour. A friendship was forming and Kitty knew, or hoped, it would last their whole lives through. Her curiosity was awakened now and she was eager to know more about Dotty's background. Tongue in cheek, she asked, 'And what does your dad do?'

'Oh, he faithfully bends his elbow every night in Flannigan's bar,' quipped Dotty before brusquely changing the subject. 'But enough of me; what about your parents?'

This terse reply alerted Kitty to the fact that jovial Dotty did not wish to discuss her father. She too did not wish to say anything right now about her dad but she did manage to mumble, 'My mum is . . . Well she passed away when I was fifteen.'

'And your dad?'

'My dad . . . ?' Kitty just shook her head and decided not to elaborate on him. Deftly she changed the subject by adopting a confidential pose and whispering, 'What is also alarming about the draconian rules in here is, and that is according to one of the second-year nurses' – Kitty paused briefly to make sure that she had Dotty's full attention before adding with a tease – 'that the Assistant Matron patrols our block here every night just to make sure we've not smuggled in any young, handsome, virile men! She also said that we would be severely reprimanded if we opened windows to admit nurses who have been out dancing and missed the curfew at ten!'

Dotty got up off the bed. 'Well I don't think I'm going to make their or my mother St Teresa's grade.' She now advanced to the door and she turned and awarded Kitty with a roguish smile before quipping, 'Not sure if I want to but what I do know is I'm too tired to resign tonight so I'm off to bed.'

Kitty too was smiling as the door clicked shut.

6

JUNE 1944

Mondays in Leith Hospital's Outpatients and Emergency department were always extremely busy. The unit was managed by a very strict Sister. Doctors, nurses and cleaners were all terrified of her. It was even rumoured that the cockroaches, when they heard her approach, flung themselves into the boiling sterilising unit as it was less torturous than being put to death by her. Nonetheless, she ran an efficient division, probably the most effective department in the whole of the hospital, and nurses accepted that being trained by her was their passport to any job that they would apply for when they graduated.

The unit attended to all the casualties that were brought from the various industries. In particular, they were kept extremely busy with workers from the shipyards and docks, where men's working conditions were far from safe.

It was into this environment that Kitty and Dotty were transferred when spring had arrived. Dotty and Kitty had been so excited to be starting their accident and emergency training. It was true that they had got used to mopping up vomit and cleaning backsides on the wards – but getting the opportunity to be on the front line, when patients who had just experienced accidents or traumas came in, just seemed so stimulating and worthwhile.

They both did very well in the Outpatients and Emergency department and were sorry when their four-week stint was over. Kitty was then transferred to the Men's Medical ward and Dotty to Men's Surgical.

*   *   *

It only took two weeks of being on the Men's Medical ward for Kitty to feel that she had no other option but to hand in her resignation to Matron. The decision to resign was not being made rashly by Kitty. In fact, when she thought back over the events leading to her taking this momentous decision, she still felt it was the right course for her to follow.

Always, she would remember that from the minute she had met Sister Irvine of the Men's Medical ward an instant animosity rose up between them. Kitty felt that even if she had stood on her head she could never have pleased the frustrated old bitch, as Kitty thought of her.

This present bright Monday morning brought everything to a head. Kitty had arrived on duty ahead of time. She did this in an effort to make sure that she did not get off on the wrong foot with Sister Irvine. She had just finished dusting the ward piano when the Sister swept up the ward and immediately ran her right index finger over the instrument. 'Do you call this dusted?' she hissed.

Kitty could only shrug. It was dusted but it would never be to the unreasonable standards of Sister Irvine.

Embarrassed, sulking Kitty then went as fast as she could to put the bedpans out before going on to wash the lockers. She should have had a trainee nurse like herself working with her but the poor lass was suffering from a sickness bug. Just when Kitty was rushing to take the bedpans in and put them into the sluice the breakfast trolley arrived. She was so pushed for time she decided not to wash the bedpans there and then but to attend to them later. Quickly, she dashed back into the ward to dish up breakfast when Sister Irvine screamed, 'Anderson, where is Mr Smith and when did you last see him?'

Looking up the ward to where Mr Smith should have been in bed, Kitty became alarmed when she noted that he was not there. 'Eh, eh,' she stammered, 'I saw him half an hour ago when I started the bedpan round. He said that he could now go to the lavatory on his own.'

'Anderson, I advised you that he was a wanderer and to keep an eye on him.'

By this time Kitty was so fed up she haughtily replied, 'Y-e-e-s and I would have kept him under surveillance but I have only one pair of hands and two eyes. And even you, Sister, could not have managed to do what I have done this morning.'

Before Sister Irvine could reply, Dotty arrived on the ward. Submissively she nodded to Sister Irvine before saying, 'Assistant Matron said I should report to you this morning as you are shorthanded on your ward.'

'Yes, we are shorthanded and what staff is available . . . is worse than useless.'

'Could you do the breakfasts, Keane?' Kitty implored. 'And I will go and finish up in the sluice.'

Dotty nodded and without another word Kitty fled to the sanctuary of the wash room.

After taking all her fury out on scrubbing the bedpans she began to wash and disinfect the floor. As she swished the mop backwards and forwards she became swamped by emotion which caused her to slump down and weep uncontrollably.

On hearing her sobs, Dotty joined her in the sluice. 'Come on now, Kitty. Don't let that old trout get the better of you. Look, it is your break time soon so why don't you go and pull yourself together.'

'I will go, Dotty, but not to pull myself together. I can't

stand the constant unwarranted criticism. It seems I can't get anything right so I'm going to hand in my notice to Matron before they ask me to resign.'

'No. Please don't do that. Besides, where would you go?'

'Into domestic service, I suppose, because I need to find a job where I would also get a roof over my head.'

'Look. Don't be hasty. We all get it in the neck. But like you I have nowhere to go so I just bite the bullet.'

'But you have your mum and dad in Belfast.'

Dotty let out a derisive chuckle before confiding, 'St Jude's laundries where they beat young lassies into submission would be an easier option. My parents live in a continual war zone and my mum, who can't get the better of my drunken dad, beats her frustration out on my brothers, sisters and myself. Go back there? No. No. At least here the abuse is all verbal.'

Kitty was due to have some time off in the afternoon but before leaving the hospital she called in at the Matron's office.

The Matron looked up when she entered and without saying a word Kitty laid the sealed envelope that held her resignation down on the table.

'Is that what I think it is, Anderson?'

Kitty sniffed before nodding.

'Then let me say something. You have the makings of one of the best nurses that have ever been trained here. You, I predict, will make a wonderful career for yourself. Yes, the training and discipline are stringent, but if we do not teach you to reach the highest standards that you can, then we will have failed you. Now do you wish to pick' – she now pointed to the envelope – 'that up, and after you have had a few hours to think things over, come back on duty tonight knowing that you are making the grade?'

Kitty shook her head.

'Right,' emphasised Matron, 'tell you what . . . I will leave that envelope lying there for a week and if in that time you have not changed your mind, I will open it and accept your resignation.'

Four hours was what Kitty was due to have in way of a break within her split shift. The writing of her resignation and the subsequent visit to Matron to deliver the, as Kitty saw it, 'surrender notice', wasted an hour of her precious time.

The three hours that were left would be spent going to her grandmother's house to visit Rosebud. This ongoing arrangement had been put in place when Kitty had become estranged from her father and Connie.

Kitty had been the only mother Rosebud had known since she was born. It was only natural then that when Kitty had started to do her training in Leith Hospital and had therefore gone out of Rosebud's life the child felt bereft.

Granny Jenny, concerned for the little girl, had then brokered a visiting arrangement, whereby on one of Kitty's afternoons off Connie would bring Rosebud down to Jenny's in Parkvale Place and Kitty would then be able to spend time with Rosebud. The compromise worked very well because Connie always made sure that she was well away from Parkvale Place before Kitty arrived.

When a breathless Kitty arrived at Parkvale Place, Rosebud was in the pathway.

'Kitty,' she called out, 'Granny says you've to hurry up as she doesn't know what to do.'

'About what?'

Rosebud shrugged before putting up her arms so that Kitty could lift her up.

Once inside the house Kitty put Rosebud slowly down as she tried to take in the scene in the house. Connie, wringing her hands and whimpering, was pacing up and down the floor. Her grandmother, on the other hand, was seated on a chair and her eyes were bulging and she too was whining like a pained dog.

'What's going on here?'

'Oh, Kitty,' Jenny whimpered, 'I think Connie's labour has started and, oh . . . Kitty, will you please, please help? I don't want what happened to your mum to happen to Connie because I might do the wrong thing again.'

Forgetting that she was not on friendly terms with Connie, a concerned Kitty went to her and automatically started to rub her back. 'How often are the pains coming, Connie?'

'The bad pains are about every quarter of an hour but I am just so, so uncomfortable.'

'Hmmm,' was all Kitty said. But she did take a long look at Connie who was extremely bloated. Indeed, her stomach was so swollen that it looked as if she was about to give birth to at least triplets.

Placing her hand over her mouth Kitty tried to think what she could do. Like her grandmother, she painfully remembered and regretted what had happened to her mother when she had given birth to Rosebud. No way did she wish to be involved in anything like that. She accepted that her inexperience had not caused problems when she had assisted Dora with her labour but Connie . . . well, her age! More importantly, she also acknowledged that even although she had not spoken to Connie for going on four months, she still cared for her, and missed her so very much.

Gathering her resolve, Kitty then said, 'Look, Connie, I have very little experience in midwifery, but from the limited knowledge I do have I think we have time to get you home. Once you're there I'll get a midwife from their base on Restalrig Road to come and attend to you.'

Connie shook her head. 'Are you saying that you think I should leave here on my own? What about the state I'm in?'

Shaking her head, Kitty lifted up Connie's coat and as she wrapped it around her she said, 'No. Not by yourself. I'm going to go with you.' Offering Connie her arm Kitty continued, 'And I will stay with you every inch of the way. So come on now, we simply can't waste time.' Turning to Rosebud she simpered, 'Darling, I'll try and see you . . . maybe tomorrow or most definitely the day after that.'

The journey from Parkvale Place took much longer than Kitty thought it would. They were just halfway up the steep Restalrig brae at the corner of Cornhill Terrace when Connie said, 'I don't think I can go any further. Please let me rest here on this garden wall.' As soon as she was seated, Kitty checked her watch and noted that Connie's contractions had intensified and were now coming every eight minutes.

Her first reaction was to panic. But one of the first things that you are taught when doing your nurse's training is that, even although you are faced with a difficulty, you do not convey your anxiety to the patient. This being the case, Kitty drew in three deep breaths to calm herself and also to give herself time to think. On the third inhalation her eyes wandered up to just beyond the Leith Provident Grocer's shop. 'That,' she almost screamed, 'is exactly what we need right now!'

It was, of course, the midwife's house and station. So all Kitty had to do was to drag a now very reluctant Connie up to its doors and all the expert assistance that Connie required would then be on hand.

'Right, Connie, you have about five minutes before your next contraction so what I need you to do is to be brave and hurry yourself up. So come on, let's get going . . .'

'Home!'

'No. Just to past the shops there on the left. What we are trying to do is . . . get to the midwife's house. Honestly, Connie, there is a lovely woman there, a midwife, Sister Fowler, and she will help us. Know something?' Kitty babbled on in the hope of distracting Connie from her plight, 'It was she, Joan Fowler, who persuaded me that I could, and should, go into nursing.'

Six minutes later Kitty was banging on the door of the midwife's house. 'Joan, Joan!' she hollered.

The door opened and there thankfully stood Joan. 'Where's the fire?'

'No fire but look there at the bottom of your steps it's my . . .' Kitty hesitated. 'My stepmother and she is about to give birth. I just couldn't carry her up the steps but you and I could.'

Joan nodded.

A few minutes later Connie was safely lying on a bed and all the expert assistance she required was on hand.

Kitty glanced up at the clock. 'Oh no,' she screeched. 'I only have twenty minutes before I'm due on duty again.'

'Do you have to go now?' Joan asked while she checked another of Connie's contractions. 'Surely not? The baby's head is visible. Look.'

'Surely yes,' Kitty called back as she began to race from the house. 'Arriving late for duty I can assure you is at the very least . . . a hanging offence!'

Kitty sprinted all the way back from Restalrig Road to the Leith Hospital. Not once did she stop to draw breath. However, valiant as her effort was, when she bounded in the hospital doors she only had two precious minutes to spare before she was due on the ward.

In an effort to be on time she found herself still pinning on her cap when she arrived at the entrance to Sister Irvine's ward. Heaving a sigh of relief, she took in a deep breath but as she pushed open the door a voice from the floor called up to her. Looking down she was surprised to see that the speech was coming from the ward cleaner, who was, as per usual, down on her hands and knees scrubbing the corridor leading into the ward.

Kitty immediately drew up short. She really liked Mrs Green, who always had a kind word for everyone. She was also a person who would ask the like of Dotty, who had no relatives in Edinburgh, home for tea and a blether.

'Sorry, Mrs Green,' Kitty said as she slipped another hairgrip into her cap. 'I didn't quite catch what you said.'

'Just that I don't know what it's all about but Sister Irvine told me to tell you that you are not to go on to the ward but to report immediately to her in her office when you come on duty.'

Swearing was something that Kitty very rarely resorted to. But, on hearing that she was to report to Sister, and not to go on to the ward, she reckoned that once more it was confrontation time. Completely convinced that Sister Irvine had an ulterior motive she muttered under her breath, 'Bloody sadist, that's what she is. Yes, oh yes, I bet the old bitch has it in for me . . . yet again.'

'Ah, Anderson,' Sister Irvine said in a voice dripping with honey, 'there have been two serious incidents in our vicinity that have resulted in multiple casualties and Matron has decided, since you did so very well when you did your spell of training in the Outpatients department, that you should report there for your evening shift.'

To say that the feet had been cawed from Kitty was an understatement. Sister Irvine, she concluded, was being so reasonable that it was one of two things. She was either delighted that she would not have to endure Kitty being on her ward, or Matron had had a word with her about the unjust treatment that she had meted out to Kitty and her moderate tone of voice was her way of apologising.

Making her way over to Outpatients, Kitty conceded that the Matron would not have had a word with Sister Irvine – it would not have been hospital politics to have done so. (Years later she did discover that, on the afternoon of the day when Kitty had handed in her resignation, Matron had invited Sister Irvine in for afternoon tea. Evidently, she had tactfully got one of the subjects being discussed around to which of the probationer nurses would, with the right training and encouragement, make the enviable grade of State Registered, Leith Hospital-trained nurses.)

It was only natural that Kitty, with limited training in accidents and emergencies, was assigned to dressing the minor injuries of the walking wounded. She was swabbing the badly grazed leg of a young lad whose treatment card told her that his name was James Henderson and he was the same age as her brother Davy. The young man was very tense and she knew that when she started to pick out the embedded grit with tweezers he would become even more so. In an effort to relax him she said, 'And how did you manage, James, to get your leg into this mess?'

Lifting up his right hand, James began to wipe his running nose and then he blubbed, 'Everybody calls me Jimmy and I work as an apprentice in the shipyards.'

Kitty drew back from Jimmy as a cold blast seemed to blow into her and chill her very bones. 'Which shipyards are you employed in?' she heard herself ask.

'Robb's.'

'And what happened and how many are injured?'

'A lot injured. You see, we had to get the ship back out on time so we had to work overtime. Going for an early tea we were. And none of us, honestly not one of us, knew that the lorry was out of control. It was at our back and just before it ploughed right into us Johnny Anderson shouted, "Jump, Davy. Jump, Davy, and the rest of you lads get out of the way too!" I turned and I flung myself to the side. Next thing I kent was the lorry's catapulting itself into the water. It wasn't on its own either; some of the lads were in the drink along with it.' Jimmy stopped and wiped his nose again before saying, 'And some were just lying on the ground moaning or even worse saying . . . nought.'

Kitty's first instinct was to go and consult the Sister and ask if she could look at the casualty list. Before she was able to do that, however, a senior nurse came forward.

'Anderson,' the nurse began, 'as soon as you've finished Mr Henderson's dressing, go into the main dressing area, where there are children who require their minor injuries dressed. Poor children were just playing innocently in the street when they were hit by falling masonry. What I am told is that a building in East Cromwell Street became unsafe and dislodged stones and rubble tumbled down indiscriminately.' The senior nurse bit on her lip before spitting, 'Fire brigade say they were not surprised as the condemned tenement probably got further damaged in the last air raid. This war! When will it ever end? Lives blighted, casualties everywhere, and not only on the battlefields.'

Still feeling that she should go and check the lists and ensure most importantly that her younger brother, whom she had cared for since their mother had died, was safe and also her father . . . Her face flushed, and she admitted that he was still her father, and whatever else, he always would be. This being the case she gladly conceded that the time she had spent with Connie today had taught her that family is more important than holding unjustifiable grievances.

On arrival at the treatment area, Kitty found there were three other nurses who were working there. Before they knew it, two hours quickly went by as they expertly dressed all the minor wounds.

When the last little girl, who had a deep gash on her forehead, was dressed, the four nurses visibly flopped. For all four it had been a learning experience as this had been their first experience of being involved when major incidents had occurred.

Rolling up the unused part of a bandage, Jane Thompson said, 'Well at least, girls, all of our patients are away home to sleep soundly in their own beds tonight – that is providing we don't get an air raid.'

'And have you any news on the major casualties?' Kitty tentatively asked, but in reality she did not wish to know.

'One from the shipyards is dead, two are unconscious and may . . .' Jane shrugged. 'And one is very lucky in that he has only had his left arm amputated from below the elbow. There is also a young eight-year-old lad from East Cromwell Street who has unfortunately lost his leg. On the bright side, two women, who were leaning out of their windows having a good blether, were so traumatised that one of them, Jessie Logan, the street gossip, who was hit a glancing blow, has said she'll never speak again.'

'Want to put a bet on that, Kitty?' teased Helen Judge.

Kitty just shook her head and her colleagues were surprised when, without uttering another word, she left the station and proceeded towards Sister's office.

She only had to knock on the door once before she heard the Sister bid her enter.

Looking up from the reports she was checking Sister said, 'You have a problem, Anderson?'

'Yes, Sister, my brother David and my father John Anderson may have been involved in the accident at the shipyards and I wonder if you could look at the casualty lists to see if they were admitted.'

'Mmmmm,' replied Sister before scanning the reports in front of her again. 'Your brother was admitted because he had been fished out of the water and we had to make sure that he had not suffered any trauma from that incident.' Sister now drummed her fingers on her desks. 'As to your father, well . . . we have admitted and operated on a John Anderson but whether or not he is your father I do not know. What I do know is that Mr Lawson – who, as you are aware is a brilliant surgeon – did manage to save the man's life although unfortunately he could not save his left arm.'

Without being given leave to sit down, Kitty sank on to

the chair in front of the desk. 'His left arm's been amputated. But . . . he requires two hands to do his job.'

Sister gave a little cough. 'Anderson, before you get yourself upset, would it not make more sense to check at the Men's Surgical ward?' she suggested with a hint of impatience. 'What I am saying is that I think that you should make sure that the gentleman who is recovering there is indeed your father.'

Giving Sister an obedient nod, Kitty stood up and then scurried away.

Even although it was June and daylight, and warmth extended well into the night, when Kitty arrived at the Men's Surgical ward she shivered.

Peering into the evening gloom she allowed her eyes to dance around the ward. Immediately she noted that there were two beds where the patients were being constantly monitored. Advancing up the ward towards these beds she felt a feeling of dread overcoming her. This alarm was added to as she noted that at the nearest bed her brother Davy was sitting.

'Davy,' she whispered, 'how is he?'

Before he responded Davy immediately stood up. He then pulled Kitty into a strong embrace. So strong was his hug that she actually felt unable to breathe properly. She was just about to plead for him to let her go when she felt his whole body convulse and collapse into her. 'Steady, lad,' she implored whilst guiding him back down on to a chair. 'Now has Dad said anything?'

Davy panted as he tried to hold back his tears. 'No. And in his delirium he was asking for Connie. I know the police went to tell her but the callous bitch has never shown up. And where's Granny? She's usually in the middle of everything.'

'Davy, Davy,' Kitty scolded, 'Connie wouldn't be able to come. When I left her this afternoon she was just about to give birth.' Kitty's hand flew to her mouth. 'Oh dear, I want to stay here with Dad but I also know that I should be going to see Connie and tell her how he is and . . . is it true, that he has lost his left arm?'

Davy confirmed with a nod. 'Aye, from just below the elbow.'

'Why?' Kitty stupidly blurted.

'He was so busy saving everybody else that when the lorry collided with him his arm was crushed beneath a wheel. Losing his arm, Kitty, will be . . .'

'You don't have to say it. I know he will be unable to cope with the fact that he will not be able to work and therefore provide for his family.'

Like a spectre the Senior Nurse had now silently floated up the ward to check on Johnny. 'Do you think he'll regain consciousness soon, Porter?' Kitty heard herself ask.

'No. Sleep is a good healer so it is best to leave him to come to naturally.' The nurse then looked at her watch as she began to check Johnny's pulse.

The Assistant Matron listened intently to Kitty's plea that she be given a late pass so that she could go and check on her stepmother. To Kitty's astonishment she was issued immediately with the necessary document.

Davy, who had waited expectantly at the hospital exit for her, was relieved when a perplexed Kitty joined him to hastily make their way to their dad's home in Restalrig Road.

If Davy had wondered where his grandmother Jenny was, as soon as he entered the living room of his father's house he found out. There, kneeling by Connie, who was huddled up in the easy chair, was Jenny. 'See there, Connie, I told you that either Davy or Kitty would come and tell us how things are with our Johnny.'

Kitty immediately went over and knelt down beside Connie. 'How are you and of course the baby?'

'Oh, doing well now,' Jenny chanted before Connie could respond. 'And the wee – well not so wee – real bruiser, who weighed in at eight and a half pounds, Jackie, is just what we need right now.'

'So you've called him after our Jack. Connie, that was thoughtful of you.'

Connie just nodded and again Jenny butted in. 'Not so much of the "him", Kitty, it's a "her".'

'A girl called Jackie?' Kitty tittered.

'Aye, Jackie – short for Jacqueline but the wee lamb is still called after Jack,' Jenny announced before Connie could get a word in edgeways.

Before anyone else could put in their tuppence worth there was a lull in the conversation. This pause allowed Connie to shout, 'Look, everyone, I know you are all delighted about the baby but could someone please, please tell me about Johnny? I am beside myself with worry and that midwife . . .'

'Joan Fowler?'

'Aye, she says I won't be fit to visit my Johnny for another week. That woman is something else, so she is.'

'Well she delivered your baby safely.'

'Aye, she did that, Kitty. Then, because the ambulances were all busy, she asked the Leith Provident bread van if he would give me a lift up the road. You know, I still can't believe that she pushed me and my newborn baby into that van.' She snorted before adding, 'Found myself surrounded

210

by six plain loaves, four high pans and a dozen rolls, so I did.'

For the first time that day Kitty laughed. How like Joan Fowler. *That lady,* she thought, *wouldn't care what she had to do to get Connie a lift home as long as she did.* And what was so terribly wrong to be arriving safely home along with the bread delivery?

Kitty now had to answer Connie's questions about Johnny. 'Well, Connie,' she began. 'Two men did not survive the accident, but thank goodness Dad did.' Kitty gulped before she added, 'Unfortunately he has had his left arm, and I stress left arm, amputated just below the elbow.'

The anguished cries of Connie and Jenny that reverberated around the room pierced into Kitty's head. She truly wished at that moment in time that she was somewhere else – anywhere at all but standing in her father's house witnessing the anguish of Connie and her grandmother.

'How is he taking it?' Connie asked through her sobs.

'Right now he's asleep and I don't think he's aware of what has happened. Tomorrow morning will be . . . well it will be . . . so . . . very difficult for him.'

'Aye, it will be that,' Jenny sniffed, 'because like his father before him he is a diligent, hard-working bread earner and I suppose now he will not be able . . .'

'To carry on as a plater in the shipyards,' Davy muttered.

'Will he?'

'No, Granny, that skill requires two hands.'

There was a long, drawn-out silence before Connie said, 'No matter. We will manage because when Jackie is off the breast I'll go back out to work.'

'Connie,' Kitty replied, 'I know that you will but a woman cannot earn as much as a man even if she is doing the same job. I wish I could help but since I started my training I'm dependent on Aunty Kate's generosity to keep myself afloat. But you know . . .' A protesting wail erupted from the cradle reminding everyone that a precious child had arrived today and Kitty then walked over and she lifted the baby up into her arms.

Looking down on to the plump little face she knew that even if her father was no longer able to work and provide for his family, that family was still truly blessed. Pressing her fingers on the child's mouth she silently vowed there and then that when she was able to do so, the lovely baby Jackie, and of course vivacious Rosebud, would be provided for.

The baby squawked again and Connie held out her hands to take her and feed her.

At five o'clock in the morning the ward lights were switched on and the night staff started to prepare the patients for the day ahead.

All night Johnny Anderson had hovered between consciousness and merciful oblivion. He tried to stretch the fingers of his left hand in an attempt to ease the agonising pain in them. These nerve-ending pains that he had never experienced in his life before were excruciating, so much so that they shot up his arm and screwed their vice-like grip into his very neck and shoulder.

Lifting his right hand he reached it over to stroke his left arm and when he could only feel a bandaged stump he cried out in terror.

On hearing Johnny's plaintive cries the Staff Nurse rushed up the ward. 'Are you in pain, Mr Anderson?' she asked.

Johnny, eyes bulging, body trembling, was now sitting

bolt upright in the bed. 'Where am I? Where is my hand? What has happened to it?' He repeated this over and over again to himself.

Drawing the screens around Johnny, the nurse then sat on the edge of his bed and, taking his right hand into hers, she quietly told him all he needed and wished to know. When she had finished he slumped back against the pillows. Utter despair engulfed him and he wished to cry out in protest. *Why,* he screamed inwardly, *has this awful thing happened to me?* The horrific realisation of what it meant to his life was even too great for tears to assuage. The infliction of a deep, black depression descended on his soul because he truly believed that he had now been rendered utterly useless.

On arrival back at the nurses' home a completely exhausted Kitty threw herself down on her bed. She should have fallen asleep as soon as her head hit the pillow but the memories of the day's events kept bouncing around in her mind.

By two o'clock, when she had been sure that sleep would evade her all night, she remembered that Connie had begged her to find some way of getting her and Jackie down to visit Johnny. Kitty had, of course, agreed that she would, but now in the stillness of the night she had wondered how she could do that.

The Home Sister clanging the bell to awaken the nurses who were due on early-morning duty also awoke a deeply slumbering Kitty. Squinting at the clock she noted to her surprise that it was now seven o'clock.

Even although she was not on duty until lunchtime she immediately jumped out of bed and started to get dressed.

Half an hour later she was seen at the porter's cubicle in earnest conversation with Michael Malone, the very helpful and obliging hospital porter, and he was pointing to the side wall where the wheelchairs were kept.

Five minutes later Kitty was seen running along Great Junction Street pushing an empty wheelchair. Two hours later at a considerable reduced rate of progress she was back on the street but the chair was no longer empty. Swathed in a blanket and holding tightly on to her baby sat a very apprehensive Connie.

Kitty was about to push the chair towards the Men's Surgical ward when Michael said, 'Anderson, will I find someone to mind the baby for you while you visit your dad?'

Kitty hesitated. It was true that children were not allowed to visit the wards, but . . . Connie had just turned her head around to look directly at Kitty and without a word being spoken she managed to convey to Kitty that rules may be rules and regulations may be regulations, but there were times that they should not be adhered to and this was one of them.

As soon as they arrived at the ward Kitty parked the chair before going to speak to the Ward Sister to earnestly plead with her.

Five minutes later Connie was sitting by Johnny's bed, willing him to open his eyes and yet afraid to disturb him if he was asleep. Gently she whispered, 'Johnny, Johnny, dear, look who I've brought to meet you.'

Slowly Johnny's eyes flickered open. The drug that Sister had administered to dull the pain had also given him a feeling of floating above everything. When Connie leant over to rub his cheek he willed himself to look at her. *Yes,* he thought, *it is her.* His heart then became so full that he thought that it would burst.

Extending out his right hand to her he mumbled, 'Connie, I was in an accident.'

Tears splashing down her face Connie replied, 'That right? Well know something? I had an accident nine months ago and yesterday I gave birth . . . Look, Johnny, it's our baby . . . Jackie.'

Johnny struggled up in bed and Kitty lifted the baby out of Connie's arms and she held the baby's face next to Johnny's. 'She's lovely, Dad. Smell her. She was all powdered with Johnson's baby powder this morning.'

'She?' exclaimed Johnny.

'Yes. Remember I told you last night that Connie had given birth to a wee girl. The spitting image of Rosebud she is.' Kitty hesitated to control her emotions before she added with a chuckle, 'Now, Dad, if that's not the stuff that nightmares are made of then I don't know what is!' Kitty glanced up when she heard the distinctive impatient tap of her grandmother's heels on the ward floor. 'Well, Dad,' she conceded when Jenny arrived at Johnny's bedside, 'it just might be that the two wee lambs take after their organising matriarchal granny.'

The afternoon visiting hour coincided with Kitty's break but instead of having a quick meal and a sit down, she dashed over to visit her dad.

To her dismay the visit from Connie and the baby had really done nothing to lift Johnny's spirits. In fact Connie saying to him not to worry as she would soon be able to go out and work just seemed to have completely floored him. Without really addressing anyone in particular he then

215

stuttered, 'On the scrap heap – the scrap heap. That's where I am.'

From the little training she already had in the hospital she knew that, if Johnny was to recover quickly, he had to have his mood lifted. She had in the past managed to help patients to see that life, although changed, was still very much worth living. She remembered how Sister Burgess, who could make young nurses buckle at the knees when she chastised them, only two weeks ago had said to Kitty, 'Anderson, you remember last week when we discharged Mr Young that I was concerned about how he would manage?' Kitty nodded, but stayed mute, as she watched Sister packing a brown paper carrier bag with food that patients' relatives had brought in. 'Now, it is evident that all these eggs, and the jam, biscuits and apples, are surplus to what our patients can consume,' Sister declared. 'So as it is a sin, a sin do you hear, Anderson, to waste food, especially now with the rationing, I wish you to nip over to Bowling Green Street and give this bag to Mr Young.' Kitty's mouth gaped. 'You see his wife died last year,' Sister confided to Kitty, 'and his only son is a prisoner of war. Mr Young is therefore all alone and requires our compassion.' Kitty dutifully nodded again before Sister continued, 'I also wish to know that he is managing to cope. Loneliness and a feeling that nobody cares, Anderson, are as much killers as disease.'

So with Sister Burgess's words ringing in her ears, Kitty knew she had to reach out to her father and have him believe that life was still very sweet.

Later that afternoon, an exuberant and smiling Kitty arrived back at her father's bedside. Before she uttered a word she was surprised to see that he already had a visitor. But then she should have known that as soon as he would be permitted to visit, Jock Weldon would be in to see his old friend and sparring partner.

'How is he?'

'Well, Kitty, I've been here for ten minutes and he still hasn't opened his eyes.'

'Aye, might be that I didnae want to open them,' Johnny drawled.

'Oh, you are really with us,' chorused Kitty, going over to sit at the opposite side of the bed from Jock.

Johnny's eyes were now wide open and he signalled to Kitty by pointing towards the water jug that he required a drink. Rising and pouring some fresh water into her father's drinking glass, she then handed it to him.

'Surely you're going to hold the glass up to my mouth for me?'

'No,' was Kitty's terse reply.

Before taking a long slurp from the glass Johnny looked at Jock and hissed, 'Calls herself a nurse, would you believe.'

Kitty was about to respond that she was a nurse, and therefore she would not be party to her father turning himself into an invalid, when Jock put up a hand to signal that she should stay mute.

'Johnny, lad,' he began enthusiastically. 'Do you know what day this is?'

'Aye, I might have lost half an arm but my brain still works so I ken fine that it's Tuesday.'

'That's right. And this day will go down in history.'

Johnny cackled. 'What for? Surely you're not trying to make a joke out of me having half my arm hacked off?'

'No. It's nothing to do with your arm, Johnny. This is the day that you and I knew would have to come. The one we've been waiting and praying for.'

Johnny became animated. He stretched out his right hand towards Jock's. 'Are you saying that the invasion has started? Overlord has begun?'

'Aye, the long-awaited invasion of France started on the beaches of Normandy before dawn.'

Flopping back down on his pillows Johnny slowly exhaled before gasping, 'Normandy. Good. Now I know there will be casualties, but . . .'

'Johnny, listen. Remember you asked me about the concrete building-like things that were in our launching harbour?'

'Aye, but they were taken away months ago.'

'That's right. And know what they were?' Johnny shook his head. 'Parts of Mulberry . . .'

'Mulberry? What in the name of Dickens is Mulberry?'

'Floating harbours, Johnny lad. Our wee shipyard built parts of the vital floating harbours that are at this minute taking our soldiers, and all the supplies that they need, on to the shores of France.'

Johnny smiled. 'Aye, our wee shipyard did more than her bit to win this war.'

'That's right. And I know this invasion is not the end of the war but as sure as hell it's the beginning of the end.'

'Right enough the end of the madness, the evil . . . the utter waste of our youth.'

Now that Jock had Johnny back to thinking about something other than himself he continued slyly, 'You're right, Johnny, we in Leith, in our own wee shipyard, did more than our bit to win this war. See when it's all over I hope that people dinnae forget that it was through sheer hard work and determination to make sure that we – by that I mean the whole of Great Britain – wasnae starved into submission and that we in Leith did our bit.' He sighed. Johnny nodded. 'And ken this, Johnny, by the time it's over we will hae repaired around 2,800 ships.'

Johnny again nodded in agreement.

'And, Johnny lad,' Jock quickly added, 'our fame is such that we are to hae a visit from their Majesties. Aye, the King and his Lizzie are coming, to acknowledge what we achieved and will continue to achieve.'

'Aye, we did work so very hard, so we did. And, Jock, our men never grumbled when they had to graft twenty hours out of twenty-four to get the ships back out and into service again.' Johnny now silently remembered some of the vessels that had come in broken and useless. Vessels like the *Cossack*, *Jersey*, *Zulu*, HMS *Tyrian*, HMS *Fame*, the two Town Class American Destroyers, the *Ludlow* and *Leeds*, to name but a few. He had to swallow hard to keep his emotions in control as he thought how all of them had been repaired and made seaworthy again by the artisans, labourers and apprentices in the wee shipyard in Leith. Sniffing and panting he then muttered, 'And, Jock, ken something else, at the height of the conflict our yard repaired one sea-going vessel every week!'

'And don't forget the fifty-plus new ships that we built,' Jock uttered jovially because he did not wish Johnny to go back to thinking about his own plight.

'I don't. The Admiralty asked us to build trawlers, corvettes, minesweepers, frigates and rescue tugs, and we never let them down. One entirely new ship was built by us and launched from the Victoria Shipyard every six weeks. Some of the ships that we created with our skills, that are second to none, then went on to fight the enemy.'

'That's right, Johnny lad.'

Kitty was listening intently to all the reminiscences. Slowly it dawned on her that Jock had an ulterior motive for jogging her dad's memories. Where this would all lead to she just didn't know. She did, however, decide to sit quietly until the course that Jock wished Johnny to take became evident.

'Remember, Johnny lad, when we used to sit and have a quiet pint in the Links Tavern at the bottom of Restalrig Road?'

'Now how could I forget our chats on putting the world to rights?' Johnny mocked.

'So you'll remember then how you would talk about how life for the working man and his family would have to change when this war is over.'

'And it will change. Dinnae forget that the Beveridge Report that was published by parliament at the beginning of December 1942 was accepted by all political persuasions.' Johnny had now become quite lively again and he was wagging his right index finger forcefully to emphasise his point. 'And they all agreed that it would be fully implemented when the war was over and a new parliament had been sworn in.'

Jock nodded. 'You're right. That is assured. Oh aye, when the hostilities end we have been guaranteed that war will then be waged on poverty and want in this rich country of ours.'

'Aye, and it will be good to see the back of them two plus disease, ignorance and idleness. Nothing seeps into and destroys the soul and will of the working man like these five evils do.'

Jock allowed a couple of minutes to pass so that Johnny could be inspired again by the hopes and dreams he had for the working man and his family. 'Mind you, Johnny lad,' he eventually said, 'the making of this Welfare State and National Health Service will take great effort on the part of good men to make sure that the government of the day doesnae water them down.'

'You're right there. We all have to remain vigilant.' Johnny was now in a state of rapture and as if just speaking his thoughts out aloud he murmured, 'Imagine it, Jock: we will see the rat-infested slums around our dock area being bulldozed to the ground. No longer will six families hae to share one lavvy. Naw, they will be able to rent one of the newly built spacious bright and airy houses and,' he emphasised, 'they will all hae bathrooms and electric light.'

'And if we get it right, Johnny lad, the likes of our children will be better educated and expect to be able to go on to university. Imagine it – our grandchildren could end up being doctors, lawyers, accountants.'

Johnny nodded and chuckled. He liked the idea of the people who created the wealth of the nation at last getting a better share of it.

Before Johnny could go on, a nurse came to check his temperature and pulse. When the thermometer was placed in his mouth it reminded him that he had not elaborated on one of his dearest dreams – a National Health Service. 'Jock,' he spluttered as the thermometer waggled up and down in his mouth, 'when we do pass the bills to create the new fairer Britain it will benefit the like of this wee hospital that up till now has depended on charitable donations and gala days to fund it.'

Kitty, who had never really taken much interest in politics, looked quizzically at her father before she said, 'Dad, are you saying that by the time I have qualified my salary will be paid by the state?'

Johnny nodded. 'And what happened to your mum because we couldnae afford for her to go into hospital to have Rosebud will be a thing of the past.'

Leaning back in his chair and rubbing his hands over his chest Jock then quietly added, 'Aye, it will be just great. But och, Johnny, you and I ken that there will be those in the government that will start hollering that we cannae afford it all. We cannae afford it all.'

'We bloody – sorry, Kitty, for my French – but we just have to afford it all, Jock.'

'You're right there, Johnny, but we will need good men on the floor of the House of Commons to make sure it doesn't get sidetracked.'

Kitty was very pleased that Jock had got her dad's thoughts away from his own worries. But she was not quite sure where all this rhetoric was taking them so she quietly asked, 'And where, Mr Weldon, do you think the country will find all these people you seem to think will be required to bring in this Welfare State?'

'Well for a start your dad here could stand for parliament.'

'Me?' Johnny screeched. 'Are you off your trolley? I left school at thirteen where I was only educated to work by my' – Johnny stopped and put his right hand over his bandaged stump – 'hands because then I had two of them.'

'Nonsense. You have more than proved your worth. You are an orator, Johnny. You know your arguments and plead your cases well.'

'That right? Next thing, Kitty, is he'll be telling me to stand as a Tory.'

'Why would I do that when you are a fully paid-up member of the Labour Party and the Tories will not form the next government after the war?'

'Of course they will. Churchill is a hero. He is the man, the only man, who wouldn't do a deal with Hitler – the man who gave us the confidence to keep on fighting when common sense was telling us to roll over.'

'I grant you that. He's the war hero and you cannae take that away from him but he's not the man to lead us in the post-war world.' Johnny was now bemused. Jock smirked. 'Johnny lad,' he went on, 'Winston doesn't understand where Britain's going. He's upper class – never been on a bus. Don't you understand he doesn't identify with the wishes and needs of the ordinary people?'

'And,' Kitty tentatively interrupted, 'what are our wishes and needs?'

'Oh, lassie, we have to say good riddance to the unjust class system – it stifles the working class. We will all hae a vote in the election and then Churchill will discover that we havnae forgotten the brutal part that he played in the 1926 General Strike when he ground the Dockers, Miners and the TUC into submission. You see, lassie, he doesn't want his world of privilege to change and for that to happen he would have to keep us, the working class, in our place. And what we want, and will get, is social reform.'

'Social reform?' Kitty mumbled.

'Aye, like your dad just said . . . seeing the Welfare State and the National Health Service being brought in. You are too young to remember the unemployment, poverty and deprivation of the 1930s – believe me it was horrendous. So what is so wrong in us wanting an end to all of that?'

Kitty could only reply, 'Nothing.'

'And as your dad is one of the best and most knowledgeable shop stewards that I have ever done business with, he would be an asset to the team that will see Beveridge's social reforms implemented.'

'And do you think that Westminster will be so hard up for members that they will be willing to take me, a one-armed disabled man?'

'Don't see why not. After all, before the war their numbers were made up with some that definitely had no heart and others whose brains were befuddled with booze.'

Johnny laughed. 'Be reasonable, as I've already said I'm not clever enough for that.'

The enthusiasm that oozed from Jock now inspired Kitty. Looking at her father she could see what Bobby had pointed out to her – that her dad was clever, self-educated, motivated and passionate. There was something worthwhile about him. He was a man who had never really had a chance to reach his potential. By standing for parliament it would not only be a thing he could do really well but would also give him a reason to live his life to the full. After all, hadn't he always more than looked after the men he represented – the workers?'

'Dad,' she faltered, 'all these doubts that you are having just now I had before I came into this hospital to train as a nurse. I thought that even although I wished to nurse people, restore them to good health, that it was an over-ambitious

The Tangling of the Web
Millie Gray
RRP £7.99 – 978 1 84502 720 9

Sally, who married young to escape her appalling childhood, is often left to bitterly reflect on the hand she has been dealt. She is, on the whole, happy caring for her handsome husband, his mother, her own three children, one of whom has a disability, and her eccentric sister. Then suddenly her world comes crashing down when her husband leaves her with no warning.

She is helped unexpectedly by a friend whose advice stands her in good stead, and by hard work and sheer determination she soon turns around a Leith pub which has a shocking reputation as a house of ill-repute. During all her trials she still finds time to care for her ever-increasing family and, having been a victim of abuse, she is always on hand to assist her many, some dubious, friends to realise their potential.

But, as Sally is to discover, there is no escape from the past, and when it comes back to haunt her she is astounded when a family friend supplies some answers to awkward questions that have troubled her all her life.

www.blackandwhitepublishing.com

When Sorry is Not Enough
Millie Gray
RRP £7.99 – 978 1 84502 778 0

In *When Sorry Is Not Enough*, the thrilling sequel to *The Tangling of the Web*, Sally Stuart's adventures in post-war Leith continue.

Four years on from discovering their true heritage, Sally and Luke have overcome their animosity to forge a trusting relationship. And now Luke has returned home from his post as a detective in the Hong Kong police force to prove the innocence of his friend Irish, who is in prison for the murder of his wife. Luke believes Irish was set up and asks for Sally's help to prove it.

But, as always, Sally has her hands full: as well as tending her flourishing business empire, she must also pick up the pieces when her family runs into trouble, from her feckless sister Josie to her self-centred daughter Margo. Moreover, she must put her own dreams on hold because the man she loves is not free to be with her.

So when Luke suggests that Sally return to Hong Kong with him to start a new life, she is sorely tempted. Will she really leave her beloved Leith behind?

www.blackandwhitepublishing.com

Eighteen Couper Street
Millie Gray
RRP £7.99 – 978 1 84502 438 3

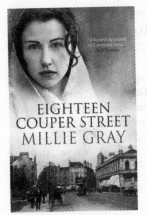

Eighteen Couper Street is the prequel to the Campbell family saga. Anna Campbell, a Leith 'worthy' in the full sense of the word, never turns anyone away from her door. The condemned tenement is the home to many families in dire poverty and Anna, known as a 'wise-woman', hatches and despatches and treats all minor ailments for her friends.

She dedicates her life to raising six children, four boys and two girls who are not her own. The girls, Rachel and Bella, remain with her into adulthood and despite her care she is horrified when fifteen-year-old Bella becomes pregnant by Gus, someone she had given shelter to in his hour of need. Gus skips the country and is hotly pursued across the world and made to return to marry Bella. The bane of Anna's life is the ne'er-do-weel Gabby, Rachel's father. Little does she realise that her continuing desire for revenge against him will have such a devastating effect on Rachel and also the rest of the family.

The families struggle to cope with daily life but there are bigger tragedies in store. The sinking of the *Titanic*, the First World War, the Gretna Rail Disaster, the Spanish flu – all have serious repercussions on the lives of the families involved, and Anna, as ever, is there to help them come to terms with them.

Crystal's Song
Millie Gray
RRP £8.99 – 978 1 84502 3409

Millie Gray returns to wartime Leith to weave another tale full of warmth and humour, hardship and survival. Living in the same neighbourhood as the Campbells of Millie Gray's previous bestsellers, the Glass family is struggling to make ends meet. With father Tam taken captive by the Germans, his wife Dinah and his children are left to fear the worst. While Dinah seeks comfort in the arms of various soldiers, the children, including the headstrong Crystal, fear for their father's and their own safety as they are forced to evacuate their beloved home.

When, miraculously, Tam returns alive, the family must face the consequences of the past in order to build an ever-tenuous future in post-war Scotland.

In a Class of Their Own
Millie Gray
RRP £7.99 – 978 1 84502 256 3

MILLIE GRAY
IN A CLASS
OF THEIR OWN

In a Class of Their Own tells the story of one family's life in Leith through the dark and difficult years of the Second World War. Like so many others, Rachel Campbell wants a better life for herself and her four children but her feckless husband Johnny isn't helping. And when he finally deserts her, Rachel is left to fend for herself and her children through the poverty and dangers of wartime.

Based on the real-life wartime experiences of author Millie Gray, *In a Class of Their Own* brilliantly recreates the atmosphere of the time with all the hardships and struggles as well as the fun and humour of everyday life.

In a League of Their Own
Millie Gray
RRP £7.99 – 978 1 84502 284 6

MILLIE GRAY
IN A LEAGUE
OF THEIR OWN

This brilliant sequel to Millie Gray's first novel, *In a Class of Their Own*, continues the story of Rachel Campbell and her family. It's October 1954 and Sam is home from his eventful National Service experiences in the Korean War. Meanwhile, Rachel's eldest daughter Hannah is due to have her second child on a remote Hebridean island and the birth is far from straightforward. Sam joins the police and he finds it particularly challenging to be competing with his more academic brother Paul.

Then, just as life seems to be settling down for the Campbells, Rachel gets news that her estranged husband Johnny has died – some fifteen years after he deserted his family. And, typically, Johnny has left a mess behind him, which Rachel has to clean up.

www.blackandwhitepublishing.com

however, did bend down to fish out a receptacle from under her desk. Still without a single sound passing between the two women, Kitty tore the envelope and its contents into shreds. There was nothing else to do now except drop the tatters into the waste-paper basket that the Matron was holding out towards her.

dream from someone from my background. Then on the day I found out you were going to marry Connie I was incensed and as I was going up Restalrig Road I met Joan Fowler, the midwife who ended up delivering your daughter, Jackie. She took me into her house, sat me down with a cup of tea and a slice of toast and she then persuaded me that I was smart enough to be a nurse and if I didn't go and apply to be trained here, in Leith Hospital, it would be something I would regret for the rest of my life. So you see, Dad, after this war we will need good men like you who have a vision of a brighter future for everybody in this country. So stop feeling sorry for yourself. All right, you have lost half an arm, but would you like to see in the future that some other poor bloke suffers an injury, like yours, and he is flung on to the scrap heap and his wife and children are then sentenced to a life of poverty and deprivation?'

Johnny shook his head.

'So you see I could be qualifying . . .' Kitty suddenly remembered something. Her eyes bulged and she started to run from the ward but as she did so she called back, 'and you could be taking your seat in the House of Commons all in two, well maybe three, years' time.'

'Where's she away to?' Jock asked Johnny.

'I think to get herself on duty right away. See there's the late-shift nurses coming on to this ward.'

The sound of Kitty knocking on the Matron's door was still reverberating when a stern voice called out, 'Enter.'

Kitty did as she was bid, but instead of standing with her hands submissively behind her back, she slid her right hand over the Matron's desk to pick up her resignation letter.

Neither the Matron nor Kitty said a word. Matron,